Praise for *New from Here*

An Instant #1 *New York Times* Bestseller
A Kids Indie Next Pick
An Amazon Best Book of the Month

★ "A compelling story that conveys the importance of showing love and kindness, especially during hard times. Highly recommended for all middle-grade collections."
—*Booklist*, starred review

"Yang deftly touches on complex issues including China–Hong Kong relations, racism, the grief of separation and dislocation, and the pandemic, all while maintaining a hopeful tone. . . . A timely and compelling family journey." —*Kirkus Reviews*

★ "A pandemic book that is also a story of the importance of family, friendship, and standing up for what is right; another knockout from Yang." —*School Library Journal*, starred review

"Narrating from Knox's approachable, first-person-present perspective, Yang adeptly maintains a sense of hope and belief in love, balancing haunting dramatic irony . . . with moments of levity as the family works to be reunited." —*Publishers Weekly*

"A strong and timely novel about a family weathering adversity."
—*Horn Book Magazine*

"This book will keep readers turning pages, if not for its recognizable elements than for its ability to transmit the love and strength of a family under duress in an unusual time."
—*School Library Connection*

"A timely mid-grade must-have and a story that needs to be told."
—*BCCB*

KELLY YANG

Simon & Schuster Books for Young Readers

NEW YORK · LONDON · TORONTO · SYDNEY · NEW DELHI

SIMON & SCHUSTER BOOKS FOR YOUNG READERS
An imprint of Simon & Schuster Children's Publishing Division
1230 Avenue of the Americas, New York, New York 10020
This book is a work of fiction. Any references to historical events, real people, or real places are used fictitiously. Other names, characters, places, and events are products of the author's imagination, and any resemblance to actual events or places or persons, living or dead, is entirely coincidental.
Text © 2022 by Yang Yang
Cover illustration © 2022 by Maike Plenzke
Cover design by Lucy Ruth Cummins © 2022 by Simon & Schuster, Inc.
All rights reserved, including the right of reproduction in whole or in part in any form.
SIMON & SCHUSTER BOOKS FOR YOUNG READERS and related marks are trademarks of Simon & Schuster, Inc.
For information about special discounts for bulk purchases, please contact Simon & Schuster Special Sales at 1-866-506-1949 or business@simonandschuster.com.
The Simon & Schuster Speakers Bureau can bring authors to your live event. For more information or to book an event, contact the Simon & Schuster Speakers Bureau at 1-866-248-3049 or visit our website at www.simonspeakers.com.
Also available in a Simon & Schuster Books for Young Readers hardcover edition
Interior design by Hilary Zarycky
The text for this book was set in New Baskerville.
Manufactured in the United States of America 0123 OFF
First Simon & Schuster Books for Young Readers paperback edition February 2023
2 4 6 8 10 9 7 5 3 1
The Library of Congress has cataloged the hardcover edition as follows:
Names: Yang, Kelly, author. | Title: New from here / Kelly Yang.
Description: First edition. | New York : Simon & Schuster Books for Young Readers, [2022] | Audience: Ages 8–12. | Audience: Grades 4–6. |
Summary: Knox works to keep his family together as they move from Hong Kong back to northern California during the initial outbreak of the coronavirus.
Identifiers: LCCN 2021016513 (print) | LCCN 2021016514 (ebook) | ISBN 9781534488304 (hardcover) | ISBN 9781534488328 (ebook) | ISBN 9781534488311 (pbk)
Subjects: CYAC: COVID-19 (Disease)—Fiction. | Attention-deficit hyperactivity disorder—Fiction. | Chinese Americans—Fiction. | Racially mixed people—Fiction. | Moneymaking projects—Fiction. | Family life—California—Fiction.
Classification: LCC PZ7.1.Y365 Ne 2022 (print) | LCC PZ7.1.Y365 (ebook) | DDC [Fic]—dc23
LC record available at https://lccn.loc.gov/2021016513
LC ebook record available at https://lccn.loc.gov/2021016514

To Tilden, Eliot, and Nina

Chapter 1

M y name is Knox and sometimes I just blurt words out. It
drives everyone in my family crazy. I don't mean to—I
just really *need* to know things. Like right now, when my
dad's trying to explain the coronavirus to us and the reasons
why we're going to America.

"It's safer there," Dad says. "They don't have the virus."

"How's it safer?" I ask.

"He just *said*!" my brother, Bowen, erupts. "Listen for a
change, Knot!"

I glare at Bowen. Ever since I was about five years old,
Bowen's been calling me Knot instead of my name, Knox, as
in Knot-from-this-family, even though I am definitely from
this family and Bowen's from planet Bully.

"Stop it, Bowen," Dad says in his stern, deep voice. A taxi
beeps loudly on the street below our apartment, as if to add,
Yeah, Bowen! Hong Kong taxis are always beeping loudly.

Dad bends down so we're eye to eye and goes over all the
risks of the coronavirus again—pneumonia, difficulty breathing, and even death. I swallow hard.

"This is serious," he says. "It could be like SARS all over
again."

When news of the virus dropped on my tenth birthday
a week ago, we hadn't even celebrated Chinese New Year

yet. The last of the Christmas decorations hadn't been taken down. That night, we all watched in horror at the footage of doctors in hazmat suits and patients lying in hospital corridors in Wuhan, China. I could hear the doctors saying in Mandarin, "People are dying! We need *help*!" No one even ate my rocket ship birthday cake, even though I worked on it with my little sister Lea for two hours and we used *so* much frosting.

"What happens if we don't leave? Are we all going to die?" I ask.

"No . . . ," Dad says, in the patient yet worried tone he uses when I ask him if my finger will melt if I hold it above a candle for a really long time. "But I think it's better if you guys go to California. If it's anything like SARS, we can't take any chances."

Lea and I look at each other, alarmed.

"What do you mean 'you guys'?" I ask. "You're not coming?"

Dad sighs. "Unfortunately, I have to stay behind and work. But Mom can take you—all her deals are on hold for now anyway."

Mom's a banker. Her office building has lots of windows and lights up Central District, Hong Kong, even at night, because people are always working.

"It'll be fun! It'll give us a chance to bond!" Mom says brightly, looking up from her work phone. We're at the kitchen table, and even though there's a no-phone policy at the table—a rule Mom came up with—she always forgets and sneaks peeks at her phone.

At the thought of not going with Dad, I groan and kick my chair leg with my foot. It hurts but I don't say "ow" in front of Bowen.

"For how long?" Bowen asks.

"Until this thing is over. A month maybe?" Dad answers. He crosses his fingers. "Hopefully, it'll be over by February."

"A whole month?" I shake my head. "No. I can't!"

I feel the tears building inside. Dad's my best friend! He's the one who tickles me to bed every night. Who picks me up from after-school soccer and my six-year-old sister up from after-school art every day. Who hasn't missed a single soccer game, even when Mom's traveling for work. Who's *always* there for us. I can't be gone from him for that many days.

"I'm not going," I say. Being stuck in America with my big brother will *definitely* kill me before the virus does. "I'll take my chances here."

Bowen immediately takes one of the surgical face masks on the counter and puts it on his face, like I'm already contagious. What a wimp.

My sister, Lea, tries to reason with me. "But Knox, we can go to your beach!"

I give her a faint smile. Knox Beach, in Northern California, is the beach I was named after. We go there every summer, and to our little house in El Tercera, which my grandma Francine left Dad. It's right outside Berkeley, where Mom and Dad both went to college. There is a hill by our house with wild horses. I like summers in El Tercera because it's really the only time we get to spend with Mom. The rest of the year, she's always so busy with work.

Summer Mom takes us to the movies and to get frozen yogurt. Winter Mom loads us up on tutors and tells us not to bug her because she's "got to reply to this." Maybe it *will* be fun. I've never been to Knox Beach in the winter.

But then I look at Dad and my excitement dissolves. I vow not to ditch him for a beach.

"Nope." I shake my head.

Mom stares at me. "Knox . . ."

"Why do you always have to be so difficult!" Bowen yells from behind his mask.

Mom orders Bowen to take his mask off his face at once and starts counting them. There are still twenty-seven left, including the one Bowen just wore for two seconds (*ewww—I'm so not using that one!*). She hugs the box of masks in her arms as she looks out the window at the long line of people waiting in front of the pharmacy downstairs. It's late January and freezing cold outside. Still, the line of shivering people snakes all the way down the street, even though the pharmacy—every pharmacy in Hong Kong—is completely out of masks.

"These are more precious now than gold," Mom reminds us in Mandarin. Mom always speaks to us in Mandarin when something's really important. The only reason we got ours was because Mom's friend Auntie Jackie, in California, FedExed them to us. Mom says that's a sign of a true friend.

I only have two true friends in the world—Dad and my friend Amir, who moved back to London. It took me nine years to find him because of my blurting-things-out problem. In the end, all it took to lose him was a raise for his dad. I can't compete with a raise! That's the thing about going to school in an international city like Hong Kong. People are always moving.

Thankfully, I still have my other best friend. And I'm not leaving him behind.

4

Chapter 2

--- ✈

Mom finally allowed me to go outside to play soccer because I was "driving her nuts." I ask Bowen if he wants to come with me, even though he's probably going to say no.

To my surprise, he says okay. He must *really* be bored at home. Even though we're still in the middle of Chinese New Year holiday week, it doesn't feel like Chinese New Year this year. People aren't handing out *lai sees* on the street. *Lai sees* are red packets filled with money, and every year around this time, I always get a bunch from strangers on the street. They can't resist me because I look so handsome.

But not this year.

I look around for Lea, but she's FaceTiming with one of her fifty thousand friends from school, even though she's only in first grade. I don't know what her secret is. She's not *that* great. As soon as I think that, I feel bad. After all, Lea was the one who insisted on mixing the yellow with the blue frosting to make green for my rocket cake because that's my favorite color. She's actually pretty great.

Anyway, Bowen and I put on our "masks" and head out. Mom didn't want to waste two of our twenty-seven real face masks, so she puts a paper towel across our nose and mouth and fixes it with a rubber band. It works okay.

We get in the elevator and use little toothpicks that the building management put out to press the elevator buttons, instead of our fingers. It's so weird to use toothpicks to press buttons, like we're eating elevator-button fruit.

On Tai Street, everyone's wearing masks instead of their traditional Chinese New Year *changshan* jackets. Even though the government hasn't officially told everyone to, people know from SARS that masks help protect us. One guy doesn't have a mask, so he puts a clear plastic water jug over his head. Bowen chuckles. The guy yells something at him in Cantonese. People are always speaking Cantonese to Bowen because he looks more like Mom and people think he's full Chinese, whereas I look more like Dad and I don't get it as much. Which is sad because I actually *know* Chinese.

As soon as we get down to the soccer pitch, Bowen takes his mask off. I take mine off too and kick the ball to Bowen. My twelve-year-old brother is a great athlete, fast and strong. He is the track star at his school, with thick legs that my *lao ye* says are like tree trunks. I run to keep up. Bowen passes the ball back to me instead of hogging it, which is nice.

I spot some kids from our neighborhood playing in the park next to the soccer pitch. I start running over to them.

"What are you doing?" Bowen calls, and chases after me. I try to outrun him, but he's too fast. He grabs my arm. "You can't play with them!"

"Why not?" I miss kicking the ball around with the other kids at school, and since the government announced school is closed indefinitely, even after the Chinese New Year holiday break is over, who knows when the next time I'll play with other kids will be? So I tell my brother to bug off. "You're not the boss of me," I tell Bowen, shaking my arm free.

Bowen steals my ball away with his quick feet.

"Hey!" I shout.

I run after him to get my ball back. When we get to Tung Lam Terrace, the small, narrow lane leading to our apartment, I kick the ball from between his legs. What's *wrong* with him?

"Why'd you have to take my ball?" I shout.

"I'm trying to keep you alive!" he shouts back.

Yeah right. Like he gives one boba about me. I hold the ball in place with my foot, crossing my arms at Bowen.

"You don't know if those kids have it or not . . . ," he says.

"What?"

"The virus! Duh!"

"They don't have it!" I say. "Would they be playing soccer if they were sick?"

"The incubation period is fourteen days, dummy!"

I hate arguing with Bowen because he's always making up stuff that I don't understand. What's an incubation period?

"People are *dying*, Knox! Over four hundred people in China!" Bowen says. "Why do you think they closed all our schools?"

"Yeah, in *China*. We're not in China!"

"But we're in Hong Kong, right next door!" Bowen says. "Do you know how many people come across the border every day? Like *millions*."

Millions? I don't think so.

I take my foot off the ball and let it roll down the hill, toward the soccer pitch. Forget Bowen. Forget the virus. I'm going to play with those kids.

"Fine! Go! Do whatever you want!" Bowen calls out to me. "But don't cry when they take you away from Mom and Dad and you have half a dozen doctors sticking long needles in you!"

I stop walking, catching the ball with my foot. *Needles?* I hesitate for a second and turn around, torn between believing Bowen and hating him. I wish I hadn't taken off my paper towel mask. It looked silly, but it was *something*. I sneak one last look toward the soccer pitch and hang my head as I follow my brother up the path to our apartment.

I hope the virus is over soon.

Chapter 3

--✈

My dog, Cody, wags his fluffy white tail when we get back to the apartment. Dad is cooking dinner. Another reason why I can't leave him. I'd starve. The only things Mom knows how to make are reservations.

Mom looks up from her computer and bolts over to us with hand sanitizer as soon as we walk inside.

"Rub your hands together!" she orders, while she counts the seconds. "I watched this YouTube video. You have to rub for twenty seconds!" We rub and rub, even when we run out of sanitizer, until we finally get to twenty.

"Now go take a shower," she says. "And remember, put the toilet seat down before you flush!"

"Why?" I ask.

"Because the virus can spread through poop," my grandmother's voice calls from the speakers of Mom's computer.

"Through poop??" Lea asks from the kitchen, horrified. She's helping Dad with dinner and drops the wooden salad spoon. She runs from the kitchen island to her room, screaming.

I chuckle at my sister. Sometimes I forget she's still six. "Hi, Lao Lao." I walk over and wave, while Bowen takes a shower first. I miss my *lao lao*. She and my *lao ye* live in Beijing. I haven't seen them since Christmas. They were supposed to

9

come down for Chinese New Year, but then the news of the virus hit. Another thing the virus cancelled.

"Hi, didi," she says, calling me by my nickname, the Mandarin phrase for "younger brother." Even though the rest of Hong Kong speaks Cantonese, we're Mandarin speakers because my grandparents are from Beijing. "You excited about going to America?"

I turn to my mom. "I thought we decided not to go!"

"We haven't decided yet, Ma," Mom says to Lao Lao.

"What if it spreads there?" Lao Lao asks.

"They have almost *no* cases," Mom tells her.

"But what *if*?"

"That won't happen in America," Mom says. "They have the most advanced medical system in the world. We'll be fine."

"Just be careful. And tell the kids they *must* wear a mask on the plane. And Andrew."

"Dad's not coming," I tell Lao Lao. "He has to stay here and work."

Lao Lao peers into the Skype at Mom. "He's not coming?! So you'd be taking the kids *by yourself*??"

"You say that like it's so impossible." Mom frowns at my grandmother.

"It is impossible!" I pipe in. "We're a handful!"

Mom gives me a look.

The last time Mom took care of us on her own was before Lea was born. And she had Lao Lao to help her.

"I'll be fine," she insists. I shake my head. I'm not so confident.

"I'd stay put and ride it out. Stock up on essentials," Lao

Lao suggests, pointing to her humongous stash of groceries in her kitchen.

"Wow. That's a lot of flour!"

Lao Lao tells me she plans on not leaving her apartment until this thing is over. Even if it takes five months. She'll hibernate like a bear. Which makes me a little sad. Are we not going to see her the whole time?

"Well, I can't do that," Mom says. "The kids need to go out and run around, especially Knox." She glances at me. "You know how he is."

How am I? I wonder. And is that the reason we're doing this? Because Mom thinks I can't handle spending five months cooped up inside our apartment in Hong Kong? I can handle it. Despite what Lily, my therapist at school, says, I *can* stay put.

I sigh a little thinking about Lily. Now that school's closed indefinitely, I wonder when I'll see her again. Mom says after next week, we're going to start online school. She says it's gonna be fun, like a video game. I doubt that. I think it's gonna be like the kind of video game where everything constantly freezes.

Lao Lao sighs and reaches out a hand to the screen. "I wish I could help . . . ," she says. "But this virus. My age."

I reach my arms out to my grandmother, wishing I could give her a hug. My arms hit the sharp corners of our bulky Mac.

"It's okay, Ma. I've got this," Mom says. "You just take care of yourself in Beijing."

•   •   •

11

At dinner, Bowen asks Mom, "Are the doctors still planning on striking?"

Mom sighs, glancing down at her phone. "I don't know, gege," she says, calling him by the Chinese nickname for "big brother."

"What's a strike?" I ask, feeding Cody a piece of Dad's chicken piccata under the table. Dad's chicken piccata is the best. He got the recipe from Grandma Francine, who got it from an old restaurant in San Francisco, before she passed away.

Dad explains a strike is when you refuse to do your job out of protest. Mom says the doctors in Hong Kong are concerned with the rise in cases and whether they'll spill over into Hong Kong. When she says that, I close my eyes and think of the virus like a glass of orange juice.

"They want the border with China to be closed so the mainlanders can't get in," Dad explains.

Main-land-ers. I open my eyes wide. It's almost a swear word now in Hong Kong. Ever since the summer, there have been protests all over the city against the government. At first the marches were peaceful, but then there were petrol bombs and tear gas. The protestors broke into the legislative building, shattering the glass doors. School was cancelled for two weeks. I saw the words *F-bomb China People* graffitied on the street. An old man was set on fire for disagreeing with the protestors.

I started wondering, am I a "China People"? My mom, my *lao lao* and *lao ye*—they were all born in China. If I am, does it mean I'm not welcome here?

"If we get sick, we shouldn't speak Mandarin in the hospital," Mom says. "So people don't think we're mainlanders."

"We're *not* mainlanders," Bowen insists. "We're Americans." He looks to Dad to make sure.

"We're definitely Americans," Dad says, chuckling as he adds, "We have the tax returns to prove it."

"It's not just the tax returns," Mom says. "Dad and I both grew up there and went to school there. We only ended up in Hong Kong because of work."

"Well, not just because of work," Dad says, looking to Mom. "You also wanted to be closer to your parents."

"The point is, we're also very Chinese," Mom adds with a smile. "That's why I named you Bowen, Lea, and Knox. After all my favorite places in Beijing, Hong Kong, and America." Her voice hitches. "But right now, I need you three to lean into the Hong Kong and American parts of yourselves . . . okay?"

I look down. I wonder if you took apart my body and sorted it all out, which parts are Hong Kong and American. My nose? My arm hair? My big toe? And which parts I would have to hide.

Chapter 4

The next day, I wake up to Dad's voice on a conference call. I forget for a second that he's working from home. When the virus news erupted, his office, like many offices in Hong Kong, had to close—I guess that's one good thing about the virus! I scramble out of bed in my pj's, excited to photobomb Dad's Zoom.

I crawl into my parents' bedroom, where Dad has set up his temporary office, trying hard not to giggle, then burst onto Dad's screen! It takes Dad a second to realize I'm behind him, and when he does, he tries to block his camera with his hands, accidentally knocking over his coffee. All his coworkers see it and they laugh, laugh, laugh.

Dad doesn't think it's so funny. One look at his face and I run outside to grab paper towels.

I hear a loud "Knox!" from their room. Dad's Zoom must be over.

I walk back inside with Cody.

"Hey, buddy, that wasn't really cool what you did," he says. "It was an important work meeting."

I look down. I can tell Dad's mad and it makes me feel terrible. I was just trying to be funny. What Dad's coworkers were saying sounded *so* boring. But sometimes when I'm trying to be funny, I go too far. I wish there were a stop sign in my head before people skip right from laughing to frowning. But my brain only has GO FASTER signs.

"Sorry . . . ," I murmur quietly.

"It's okay." Dad's face softens. I help him clean up the coffee as Cody curls up for a nap. "I know it's hard to get used to, me working from home."

I look up from the coffee mess. I shake my head—that's not it. I *love* having him here. But I'm not sure when I can play with him and when I can't. . . . The boundary is so confusing.

Dad must have sensed my frustration because he wipes his hand, puts the paper towels down, and asks, "How about we play some soccer?" He throws a pillow at me from the bed.

Cody lifts his fluffy head excitedly. I give Dad a funny look. "Here?"

He gets up and moves all the fragile items out of the way. Then he starts rearranging all the pillows. Before I know it, he's built a pillow soccer pitch for me on his bed! I grin. Dad says I can't kick an actual soccer ball, so I run out and grab my dog Cody's squishy green rubber ball instead.

"Score!" Dad exclaims when I kick the ball between the two towers of Thai silk pillows.

I throw my arms in the air and run around my parents' bed for the fans, pretending it's a stadium. Cody chases me. Dad tries to score a goal too and lands with a loud thud on the carpet. I giggle. It's so fun playing bedroom soccer with Dad.

After I score a few more points, we sit down on the bed to catch our breath. Dad's holding the squishy ball. I'm still thinking about what we discussed during dinner last night. "Hey, Dad . . . what do you think Hong Kong should do?" I ask him. "Should we close the border to mainlanders?"

Dad leans over. A pillow from the fort falls down.

He considers the question carefully. "I think it's important to contain the virus and protect people," he says. "But I also think that we should not use this as an excuse to be hateful toward people just because of where they came from. In moments of human tragedy, we need to show compassion and kindness."

I nod. *Not just during human tragedy,* I want to add. *During regular times with your little brother, too,* still thinking about yesterday at the soccer pitch. But I don't say that to Dad. Instead, I ask him another thing that has been bothering me.

"Why did Mom tell us to stop speaking Mandarin?" I ask Dad. All my life, my mom's been pestering me to speak more Mandarin. That's why my grandparents are always coming down to Hong Kong and watching us, and she even got me a Chinese tutor—so my Mandarin would be native.

"Oh, no . . . she didn't say stop speaking it altogether," Dad says. "Just not in the hospital in Hong Kong."

"Why?" I ask.

"She's worried you won't be treated as well by the nurses and the doctors."

I look down. "People hate us, don't they?" I mutter in a small voice. "That's why they burned that old man. . . ."

Dad puts the squishy ball down. He looks into my eyes, his face serious. "No," he says. "They don't hate you. It's complicated," he explains.

I frown.

Dad sighs and says, "The Hong Kong people just want more autonomy."

"What's autonomy?" I ask.

Dad thinks for a minute. "They want to be able to decide their own matters," he says finally.

That sounds good. I smile and say, "I want more autonomy in my life too!"

"I'm sure you do," Dad chuckles. His voice trails off. He adds gently, "Actually, if you go and live in America . . ."

Here we go again. The thought of going to America and leaving my dad puts a pain in my chest so sharp, I worry I've caught the virus.

"I don't want to talk about it," I say to Dad.

"It wouldn't be forever, only for a little while. Until the virus is over. Then you can come back."

"But what if you get sick?"

I take a pillow and hold it up to my face to block my eyes. I don't want Dad to see me cry. I want him to see I'm just as strong as Bowen—which I *am*.

Dad takes my pillow and pulls it down gently. "I won't get sick," he promises. He lifts his arm and flexes his muscle. "Power of attorney!"

I laugh. Dad's a lawyer, so he loves to say "power of attorney." I don't really know what it means, but I always laugh anyway.

Dad puts a hand on my back. "I appreciate you worrying about me, buddy, but I'm a survivor," he says. "I got through SARS and malaria!"

Dad sure has survived a lot of viruses. Born in San Francisco, he's lived in Europe, Africa, and all over Asia. That's why our parents decided to raise us in Hong Kong: so we can see the world.

Now all I want to see is the clear blue sky again without a mask. And for my family to be safe and sound, together. Doesn't matter where we are.

Chapter 5

---✈

Mom and Dad call a family meeting in the kitchen later that day. Mom's holding the small whiteboard, which she only ever uses when I get a *very* bad grade in school and she tries to reteach me everything I was supposed to learn but can't remember because I was too busy bouncing in my seat.

"A homemade bomb just went off in the public hospital," Mom says. "We have to leave. Now."

The spoon drops from my sister Lea's hand and yogurt pools on the floor.

"Now?"

"We can't risk staying here any longer. If the virus spreads and we can't even go to the hospital . . ." Mom's voice trails off.

"What about school?" Lea asks. "I gotta say goodbye to my friends!"

"You'll do online school when we get there," Mom points out. "You'll still be able to see your friends."

"Forget about friends. What about Dad??" I ask.

Lea immediately grabs Dad's leg and wails, "Daddy . . ." The tears pool in her eyes.

"I'll be fine here. So long as I know you're all safe, I'll be okay," Dad insists.

"In America, at least we'll get treated," Mom adds. "No

one will mind us speaking Mandarin in the hospitals."

"We don't *have* to speak Mandarin!" I remind Mom. "We can stay and hide it!"

Mom looks away, her face full of hurt.

"I don't *want* you to have to hide who you are," she says. "That's not why we moved to Asia and raised you here."

Dad squeezes Mom's hand.

As Mom struggles to regain her composure, Dad turns to us. "Hey, I know it's not ideal to be separated. But it's an emergency. And sometimes, in emergencies, we have to do what's best for the family."

Yeah, the family. The *whole* family.

"We'll be back in time for my birthday, though, right?" Lea asks.

I can't believe Lea's still thinking about that. Her big seventh birthday is not until April 26. She's already planning a massive sleepover with all her friends.

"Hopefully, the virus will be over by then," Dad says.

I can tell by his heavy eyes how badly he wants it to be so. I want to tell Dad if it's not over by then, I'm coming back anyway. I'll hitchhike to the airport and sneak into someone's luggage flying United. Mom won't even notice. She'll be too busy bragging about all the As Bowen got in online school.

"You have to come over if it's not gone by then," Lea tells Dad.

I nod in agreement. "You can't let Mom do this all by herself! She's going to get stuck on a conference call and forget to feed us!"

"I will not!" Mom protests.

Lea turns back to Mom. "Remember the time you took

us to Thailand and you almost lost Knox at the water park?" she asks.

"Or the time you *burned* Lea's jacket in Japan because you stood too close to the heater?" Bowen continues.

Mom puts her hands up. "Okay," she says in Mandarin. "Enough. I get it."

"I promise I'll come over the first chance I get," Dad says.

I look to my siblings. Hesitantly, we each extend a hand and shake on it with Dad.

"Deal," we say as Mom holds up her phone to show us the e-tickets.

We lean in and stare at our names: Knox Wei-Evans, Bowen Wei-Evans, Lea Wei-Evans.

It's really happening. We're leaving tomorrow. I catch Dad's moist eyes as he hugs us around the kitchen island.

Chapter 6

--✈

That night, Mom goes into full commander mode, scribbling on the glass kitchen wall with her marker as she walks us through our trip to America. It's a trip we've done a thousand times before, but this time, everything feels different. The tickets Mom bought are one-way.

I look up at Mom's words on the wall.

AT THE AIRPORT:
-FACE MASK
-DON'T TOUCH ANYTHING!!!
-DON'T TOUCH FACE.
-HAND SANITIZE AFTER YOU TOUCH ANYTHING!
ON THE AIRPLANE:
-FACE MASK AT ALL TIMES EXCEPT WHEN
    EATING YOUR MEAL.
-DO NOT GO #2 ON THE PLANE—REMEMBER,
    IT CAN SPREAD THROUGH POOP!
-DO NOT TALK TO ANYONE.
-DO NOT TOUCH ANYTHING ON THE PLANE
    THAT HASN'T BEEN WIPED BY MOM WITH
    ALCOHOL WIPES.
-AFTER YOU GO TO THE BATHROOM, YOU HAVE
    TO SANITIZE YOUR HANDS WHEN YOU GET

BACK TO YOUR SEAT. I DON'T CARE IF
YOU'VE ALREADY WASHED YOUR HANDS.
IMMIGRATION AND CUSTOMS:
-WE SAY WE ARE AMERICANS AND WE ARE
COMING HOME.

I scribble down Mom's words into a notebook, like Lily taught me at school. Bowen points to the last line and asks, "Is that true? Are we *moving* there?"

"I don't know," Mom says, looking at Dad. They stare at each other, their eyes having a long conversation we can't hear.

"The important thing is when they ask if you've been to China in the last fourteen days, you say no," Dad tells us.

"And if they ask if you've talked to anyone from mainland China or interacted with anyone Chinese, you also say no," Mom adds.

"But Mommy, you're Chinese," my sister points out.

Mom scoops Lea up in her arms. "Oh my bao bao," she says, calling my sister the Chinese affectionate term for "sweetie." "I know I am. But I'm also American. And the people at Immigration and Customs are very afraid of Chinese people right now."

Well, I'm not afraid of you, I want to tell my mom. No matter what she is, I'll always love her. I don't care what anybody says.

Instead, I walk over and point to the part about not pooping on the plane and tell her not to worry.

"I never go number two on the plane," I assure Mom.

The next few hours fly by. Mom tears the apartment apart, searching through all the things we can possibly need for the next six months—that's how long my parents now say the virus could last.

It's weird packing for minimum six months, maximum forever.

I feel very sad to be leaving my home. I walk around the apartment, waving from the window at the busy streets, always bustling with people. I'll miss the scaffolders, who climb up and down the outsides of buildings putting up bamboo scaffolding so fast, I call them Spider-Men. I'll even miss the taxis honking. It's always so quiet in America. Too quiet.

Mom says it's because everyone's always in their houses. I guess that's true. I just hope they have time to come out once in a while and make a new friend. I know I'll be ready. I'll be playing soccer or pulling out the weeds with Grandma Francine's gardening tools. I've never met her—she passed away when I was still in Mom's belly. Dad said she was a single mother who worked at city hall as an assistant planning director.

I wonder if she'd like me. With old people it's hit or miss. Some love me, like the ladies who dance at the park in Hong Kong for exercise. I always join them when I can, to Bowen's great annoyance. Others think I'm too loud and crazy, like our downstairs neighbor, who shouts "Aiya!" at me and slams his window.

That's one guy I'm *not* gonna miss. As we drag suitcases across our rooms, cranky Mr. Lo whacks his ceiling with a hard object—probably a broomstick—protesting our loud packing. Lea and I roll our eyes.

"We're outta here tomorrow!" Lea shouts, stomping the floor. "You won't have to deal with us ever again!"

My eyes flash wide. *Ever again?!* Lea puts her hand over her mouth like, *Oops.* But it's too late. It's already said.

Later, Bowen comes into my room. I'm packing my soccer ball in my suitcase, trying to find space for my soccer shoes next to my favorite rocket. Bowen walks across the room, reaches inside, and throws my ball out.

"What are you doing?!" I cry. It lands on my computer keyboard with a thud.

"It's inflated, fool," he yells back. He takes the ball and sticks a needle in the valve.

As Bowen deflates my ball, I sit down in the middle of my suitcase. I wish I could pack myself inside and Dad could take my ticket. Then we could all go.

"Quit sitting in there. You're gonna break it," Bowen says.

I cross my arms, wondering, *Is this what it's gonna be like for the next six months?* Bowen bossing me around??

Just to annoy Bowen, I lie down on the suitcase—all the way back—until I hear a crack sound. Uh-oh.

"Nice," Bowen laughs.

I jump up and stare at the crack in the plastic cover. "I'll just put some tape on it," I say, getting some Scotch tape from my desk. "Mom won't even notice."

"Well, I'm going to tell her," Bowen says, walking out of my room.

"Stop!" I cry out. Frantically, I try to level with him. I remind my brother it's just us now and when we get to America, we're gonna have to share a room together. Cautiously I hold out a hand. "Truce?"

Bowen doesn't take my hand. Instead, he grabs at his hair,

suddenly remembering our house in California only has three bedrooms. "We have to share a room! *Ugh!!!*" He immediately starts angling to get a room all to himself. "Can't you share with Lea? How about this—I'll move the bunk into her room."

"Nope, not happening," I tell Bowen.

"Why not?"

"Because Lea has more stuffed animals than an airport gift shop. It takes her forty-five minutes to say good night to them! Every night!" I say.

"So?"

"So I need my ten hours so I can rest up and be a soccer star."

"Yeah right—like that's gonna happen," Bowen says, putting my deflated soccer ball over his head like a hat.

I fume, getting shaking mad, or what Lily calls my "volcano mad." I can feel the lava bubbling inside. "It'll happen before you get your own room!"

"Fine," Bowen says. "But if you rustle in the middle of the night, I'm going to take your blanket and move it to the garage."

I frown at my new roommate.

My dog, Cody, walks in and puts his head in my lap, as if to try to break up the fight. And we both put our hands around Cody's furry face.

"We'll be back, Co-Co," Bowen says. "And we'll bring you lots of treats. Real big ones! American dog treats!"

"Are they really bigger there?" I ask.

"Everything's bigger and better in America!" Bowen replies.

I smile as I look into Cody's eyes. Dad got me Cody when

I couldn't make any friends at my old primary school. It was one of the fancy ones in Hong Kong with a waiting list, and kids who went there all had their own nannies. I could tell by the third day, it wasn't the school for me.

Still, it took a whole year of forms and interviews and tests for my parents to finally find me a spot in a new school. Cody and I, we've been through some lonely times together.

I wish I could take Cody with me. But I know Dad needs him more—he'll be all Dad has once we leave. I tell myself I won't be lonely in America. I'll have my siblings.

Still, I know from experience, just because you have a lot of people around you doesn't make you less lonely. It just makes your loneliness more squished.

Chapter 7

O n the day of the flight, things are very eerie. Mom reminds
Dad every eighteen seconds as she runs from room to
room, gathering all our carry-ons, to please hand sanitize, even though we're the ones going on the dangerous journey. Dad says he will and reminds my mom of the things about
each one of us that my mom, being on the road all the time,
doesn't know.

"Lea will only eat cucumbers with the skin peeled off,"
Dad says, helping Mom drag Lea's suitcase to the living room.

"Got it," Mom says, tapping a reminder into her Notes
app.

"Knox needs to put on lotion every day or his eczema
starts flaring up. I've packed some in his suitcase."

At the mention of my eczema, I immediately start scratching. I'll bet Mom will forget. I'll bet I'll look like a red lobster
by the time I get back. I better remember myself, and I make
a note of it in my brain, hoping it's more reliable than Mom's
app.

"Lotion every day, on it," Mom says, tapping with her fingers.

"*Special* lotion," I add. "It can't have any fragrance in it, or
I'll itch!"

"I *know*. I look at the credit card receipts." Mom gives me a look. I back off. "Speaking of credit cards, I set ours up so it auto-pays from our joint account," she says to Dad.

"Great!" Dad says. "I should be getting my bonus soon. That is . . . if they're still giving it to us."

"Relax, this virus won't affect bonuses or salaries," Mom says.

When the last of the suitcases have been zipped up, we carry our luggage—plus Bowen's skis—to the car. I can't believe Bowen brought his skis. What does he think this is—a trip to Tahoe? Dad insists on driving us to the Airport Express, the direct train from the city to the airport. Somehow, we manage to squeeze all our stuff into our minivan. Cody whimpers when he sees the three of us kids pile into the car. My heart breaks hearing my labradoodle crying. Dad's does too, because he lets out a sigh and opens the back door for Cody.

"All right, Cody, you can go with us, but *just* to the train station," Dad relents.

Cody jumps inside and gives my face a huge lick. I'm going to miss him so much.

Dad turns to Mom. "You sure you want to do this?" His soft blue eyes pierce into Mom's deep brown ones.

"It's the safest option for the kids, Andrew . . . ," Mom says, wrapping her arms around him.

Dad swallows hard, then nods. "You're right."

My parents get in the front and Dad starts the car.

When we arrive at the Airport Express check-in counters, they're completely empty. Even Cody thinks it's weird. He runs up and down the hall. I've never seen the Airport Express so deserted. I look up at the big board, at all the flights cancelled or postponed due to the virus.

Mom walks up to the United counter and is relieved to hear our flight's still happening. She presents them our tickets and passports. Bowen asks to borrow a pen from the woman at the United counter for the luggage tags. "Sorry," the woman says. "I can't lend out my pen due to health and safety reasons. You have to use your own pen."

That's when it *really* hits me, how serious the virus is.

"Here, Bowen, use this," Mom says, digging a pen out from her purse.

As Bowen scribbles our address and number, I run around the Airport Express doing helicopter arms, like I always do, except this time I get no funny looks because the hall is too empty. Cody chases after me. We both stop in front of the Airport Express bakery and take in the scent of freshly baked egg tarts. Cody wags his tail. I bend down and our tummies rumble together. And for a second I am overcome with an intense desire to run in and grab them all and stuff them in my mouth, because I don't know when I'll ever eat traditional Hong Kong egg tarts again.

Dad walks over and asks me what's wrong. I tell him my fear of never eating egg tarts again. Every Sunday, my dad used to take us to city hall, where we would order little plates of dim sum off carts rolling by. Bowen would get the barbecue pork buns, Lea would get the spring rolls, and I would get the *har gao*—shrimp dumplings—and egg tarts for dessert. It was the one time each week my brother and I did not argue.

"They have dim sum in San Francisco," Dad assures me.

True. But there's something they don't have in San Francisco. As Dad puts each of our tagged suitcases onto the scale, I fight the tears welling up in my eyes.

When the last of our bags have been checked in and all the boarding passes issued, Dad walks us to the train that will take us to our gate. It's time for our goodbyes.

"I can't believe my family's leaving me!" Dad says, wiping his eyes. "What am I going to do with myself?"

"You can play with Cody!" my sister suggests.

Dad laughs. "I'll tickle him every night and pretend it's you."

"But don't give him *all* the tickles. Save some for me," Lea says.

"Don't worry, mochi. I will save all my best tickles for you," Dad promises, leaning in for a kiss.

"We'll call you as soon as we land," Mom says.

"How are you getting to the house?" Dad asks.

"Uber," Mom replies. "Don't worry, I've got this."

"I know you do," Dad says, kissing Mom on her cheek, over her mask. "Thanks again for doing this. I love you."

Mom's eyes glisten as she whispers from behind her mask, "Love you, too. Take care of yourself."

Next it's my turn. There's so much I want to say to Dad—like that the combination on my lockbox in my room is 1-4-6. Dad can look inside but he cannot under any circumstances show any of the contents to Bowen if they FaceTime. Oh, and to water my basil plant every day. (My old friend Amir got it for me, and it's the only thing from him that I have left.) And not to forget to keep practicing *stay* with Cody.

In the end, all I can manage is, "Don't die."

"I won't," Dad promises. He kneels down and opens his arms, and I run into them. Cody jumps on both of us, trying to get into the group hug. Dad whispers into my ear, "I'm going to miss you the most, buddy." And I try my best not to cry, because I'm wearing one of Mom's precious twenty-seven masks and I don't want to get it wet.

"Be good," he says when we pull apart. I nod, a stone lodged in my throat.

Finally, he stands up and turns to Bowen. At five feet ten, Bowen is extra tall for a twelve-year-old. He's almost as tall as Dad now. In spite of his best efforts to hide his feelings, I can see Bowen's mask trembling slightly.

"You're the man of the family now," Dad tells Bowen. "Take good care of your mom and your siblings, you hear?"

Bowen nods and tells Dad he will. I gaze at Bowen's eyes. He looks earnest while he says it. And I want to believe he's gonna be different in America. I *really*, really do, even though part of me thinks he won't.

We hug one last time as a family, as Mom reminds us, "Don't cry! Don't cry! Don't cry! You'll waste a mask!" even as the tears stream down her own face.

Cody whimpers so bad I have to bite the inside of my cheeks to keep from bawling.

The train comes and the Airport Express speaker announces that we have four minutes to get on.

"Bye, Dad," I say one last time. "I love you."

"I love you, too, buddy," he says, waving at me and holding Cody still as I follow my siblings and Mom to the train. "Stay strong."

I turn around and flex my right arm. "Power of attorney!"

31

Chapter 8

---✈

On the airplane, everyone is wearing masks. Even babies are wearing masks. Walking down the aisle, I see all shapes and sizes and colors—pink masks, blue masks, even ski masks. The people sitting in the row behind us, they're wearing *gas masks*. The kind with eye goggles and a giant ventilator for toxic gas, that goes *VUUUM* when you breathe. You'd think we were fleeing from a nuclear war. Mom takes a pic and sends it to Dad.

A second later, Dad texts back, That's wild! Ask them if they know Darth Vader!

Mom shows Dad's text to me and I smile. It feels like Dad's here.

I pretend that Dad just went to the bathroom and he'll be back in his seat in a minute. Which lasts all of two seconds as reality comes crashing down next to me and Bowen's butt lands where Dad's supposed to sit.

"You better not kick the person-in-front's seat, or I'm going to pretend I don't know you!" Bowen says.

I knew his promise to be nice would last only five seconds.

"I already pretend I don't know you," I inform him. "I've been pretending since I was five."

Mom scolds us, "Knock it off, both of you! Let's get there *peacefully* before we start killing each other—can we do that??"

Bowen mutters, "Whatever."

Behind us, an old man is gleefully talking on his phone as he takes his seat. "You won't believe how hard it was to get a flight out! I got one of the very *last* tickets! I'm the luckiest man alive!"

He makes it sound like we just boarded a lifeboat off the *Titanic*. Is this what this is . . . a lifeboat taking us to America?

As the plane takes off, I gaze outside, putting my hand onto the window.

Bye, Dad. I hope you get on a lifeboat too.

Mom doesn't eat anything on the flight, so Bowen devours her sandwich and his own while Lea and I watch movies. If I look straight ahead, I can almost pretend it's a normal flight. It's only when I turn around and see the rows and rows of people wearing masks that I remember this isn't normal.

Every time any of us goes to the bathroom, Mom's waiting with hand sanitizer when we get back. By the end of the flight, my hands are completely cracked.

Finally, twelve stressful hours later, we touch down at San Francisco International Airport.

There's a triumphant cheer when we land. "We made it!" people call out. Neighbors turn to each other and shake hands, then remember we're not supposed to shake hands. Some habits are hard to break. We squirt hand sanitizer like crazy.

Bowen, Lea, Mom, and I are all smiles as we walk out. Bowen takes off his mask when he steps into the terminal, and Mom immediately orders him to put it back on.

"Why??" Bowen asks. "We're safe now!"

"No, we're not!" Mom says. "We still have to get *into* the country."

Bowen shakes his head. "Well, I'm not doing it."

He tosses his mask into the trash and continues to walk through SFO without a mask. I look to my mom, confused. Should I take mine off too? Mom shoots me a look, like *don't you dare.*

She catches up with Bowen and yells at him for wasting a mask when we brought so few with us. We left most of Auntie Jackie's masks in Hong Kong for Dad. "Put it on now!" Mom says, thrusting a new mask at Bowen.

It's strange hearing Mom use the tone that she only ever uses on me when she's gotten a *Knox is about to fail!* call from my teacher. Bowen sighs but says, *"Fiiiine."*

At immigration, we file into the US citizens line. Mom gets out all our US passports. Most of the people in line, like us, are still wearing masks. Mom tells us she's going to be the one doing all the talking when we get up there and that we shouldn't say anything.

"By 'we,' she means you, Knot," Bowen says.

I glare at Bowen and nod to Mom.

The line drags on and on, barely moving. I notice the immigration officers ask many more questions to the Chinese people than the white people, even though it's the US citizens line and we're all US citizens. I overhear one officer asking an elderly Chinese man to name all the times he's been to China.

I start panicking. If they ask me that, what do I say? I think of all the birthdays, spring break trips, long walks on the Great Wall, and Chinese New Years when my relatives showered me with *lai sees*—there are too many to count. And if I tell them about all that, does that make me less American? Will they still let me in?

The anxiety builds and builds inside me until I am wiggling and squirming and itching, about to pee in my pants.

"Next!" the immigration officer calls.

My mom steps forward, with Bowen, me, and Lea. I stand at the counter, trying to hold in my pee, staring down at my cracked hands. *Don't say anything!*

Mom presents our passports and puts on her chatty, cheery voice. "Hi! How are you doing this morning?"

The officer runs our passports through her computer and says, "Where are you coming from?"

"Hong Kong," Mom tells her.

I glance over at the counter next to us, for visitors, and see a woman getting turned away. *"Please,"* the woman begs the officer. "I need to see my daughter. She lives in California."

Our immigration officer turns to my mom and asks, "Have you been to mainland China?"

Of course! Who hasn't? I want to say. *No, don't blurt* that *out!* There's a fistfight going on in my head.

I grip the counter harder and try to think of Lily, my therapist at school. What would Lily say? She would tell me to imagine the future. What does my future look like if I blurt these words out? I close my eyes and imagine a total apocalypse with corpses everywhere. My dying family coughing up a lung as they gag, "It's all because of you, Knox. You just *had* to blurt it out."

Mom shakes her head and assures the officer, "Not recently. Right, kids?" She looks at Bowen, who nods on cue.

The immigration officer perks up, pleased with our

answer. She instructs each of us to look into the camera.

Is that it? Did we pass? I hold my breath as the officer punches in a few keys on her computer. I glance at the woman at the next counter, getting escorted away from the airport exit. My jaw drops: she's getting kicked off the lifeboat, and I'm overcome with guilt. My eyes fall on a squishy gel apple our immigration officer has next to her computer. I make myself stare at it and not at the woman. It's the kind I have at school to help me focus. I really want to touch it, but it would probably not be okay with Mom. Or with the officer.

Just as I'm about to turn purple from holding my breath, the officer hands us back our passports. "You're all set. Welcome home."

Mom nearly bursts into tears. Blinking her eyes rapidly, she replies, "Thank you. It's good to be back."

Chapter 9

--✈

Bowen rips the mask from his face when we get outside and screams at the clear blue sky, "Oh America, how I've missed you!!!" Mom laughs, scooping Lea up into her arms and then holding out her free hand to grab mine.

I reach up and take my mask off too. For weeks, I've been breathing in the vinegary smell of the triple-layered face mask. It almost feels weird to breathe fresh air again. I take in a long, deep breath. *Ahhhhhhhh.* I wish Dad could smell this.

Bowen pushes the cart to our waiting Uber and helps the driver with our luggage. Bowen always helps Mom with the luggage, anytime we travel. I guess he's not 100 percent useless.

When the last of the luggage has been loaded, we get into the minivan. Mom tells us to put our masks back on, out of respect for the driver.

"So where are you guys coming from?" the driver asks as he turns onto the freeway. The driver is not wearing a mask, and I stare and stare at his smile, taking it in. Since all the mask wearing in Hong Kong began, I've almost forgotten people can smile. I activate my own smile too.

"Hong Kong," my mom tells him.

The driver's smile disappears. He starts scooting in his seat, inching away from Mom. Bowen notices it too.

"We don't have it or anything," Mom tells him from under her mask. "There are very few cases in Hong Kong—only about nine."

"That's still nine too many," the Uber driver says.

"If you want, we can get out and take a taxi," Mom says. "If that'll make you feel more comfortable."

"We're already on the freeway," the Uber driver replies with a frown. I settle back into my seat, thinking that's the end of it.

But the man drives us a bit farther and changes his mind. "Actually, yeah, if you wouldn't mind."

The driver takes a sharp turn off the highway, pulls into a random Walgreens parking lot, and drops us off in the middle of some town we don't know with all our luggage. Before our heads can even stop spinning, he speeds off.

Great.

Chapter 10

---✈

It takes us two buses and three BART trains to get to our East Bay house. On the BART ride passing through downtown San Francisco, every seat was taken except for the seats next to us. It was like we had our own little bubble everywhere we went. A bubble of fear thanks to the virus. And whenever I got up—to look at the map, not even to do helicopter arms!—everyone darted in the other direction.

At least we got seats. And they didn't kick us off. By the time we finally make it to our yellow house, we are about ready to collapse.

Thankfully, my grandmother's sunny house greets us without any judgment or fear when we walk inside.

"Good old house!" I beam.

Lea runs up to her room to sort out her stuffed animals.

I take my suitcase and lug it into my room with Bowen. I gaze at our bunk bed. When we were little, we'd always rock-paper-scissors it to see who got the top bunk. But now that Bowen's bigger, he doesn't seem to care about it as much. Which makes me happy, but also makes me sad. I take the top bunk.

When all the luggage has been moved inside, I go down to the kitchen and ask Mom, "Where should we go? In-N-Out? The taco place? Knox Beach?"

Mom takes off her mask and chews her lip, hesitating. "Should we be going out?"

"Oh, *c'mon!*" Bowen erupts, throwing his arms up.

I'm with my brother on this one. Mom can't possibly be thinking of quarantining us here in the US, too!

"Just in case . . . ," she says. "We've been on a plane. They say the quarantine period is fourteen days. Maybe we should stay home, to be safe. . . ."

"For fourteen days??" Bowen asks, reaching into the cupboard and pouring himself some water with Mom's UC Berkeley glass. "No, that's not happening."

Was it the Uber driver? Did he spook Mom? I put my hand on my belly. "I'm starved . . . *please* . . . can we go to the taco place??" I ask Mom.

"I'll order some stuff on Uber Eats!" Mom offers. "We wouldn't want to expose anyone."

"To what? Our stomach pangs?" Bowen asks.

But Mom's already got her phone out. Bowen, Lea, and I let out a collective groan as she places the order. We stomp upstairs. It seems especially cruel to have to stay indoors in America, when there's so much to do here! Target, mini golf, Jamba Juice. Don't even get me started on Best Buy . . . they have *every* type of video game Mom refuses to let me get!

"At least there's the backyard!" Lea points out.

True. I glance out the window at our small backyard. It's overgrown with weeds, but at least I could still kick around a soccer ball. I smile a little.

"*And* we don't have to be afraid of the virus here," Bowen says.

Yeah. Except everyone's afraid of us.

Chapter 11

--✈

Bowen selfishly hogs the only dresser in our room, leaving no space for me. I don't know why he brought five thousand T-shirts with him, especially since we can't go anywhere.

"Where am *I* going to put my stuff?" I ask.

"Just keep it in your suitcase," he replies.

I go and find Mom. She's in the kitchen, trying to get the smoke alarm, which needs new batteries, to stop beeping. Whenever we come back to America, it's like this. *Beep, beep, beep.*

"Bowen won't share the dresser," I tell Mom.

"There's not enough space?" she asks, getting down from the chair. "Should I order another one from IKEA?" She starts tapping on her phone.

I shake my head. She doesn't get it. It's not about a *new* dresser. If a new dresser arrives, Bowen'll just find more stuff to put in it and claim it as his too.

"Why do I have to share a room with Bowen?" I ask Mom. "Can't I sleep in the living room? Our room is way too small for the both of us."

Mom looks up from the IKEA website. "Hey," she says gently. "You're starting to sound a little . . . privileged."

I look down, feeling the guilt pool up inside me. I know we're lucky to be able to have this house at all, even if it is small and beeps, but I really miss our home. And the guy who's still there.

"It'll be fun being roommates," Mom says. "You just have to get used to it."

I turn and walk back upstairs, not at all convinced. I reach for the phone to call Dad, but then remember it's his middle of the night. I take out my laptop and email him instead.

Dad, tell Bowen not to hog the dresser. I have stuff too. Can I have my own room? Knox. P.S. Don't get the virus!!!!!!!

I press send.

Dad emails back and says I can't have my own room, but he'll try to talk to Bowen. And if that doesn't work, he'll get me a dresser. I stare at the email, at the line *And if that doesn't work.* I can't believe it. We've been here less than twenty-four hours and both my parents have given up on controlling my brother. Pretty soon I'm going to have to sleep in the backyard.

For the next couple of days, while Bowen screams at me whenever I put a sock in "his" dresser—I am counting the days until my new dresser arrives—Mom sets up all our online learning stations so we can continue going to our schools in Hong Kong from here. Bowen's working from our room and Lea from hers. And I get stuck downstairs in the corner of the living room, with Mom.

"Why do I have to do my work downstairs?" I ask Mom.

"So I can keep an eye on you!" she says.

I frown. *Great,* now I can't even go on Fortnite during "school."

"Please. Let me work upstairs," I tell Mom. "I won't distract Bowen, I promise."

"No way, Mom, you know how he is!" Bowen protests from upstairs, poking his head out of our room. "And I've got to concentrate—I've got some really important projects!"

He's *definitely* going on Fortnite.

Mom insists the living room's going to be great and sets up my new desk by the window. While she's at it, she orders an extension cord for my computer charger, replacement smoke alarms, and new lightbulbs for my desk lamp, plus groceries and four big bottles of hand sanitizer. She *tries* to order face masks too, but they're all out.

"I don't get it. We're in the US already," I say to Mom.

"You can never be too prepared," she says.

I look down at the total on the receipt—382 *US* dollars! Good thing she still has her job in Hong Kong, though I don't know how she'll keep doing it from America. She's gonna have to stay up *real* late.

Speaking of the time difference, I ask Mom, "How can we go to online school if we're fifteen hours behind?"

"Don't worry, I emailed the school before we came. They said as long as you finish all the assignments, you're fine. You don't have to be on the Zooms. . . ."

"What's a Zoom?" Lea asks.

"It's this thing where adults sit around in their underwear and mute each other," I tell her.

My sister starts giggling uncontrollably, even as Mom insists that's not what it is.

"That sounds GREAT!" Lea exclaims.

Chapter 12

---✈

I t turns out online school is not great at all. On the first Monday of February, we officially start. Our school emails us our schedule—every minute of our day is planned out for us, but it's so hard to stay focused. According to my teacher's schedule, I'm supposed to be working on mental math from 10:15 to 10:20, but I'm busy eating blueberries.

I try and multiply by two in my head while I'm eating.

Two blueberries, four blueberries.

I finally give up at fifty-six blueberries and swivel in my chair. Mom glances at me every time I swivel.

"Are you working?" she asks, looking up from her own laptop.

I roll my eyes. This would be so much easier if she weren't here. "Yes!"

She doesn't believe me and walks over to check on my work. She sees a picture of Bowen on my computer—I'm right in the middle of coloring his hair blue—before I can click away.

"C'mon, Knox, you're supposed to take this seriously!" Mom frowns.

"I'm sorry!" I exclaim. "It's just . . . it's so hard!" I point to my screen at one of my teacher's *many* assignments. "It says here, write a haiku! I don't know what a haiku is. . . ."

Just as I'm saying this, Lea calls out from the top of the staircase in a small voice. "Mommy? Can you help me? What's 'buoyancy'?"

Mom looks at me, then up at Lea, and sighs. Finally, she gets up to head upstairs to help my sister but calls to me, "Continue coloring Bowen's hair. I'll be right back."

By the time Mom's back, I've given Bowen a spiky, multi-colored Mohawk. He looks kind of like a sea urchin. I send the pic to Bowen, who emails back five minutes later.

WHAT'S WRONG WITH YOU???!☹

Maybe it wasn't such a good idea to email it to him.

"Okay, so where were we? Haikus?" Mom says, sitting down on the couch. I can tell she's tired of bouncing from room to room being teacher.

Mom's phone dings. Distracted, she tries to explain what a haiku is while replying to an urgent text message from her colleague. Her explanation is long and jumbled and makes even less sense than my teacher's instructions.

As Mom gets up to make a call, I turn back to my computer and type:

I want to learn,
From a human, not a box.
Because a human cares,
And a box stares.

I press submit and jump up from my desk. Recess time!!!

Chapter 13

By the fourth day of virtual school, my eyes are melting from staring at the screen all day. It makes me anxious turning in assignments, having no idea if I'm even on the right track. With the time difference, there's no way to ask my teacher any questions in real time, or to even talk to Lily. I always have to wait.

I hate waiting. Maybe if I was in Hong Kong on Zoom, it wouldn't be so bad. But being fifteen hours behind, it makes me feel like day-old bread.

"I don't think I'm cut out for this," I tell Mom. "I'm barely cut out for regular school. . . ."

Mom places her phone down, comes over, and puts her warm palms around my cold, sad chin. The first sign of Summer Mom since we got here. "Awww, sweetie, of course you are," she says. "I know it's frustrating. I totally get it. This is hard for everyone, believe me."

I gaze up the staircase. Not for my siblings. They've been asking for Mom's help less and less. It embarrasses me that even my little sister is getting it and I'm not. I don't know how she can sit so quietly at her desk for so long. I have to jump up from my desk every two seconds to keep my butt cheeks from going numb.

"Hey, why don't we take a break?" Mom suggests. "Help me look for something in the garage?"

I nod eagerly. Finally, Mom and I get to do something fun together! I follow my mom over to the garage. It's cold and dusty in there. Moldy brown boxes line the sides of the garage. Mom tells me most of the boxes are full of Grandma Francine's old stuff, and to be real careful.

"What are we looking for?" I ask.

"Old masks, left over from SARS. . . . There might be a box or two still here," Mom says. "We can send them to Dad. He's gonna need more soon. . . ."

I help Mom search through the boxes in the garage. We don't find any masks, but we do find a box of old black-and-white photos. I sit down on the cold garage floor and start looking through the photos. They're pictures of people I don't recognize, wearing funny-looking hats and clothes.

I look closely at the photos, and that's when I see it. They're all wearing masks!

"Mom! Look!" I exclaim.

I show Mom the photos. She marvels at them. "Wow." She turns one of the photos over. There's a light pencil scratching on the back—*1918*.

"These must have been your great-grandmother's," Mom says, pointing a finger at a woman who appears in several photos.

"But why's she wearing a mask?" I ask.

"Well, because it was the pandemic of 1918," Mom says.

"Oh yeah! There was a Netflix special!" I say. "It wiped out fifty million people!"

Mom chuckles. "It wasn't just a Netflix special," she says, putting the photos back in the box. "It was reality. And it was pretty devastating. . . ."

Mom's serious face scares me a little. I think about Dad back in Hong Kong all alone. . . .

Then Mom puts a hand on my shoulder and says in Mandarin, "Hey. It's okay. This time's different. We've evolved. We learned. And now we take these things very, very seriously. You'll see, this virus is going to be over superfast."

I nod, wanting to believe Mom. Yet wondering, deep down inside, if she *really*, really believes that, why are we in the garage . . . looking for masks?

For dinner, Mom puts a frozen pizza in the oven. I set the table, four places, plus one for Dad. Just because he's not here physically doesn't mean he can't eat with us! That gives me an idea. I reach for my iPad and place it at the head of the table. Every night, when we have dinner, we can Skype with Dad!

Except the Wi-Fi downstairs is pretty weak. Mom starts pacing the kitchen with her phone, trying to get a signal. "Shoot, I really need to return this work email!" she says, shaking her phone.

As Mom paces, Lea wrinkles her nose.

"What's that strange smell?" my sister asks.

I sniff the air. It smells like burnt bread.

"The pizza!" I exclaim, jumping up from the table. Mom forgot to set the timer. She immediately jumps into action, putting her phone down and turning off the oven. As she opens the oven door, hot burning steam blasts our faces. When the steam clears, we see our overcooked pizza, turned to charcoal.

"It's not that bad!" Mom insists. "It's just a little well done. Part of the cooking process . . ."

Over burnt pizza and a salad, we Skype with Dad.

"Oh, I tried to find you some more masks in the garage, but I couldn't find any," Mom says, munching on a cucumber. She helps Lea slice the cucumber peel off hers.

"It's all right," Dad says. "I still have some. And after that, I plan on wearing a ski mask."

"A ski mask???" I ask, nearly spitting out my water.

"How many cases do you guys have now?" Bowen asks Dad as Cody walks over on the screen and wags his tail.

"About twenty, but the government's going to start quarantining everyone who's been to the mainland," Dad says.

"We haven't even *been* to the mainland and Mom's quarantining us," I tell him. I take a bite of my pizza. The burnt crust crumbles in my mouth like soot.

"What's wrong?" Mom asks, when I put it down. "It's just like Dad's—mozzarella cheese with pepperoni!"

"It's *so* not like Dad's!" I blurt out. "It tastes like toasted eraser!"

Bowen jumps to Mom's defense. "Like you can do any better! You don't even know how to cook!"

I cross my arms at him. Bowen thinks that just because he learned how to make long life noodles from Lao Lao last Chinese New Year, he's a chef now.

Mom looks at Dad on Skype, embarrassed. She takes the scorched pizza, breaks off all the blackened crusts, and tells me to eat it.

"Don't waste," she says in Chinese.

I gaze down at Mom's offering, pressing my finger down on the bouncy cheese.

"I'm sorry I can't be there to cook for you guys," Dad suggests gently.

"I'm fine. It's *fine*," Mom insists.

There's a long, awkward silence.

"How's online school?" Dad asks, changing the subject.

I groan loudly and make a face.

"That bad, huh?" he asks.

Lea chimes in. "All we do is sit there and do a bunch of assignments. I can't even see my friends!"

"How long do we have to do it for?" Bowen seconds. "Why can't we just read and do some Khan Academy and that's it?"

"Because there's a lot more to going to school than that," Mom says.

"And we're *not* doing any of the other stuff . . . ," Bowen reminds her. I nod. Finally, something we can agree on!

Mom thinks about this for a long while. Then, ever so softly, she says, "Maybe I can call up some of the schools here. See if they can take you . . . ?"

I jerk my head up from picking off the pepperoni from my pizza. *What?*

Before I even have a chance to react, my sister waves her arms in the air and yells, "YAY!"

"Really? I'll get to run in a real track stadium! American high schools are *enormous*!" Bowen says.

"And I can invite all my new friends to my birthday party!" Lea says.

I take in my siblings' enthusiasm. Have they forgotten all about Dad already?

"I thought you guys said this was temporary!" I say.

"Relax," Mom says. "I'll just give them a call. You three can't do distance learning from another country forever. It's unsustainable, especially for you, Knox."

I flush. It's probably true, but I don't want Mom to say it out loud. And I don't want her to do something about it either. Because her solution isn't going to make it better. It's just gonna make me scared-er that I'll be separated from Dad forever.

I get up and bolt for my room.

Chapter 14

--✈

I run up the stairs and lock myself in Mom's closet. As I sit there, squished between her soft sweaters and summer dresses, the questions swirl in my mind. What if I can't stop Mom? What if I don't like my new American school? What if the teachers put me in a corner and scream at me all day long to "sit *still!!!*"?

On the other hand, I wonder if my new American school will have a therapist like Lily at my old school. I do miss talking to her.

Mom knocks on her closet door.

"You okay, bao bao?" Mom asks as she opens the door.

I nod from under the igloo of sweaters. Mom starts peeling her clothes off me. "Tell me what's wrong," she asks. With each sweater she peels off, I mutter a fear.

"What if the other kids at the new school don't like me?" I ask.

"Of course they'll like you," Mom assures me. "You've got a wonderful sense of humor and you're smart. You always make such interesting observations."

I give Mom a funny look. *I do?*

"And you're unstoppable on the field. Any school's soccer team would be lucky to have you."

That's true. I do miss playing on a soccer team.

"Will they have after-school sports?" I ask.

"I'm sure they will . . . ," she says. "I'll see if I can sign you up."

"But if I go to school here, it'll mean I'm here permanently. And I don't want to be away from Dad permanently," I confess to Mom, the tears collecting in my eyes.

Mom pulls me into her arms when she hears that.

"Oh, sweetheart," she says, kissing my head. "Me neither. But it doesn't mean that. All it means is you're going to give things here a chance . . . like school. And it'll be amazing, I promise you."

That's easy for her to say—she was top of her class at Berkeley. She has the glass downstairs to prove it.

Mom reaches for my hand. "Hey, I only suggested it because you said online school isn't working for you. But if you don't want to do it . . ."

Her voice trails off. And I sink back into the fort of sweaters, thinking back to my haiku. It *would* be nice learning from a human again, instead of a box.

"No . . . ," I say, mustering up the courage.

Mom smiles. "I know you're scared, but we can't refuse to do things just because we're scared."

"Says the woman who won't let us outside," I mutter.

Mom laughs and throws a fuzzy scarf around my neck. I lean against the soft scarf and smile.

That night, I can't sleep. Jet lag always hits me the hardest. It doesn't help that Bowen's snoring like his own BART station beneath me.

I climb down from my bunk and walk out of our room.

53

Mom's on a work call. I sit down on the staircase and listen.

"We talked about this, remember? I'm in California with my kids," Mom says into the phone. "Tell the client he's just going to have to wait. How am I even supposed to get to Shanghai? All the flights have been cancelled."

My stomach knots in a panic. *Oh no. Is Mom leaving?* We just got here! It's only been a week and a half!

"I know I can go through Japan, but it's a matter of getting back," Mom says. "I have a responsibility to my family right now."

There's a long pause. I wonder if that's why Mom's been so stressed out.

"Alex, you know it's not like that. I'm *committed* to my job, but these are extraordinary circumstances. I wouldn't be here if I had any other choice. Please, Alex, you have to understand!"

Mom bites her lip, waiting, and I bite mine, too. I wish her boss, Alex, would give her a break—I've barely seen Summer Mom since we got here! But what if he doesn't? Does that mean we have to go back? I think of the lady at immigration who boarded a lifeboat and came all the way to shore, only to have to turn around.

Her boss mutters something on the other end that makes Mom close her eyes and push her lids with her fingertips. Is she . . . crying?

"I understand."

As she hangs up with her boss, Mom sinks back onto the couch. The look on her face is so sad that I whisper, "Hi, Mommy," from the top of the stairs.

Mom looks up at me, surprised.

"Is everything okay?" I ask her.

Mom wipes her tears and puts on a brave smile. "Yes, sweetie," she assures me. I walk down the stairs and sit next to her. She lets out a long, heavy sigh, and I wish I hadn't made fun of her pizza. It wasn't *that* bad.

"Thanks for making dinner," I say to her. "It didn't taste like a toasted eraser. It tasted . . ." I think for a second. "Like a toasted nut."

Mom ruffles my hair and manages a chuckle.

"Thanks, bao bao," she says, putting a throw blanket over me. "I can live with that."

"I can live with it too."

I smile and snuggle up to Mom. Whatever happened on the call, I'm glad I got a laugh out of her. Things might not be perfect here, but Mom's trying. Hard. Maybe I can try hard too.

Chapter 15

--- ✈

Self-imposed quarantine finally ends on our fourteenth day in America with me jumping out of bed. My soccer medals—which Bowen still won't let me put on top of "his" dresser—jingle like wind chimes on the wall next to my bunk.

"No more quarantine! We're finally free!" I run to Mom's room. "Plus it's Monday morning, which is like the middle of the night in Hong Kong! *Please* tell me you'll take us out today—somewhere, anywhere, I don't even care!"

My happiness is interrupted by the TV in Mom's bedroom, declaring that the virus has officially surpassed the death toll for the SARS epidemic in China. "In Hong Kong, the first death from coronavirus was reported last week. There are now over forty cases in the city."

"*Forty* cases?? How did it get that bad?" I ask, shocked.

Mom's on the phone with Dad. "I'll have to call you back," she says.

"Is that Dad?" I ask. Before Mom can answer, I grab the phone.

"Dude, you have to come here! Forty cases?! You're gonna get it if you stay!" I tell him. "Please, Dad, you must!"

"I wish I could, but I have to stay here for my job," Dad says.

I will myself to calm down, but I can't. I keep thinking about Dad all alone in our apartment, with no one to even help him if he gets sick—Cody can't pick up the phone and call 9-9-9! Dad *has* to come! Even if it means we go through quarantine again, I'll do it! But Dad says it's out of the question.

"Businesses here are down—the economy is suffering badly. I'm lucky to still have a job," Dad says.

There's that word again . . . "lucky." I know I should be feeling grateful, but why does it feel so crummy sometimes?

Mom takes the phone from me. She asks me if I'll give her and Dad a minute to talk about some grown-up stuff. I nod and go downstairs to make myself breakfast.

I find my sister in the kitchen, eating chocolate bars for breakfast. Solid Hershey's chocolate bars!

"Lea, seriously?" I ask.

"What?" she asks with a mouthful of chocolate. "New country, new rules!"

"No, not new rules!" I grab the chocolate bar from her and put it back in the fridge. I pour my sister some cereal instead. She groans and says, "I can't eat this. We don't have any chocolate milk!"

"Well, you still have chocolate on your teeth." I point at her. "Just mix it up in your mouth."

Mom walks into the kitchen as Lea is shaking her head no.

"Can we go to the beach today??" I ask.

Mom looks like she's still unsure.

"Oh, please? Please?" Lea asks eagerly. "I can hardly remember what a bird looks like!"

"I need this," I tell Mom. All I want is to stand at the beach and look out to Dad on the other side. It'll make me feel closer to him—I know it will! Lea and I put our hands together and do our best to make sad, daylight-deprived quarantine eyes. I can feel Mom's willpower waning.

"All right." Mom caves at last. "But I still want us to wear a mask when we're out."

"Wear a mask?!" Bowen asks, overhearing us as he comes down the stairs. I'm glad the grizzly bear has finally awoken. "Look out the window! *No one* is wearing a mask. It'll look so weird!"

Mom crosses her arms at Bowen, frowning. "What's more important—not looking weird or being safe and protected?"

"Not looking weird," Bowen decides.

Mom's frown deepens.

"I don't care what we wear, so long as we get to go to my favorite place in the world!" I holler. "Knox Beach—here we come!"

Lea, Bowen, and I dash upstairs to change into our wet suits. We bought them last year at a garage sale because the water in Northern California is always so cold. When we get downstairs, Mom has all our sand toys and beach towels ready. I smile. How I've missed Summer Mom!

Chapter 16

---✈

It takes a while to get our Honda minivan started. Dad bought it a few summers ago. Bowen rides up front next to Mom, where Dad usually sits. I resent him for taking Dad's seat, so I kick him with my knee.

"Quit it!" he yells at me.

Mom gives me a look and I stop, because she's being nice taking us to the beach. I don't want her changing her mind.

As Mom backs the car out, Auntie Jackie calls from the car speakerphone.

"Guys, say hi to Auntie Jackie!"

"Auntie Jackie! You saved us with your masks!" Bowen says to her.

Auntie Jackie laughs. "What are friends for?" she asks. "Speaking of which, are we going to see you?! Maggie misses Lea."

"I miss her, too!!!" Lea calls from next to me.

"You guys still doing your self-quarantine thing?" Jackie asks. "Nobody has it here. You're good!"

Bowen makes dramatic gestures with his hands as Mom drives down the freeway. "See! Even Jackie says we're good!"

"It's over today," Mom says. "In fact, we're heading to the beach right now."

"Fun! What are you guys doing for dinner tonight? I know a great pizza place!"

I throw my arms up excitedly. *Finally* some decent pizza, not the frozen burnt ones from Lucky's!

"Actually, do you mind if we just stay in? We're still a little spooked because of the virus. . . ."

"I think you guys were *way* overdoing it, but sure, if you want, we can have dinner at my house," Auntie Jackie offers.

Mom hangs up the car speakerphone as she turns off the freeway. It's a short drive to my beach. As we pull into the beach parking lot, we gaze out at the beautiful blue waves lapping onto the golden sand. I marvel at the moving water . . . and my dad on the other side.

Mom instructs us to put on our masks before we go out. "It's going to be a little uncomfortable sometimes. But it's the price we have to pay for safety."

As we put on our masks and open the car door, the powerful whiff of the salty ocean air hits us. I breathe it in deep and smile at Mom, but the mask covers my smile.

"Thanks for taking us here, Mom," I say instead, putting a hand on her shoulder. Mom reaches and puts her hand over mine.

"You're welcome. I'm glad we came . . . ," Mom says.

I gaze out into the horizon. If I look real closely, I can see Cody wagging his tail on the other side.

"It's beautiful, isn't it?" she says.

It really is.

Chapter 17

--- ✈

When we get home, a package is sitting outside our house, waiting for us. It's my new dresser from IKEA!

"Finally! Now I can stop living out of my suitcase!" I cheer.

Bowen and Mom lug it inside, while Lea and I bring in all the sand toys. Turns out, it was too cold to play at the beach for too long. Still, I was glad we went. We quickly change out of our wet suits into our pajamas. It's amazing without in-person school—every day is pajama day! We open up the package to find thirty-six pieces of wood and a bunch of little screws.

As Mom sets out trying to build the dresser in the living room, I glance at the clock. We have about two hours before we have to leave for Auntie Jackie's. I hope we're done by then.

"It'll be a cinch!" Mom says, laying out the screws and bolts, even though it's usually Dad who builds our IKEA furniture in Hong Kong. "I used to do this all the time. When your *lao lao* and *lao ye* and I first came to this country"—she glances at Lea with a smile—"I was not much older than you, Lea."

"Really?" Lea asks, picking up one of the pieces of wood and nearly dropping it on her foot, it's so heavy.

"Careful!" Mom exclaims. "We don't have any health insurance here yet!"

Wait . . . what? "Why don't we have any health insurance?" I ask.

"It's . . . complicated," Mom replies. "I'm working on it."

Bowen helps Mom arrange all the screws and the wooden boards in order on the floor. He's even organized with furniture.

"What was it like, when you first moved to America?" Lea asks Mom as she works.

"It was great. I made lots of new friends. I didn't have as much homework, compared to in China," Mom says.

I smile—I like the sound of that!

"It was just me, Lao Lao, and Lao Ye, so we learned to rely on each other." Mom looks up and smiles. "Just like the three of you will."

Bowen, Lea, and I share a glance—*Yeah right.*

"The only person I'm relying on is myself," Bowen informs Mom as he tries to put in one of the metal screws. But they're too small and he keeps dropping them. After three failed attempts, he throws the screwdriver down. "This is gonna take forever!"

"Have patience!" Mom urges. "How else are you going to get through American school? You might have to take woodworking in high school."

"Oh, did you talk to them??" Lea asks excitedly. "Are they going to take us?"

"I've been emailing with the district," Mom says.

"Well, I'm not taking woodworking when I get to high school," Bowen says. "This isn't the Stone Age. I'm taking robotics and economics—that looks *way* better on college applications."

"It's not all about what looks good, gege," Mom says. "It's also about what you're interested in."

"Well, I am *not* interested in wasting my time in classes I'm never going to need." Bowen looks around. "Shouldn't we use like a drill?"

"I think we have one in the garage. I'll get it!" I say, scrambling up.

Mom shakes her head and tells me there's no need. "I don't know how to use one."

"I can do it!" I volunteer.

Mom and Bowen both shout "No" at the same time with such intensity that I shrivel a little next to the heap of wood.

Geez, okay!

While Mom and Bowen struggle with the dresser, Lea and I write a story about our day at the beach and submit it to our teacher in Hong Kong. Mom says until we officially enroll in American school, we still need to do online school. We press turn in and start to get ready for dinner at Auntie Jackie's house. I go upstairs to take a shower.

Mom's clenching her teeth trying to get in a stubborn screw when I come out of the bathroom. Lea walks into the living room in her bathrobe. "Mommy? I don't have any more clean underwear."

"What?" Mom asks. She gets up and wipes her brow. "Are you sure? Did you look in all your drawers?"

Lea nods.

Mom ditches the dresser to go to the laundry room in search of clean underwear. "I could have sworn I did the laundry. . . ."

I follow her and my siblings in my towel, dripping wet puddles all over the floor. We gasp when we walk inside the laundry room. There, in four giant lumps, is all our dirty laundry from the past two weeks!

"Oh my God," Bowen shrieks.

"It's like an underwear bomb went off in here!" Lea giggles, picking up one of Mom's underwear. Mom grabs it and throws it into the machine.

"What are we going to do!? We can't go to Auntie Jackie's dressed like this!" Bowen says, gazing down at his pajamas. I look down at my own *Cars 2* towel, soaking wet.

Mom jumps into action, tossing dirty socks, shirts, whatever she can find, even hair ties, into the washing machine.

Bowen points to the clock. "It's not going to dry in time! We have to be over there in less than an hour!"

"I'm so sorry . . . I just . . . I was going to do it yesterday but I . . . ," Mom says. She chews her fingernail as she gazes at the mound of dirty clothes.

"I know what we can do!" Lea exclaims, holding up a finger.

She bolts to her room.

Chapter 18

--✈

Lea's idea was to quickly wash our underwear with soapy water in the sink and dry them with the hair dryer. As we each held up our underwear in front of our faces, Mom blasted us with the hair dryer. I squeezed my eyes shut, hoping my hair wouldn't smell like underwear.

Forty-five minutes later, we're in the car on our way to Jackie's, wriggling in our seats. Bowen sniffs his dirty shirt in front of me—unfortunately, Mom did not have time to hair-dry our clothes, too.

"No one's going to even notice, Bowen," Mom tells him. "They're there to see us, not smell us."

"*I'll* still smell us," Bowen mutters.

"You know what? Then *you* do the laundry," Mom says.

"Fine, I will," Bowen says. With that, he takes out his phone. I lean forward as he sets a reminder for every day—*DO LAUNDRY OR ELSE!!!*

Mom explains as she drives that it's not so simple, you need to separate the whites from the colorful T-shirts. And different types of clothing need different temperature settings. It's kind of like the dresser that's still lying half-done on the floor in our living room, like a dusty construction site. It *looks* easy until you try it.

"I can handle it," Bowen says.

"And you have to fold it too," Mom continues. "After you take it all out of the dryer."

Bowen scrunches his face. Lea and I exchange a glance.

"I'll do the folding," my sister volunteers.

"And I'll put everything back," I add. I can't wait to put all my freshly washed clothes in my new dresser—*if* we ever finish building it!

Mom smiles at us in the rearview mirror. "That's the spirit!" she says.

As Mom drives, I can hear Lea's tummy rumbling next to me.

"What do you think Auntie Jackie's making for dinner?" I ask. I hope it's something delicious, like Dad's lasagna or chicken-and-dumplings stew. Basically anything of Dad's.

"I'm sure it'll be really good," Mom says. "Auntie Jackie was always a good cook. Even back in college."

"Is that how you two met?" Lea asks.

Mom nods. "We were in the same dorm. She was the only one who didn't want to eat the cafeteria food and made stuff in her room. I followed the delicious smell down the hall. And the rest is history."

I smile thinking of young college Mom, eating like a champ and kicking butt in her classes. We pull up in front of Auntie Jackie's house in Walnut Creek. Everything in Walnut Creek is so much nicer than in El Tercera. Even the grass is nicer. As I step onto the lawn, so green it looks like it's been shampooed with food coloring, I want to lie down and roll in it like a dog. I wish Cody were here—he'd *love* this lawn.

"You guys made it!" Auntie Jackie says. "Welcome!"

I give Maggie and Noah, Auntie Jackie's kids, a hug. Maggie is Lea's age, and she and Lea giggle as they run inside the house. I've been to their house a bunch of times over the summers. Still, every time I walk inside, I always marvel at how much bigger—and cleaner—it is than our house. At our house, there are unmatched socks on the floor and chargers all over the couch. Here you can actually see the floor. I notice they got a new air hockey table and immediately run over to play with it.

"When'd you guys get this??" I shriek. "Bowen, you want to play?"

To my surprise, Bowen says, "Sure!"

We turn on the air hockey machine and put our fingertips on the table, feeling the cool air. Noah wants to play too, but he's still too short, so Bowen lifts him up. I stop and stare for a second at Bowen holding Noah, feeling a pang of jealousy. He's always so much nicer to other people's little brothers.

"We got it over Christmas," Auntie Jackie says, handing us each a glass of homemade lemonade.

"Did you put it together yourself?" I ask her, impressed.

"Sure, it's easy." Auntie Jackie shrugs. "All you need is a drill."

Bowen looks to Mom—*Hear that?*

Lea grins. "I know how to use a hair dryer! And you wanna know what I did with it today?"

Mom puts a hand over Lea's mouth before she can spill the beans and laughs nervously. "Uh . . . do you need any help with dinner?" she asks Jackie.

"Oh, no, it's all done. I just whipped together something simple," Jackie tells Mom.

"Something simple" turns out to be garlic rosemary pork

chops, with organic cranberry apple salad, mashed potatoes, and creamed corn. And not from the can, with *real* corn. We gobble it up like starved convicts who haven't eaten in days.

"This is *so* good," I say, piling on the mashed potatoes. They're just like the ones Dad usually makes, except Auntie Jackie put little pieces of chives in hers. Lea's so hungry, she doesn't even mind the chives.

Auntie Jackie laughs. "Thanks!" She brings out the garlic bread and passes it around. I load up my plate with so many pieces, Mom gives me a look, like, *Do you really need that many?*

And yes, I do.

"So have you started looking at schools?" Auntie Jackie asks Mom.

"I'm talking to the district," Mom says, and bites into a piece of garlic bread.

"You should really move here. The public schools are much better in our area," Auntie Jackie says, turning to Maggie and Noah. "Right, kids?"

Maggie and Noah nod.

"We have a swimming pool at our school!" Maggie tells us.

Mom smiles. "I'll bet you do!" She turns to Auntie Jackie. "But the houses here are all like two million dollars. . . . There's no way we can afford that. Not with the virus and everything going on. Asia's in complete free fall right now."

"How's Andrew doing?" Auntie Jackie asks.

Mom looks down. "He's hanging in there. They're downsizing at his company."

I look up. They *are*?

"He didn't get cut or anything," Mom quickly adds. "He's

okay for now, but"—she lets out a heavy sigh—"it's really hard. He misses the kids."

"I'll bet," Auntie Jackie says. "He should just fly over and work here. We have plenty of jobs." She beams. "No economic free fall here!"

That would be *amazing*! Then Dad could cook us delicious meals! And take me to all my soccer games! I look to Mom eagerly. Maybe Auntie Jackie can get Dad a job.

"We'll see. I can't think too far ahead right now," Mom says. "I'm just trying to get through the day. It's not easy single parenting three kids." She reaches over and gives my hair a playful tousle. "Which is why I'm signing these three rascals up for school!"

"How is the district? Have you checked on greatschools.org?" Auntie Jackie asks.

Bowen stops shoveling food into his mouth. "What's that?"

"It's a website where you can find out how each school in your area ranks." She puts a hand on her chest. "Personally, I wouldn't go anywhere rated seven out of ten or below."

Bowen immediately pulls out his phone and starts checking, but Mom tells him no phones at dinner. He puts it away. "Look, I know you're in real estate and that stuff matters a lot to people," she tells Auntie Jackie. "But I went to some of the poorest public schools in California and I did okay."

Auntie Jackie points a finger at Mom. "You, my friend, are the exception."

The front door opens and I turn around, half expecting my dad to walk in. Instead, it's Uncle Joe, Auntie Jackie's husband.

"I'm home!" he calls out.

"Daddy!!!" Maggie and Noah cry out.

As Maggie and Noah jump out of their seats and run into Uncle Joe's arms, I feel the mashed potatoes harden into a lump in my throat. I didn't know it was possible to miss Dad even more than I did, but in that moment, as I watch Uncle Joe pick Maggie and Noah up and give them a big tickle, I want to curl up and hide in the bread basket.

Chapter 19

---✈

During the car ride home, I count the time difference on my fingers, wishing Mom would drive faster so I can get home and catch Dad before I go to bed. I want to tell him all about Auntie Jackie's delicious dinner—but that his mashed potatoes are better.

"Did you guys enjoy dinner?" Mom asks. "What was your favorite dish?"

"The garlic bread," I say. "Definitely the garlic bread."

"Garlic bread isn't a dish," Bowen argues. "Now, the pork chops—*those* were amazing!"

Lea nods eagerly.

"And I can't believe she has an air hockey table!" I add.

"Auntie Jackie's house is *so* nice," Lea agrees.

"That's because she works in real estate," Mom says.

"But it's not just nice on the outside, it's nice *inside*!" Lea tells Mom. "I went to the bathroom and they have these little mini roses on top of the toilet. I sat there and smelled their toilet for ten whole minutes!"

"*Ewww.*" Bowen wrinkles his nose.

Mom gazes at us in the rearview mirror, looking a little bit sad. "Hey, I know things aren't perfect right now, and I'm so sorry about the laundry today, but I'm really trying."

I look up at Mom and instantly feel ashamed to have

made her feel bad. Auntie Jackie's house is not *that* nice.

"Guess I'm not used to it being just me." She sighs as she adds, "There used to be two of me—me and your dad. But now there's only one of me."

Mom's heartfelt apology sends an air hockey puck to my gut.

"It's okay, Mommy," I say.

"Yeah, Mommy, you're doing good," Lea chimes in from her booster seat, giving her a heart sign with her little hands in the rearview mirror.

Mom lets out a weak smile.

"Who needs an air hockey table anyway?" Bowen adds. "Knox will probably break it in two seconds."

"I'll *definitely* break it," I promise.

Mom laughs. She tries to make a heart sign back for Lea but can only manage half a heart with one hand, because she's driving. I picture Dad making the other half in Hong Kong.

That night, as Mom is tucking me and Bowen into our beds, Lea walks in with her fuzzy slippers and a magazine in her hand.

"What's that?" Mom asks.

Lea holds up the magazine. It's an old issue of the trade magazine *Hong Kong Banker*. Lea flips to the page that has a picture of my mom on it.

"Now there's two of you, Mommy." Lea beams, holding up the picture.

You'd think that a thing like that would make Mom smile. She sits down on the bed and takes a deep breath.

"Guys, there's something I need to tell you," she says. "I . . . I lost my job."

I pull off the covers. *What??*

"When?" I ask.

"A few days ago. My boss didn't think it was possible for me to serve my clients from California, even though he was okay with it before I left. I tried to reason with him, but . . ." Her voice breaks. She can't get the last part out. Finally, she mutters, "He decided to let me go."

Lea wraps her arms around Mom.

"I'm so sorry, Mommy," she says.

"How can he punish you for being here?" Bowen erupts, fuming. "It's not your fault! What about our health and safety?"

Mom shakes her head, not having an answer to either of those questions. She gazes down at Magazine Mom smiling back at her.

"It's okay. I'll find something else. I've already started looking."

I suck in a breath, thinking of all the stuff we've been ordering online, including my ridiculous dresser, still unassembled downstairs. And how we're going to pay for it all. "We can return the dresser tomorrow. I don't really need it."

Mom glances at me. "Are you sure?"

"Yeah."

She mouths, *Thanks, bao bao,* and squeezes my hand.

"Everything's going to be okay," she promises as she turns off the light and walks to the door. Lea leaves with her.

I notice Mom didn't take the magazine.

I wait until Bowen's asleep before crawling down and

getting Magazine Mom. Carefully, I tear out the page in the moonlight. Against Bowen's strict warnings never to tape anything up on our wall because it'll ruin the paint, I tape it up next to my bed.

Mom might not be good at building dressers or doing the laundry. But she's pretty great at a whole bucketful of other things, and we shouldn't forget that.

Chapter 20

-- ✈

I wake up on Tuesday to the sound of Bowen yanking his dresser drawers open and slamming them closed.

"What are you doing?" I ask, rubbing my eyes.

"I'm giving you two drawers—that's it," he announces.

I rub my ears, shocked. *Did I hear that right??*

"And only until Mom gets a new job and we have some money to buy more furniture. Then I'm taking them back."

Still, this is unbelievably generous coming from Bowen, and I want to jump up and throw my arms around him, but I tell myself to play it cool.

"Thanks, gege," I say. "You think Mom's going to find something?" I climb down from the bunk.

"Of course Mom's going to find something," Bowen says matter-of-factly. His confidence gives me hope. "She's the best there is."

I nod, feeling the conviction of his words as I put my clothes away. They're so powerful and sure.

"But if she finds a job here, then we'll *really* be here. Like be here, be here," I say.

Bowen stares at me blankly. "So?"

"So what about Dad?" I let out. I know I've been saying it over and over, but the fact that no one even seems to have a plan to reunite us is worrying me. Are we *ever* gonna be a family again?

"You heard Mom—she just lost her job. We can't afford to fly back and forth right now."

I look down. Bowen's probably right. Mom was the main breadwinner of our family.

"Maybe we have savings!" I say, wishing I'd brought my lockbox.

Bowen shakes his head. "I took a look at Mom and Dad's bank account once. There was only checking."

"Only checking?" I ask. That sounds awful. "Where'd all their salary go?"

"Duh. Taxes," Bowen responds.

Oh yeah. Taxes are like wedgies for adults.

"No way can we afford a flight now for Dad. The price has gone *way* up—it's now three thousand dollars a ticket! I looked it up."

"So you *have* been thinking about it!" I grin.

"'Course I've been thinking about it," Bowen concedes. "But we're gonna have to wait."

I frown. Waiting stinks.

Bowen walks over and puts the last of my underwear in my dresser drawer.

"We can't always get what we want, Knox," Bowen says, pointing to the dresser. "Case in point."

Chapter 21

---✈

In the shower, I do the math in my head, trying to figure out how many lawns I could mow to raise $3,000 for Dad to come over. *If* I knew how to mow lawns. I get out and put on my special eczema lotion that Dad packed for me, proud of myself for remembering. That's one less thing for Mom; she has enough to worry about.

I find Mom at the dining room table, with her laptop open, sleeping at her computer. I quickly unplug her laptop charger to save energy. At the thought of Mom not having a job anymore, I glance at the fridge, suddenly worried we won't be able to do Uber Eats anymore or buy frozen pizza. *Stop,* I tell myself. She'll find something. Everything's going to be fine.

I glance at her screen—she's on something called LinkedIn. I inch closer to try to get a better look.

"What time is it?" Mom wakes up, yawning.

"It's eight," I tell her. "What's LinkedIn?"

"It's a website where you can look for a job," Mom explains.

"Have you applied for anything?" I ask excitedly, glancing at Bowen, who is making himself a smoothie.

"A few things," she says. "I still need to rack up my endorsements."

I look at Mom, puzzled. "What are endorsements?" I ask.

She smiles. "It's when people you know say you're good

at something. Like if you put all your dirty dishes in the sink. Hint, hint," Mom says to Bowen, pointing at all the bowls and cups he's using for his smoothie.

"So it's kind of like a report card," I say to Mom.

"Something like that!" she says. "The more endorsements you get from people, the better."

"We can give you endorsements!" I suggest.

Bowen nods eagerly, rinsing his mixing bowls before placing them in the dishwasher.

"I'll give you straight As, Mom, if you let me play *Call of Duty: Black Ops*," Bowen begs, putting his hands together.

Mom chuckles. "Nice try," she says. "They can't be from your own family."

Oh.

"Speaking of report cards, I thought we'd go and check out the schools today!" Mom says brightly, getting up and pouring me a glass of orange juice.

Lea strolls into the kitchen in a shorts-over-long-leggings and cape combination. Now that she's no longer wearing her school uniform, every day she looks like a different character from *Frozen II*.

"What do you say?" Mom asks, glancing at her watch. "Have your backpacks ready in half an hour?"

"Wait, what? We're starting *today*?" I ask.

"If they have space."

"What about online school??" I ask her. It seems completely mind-boggling that we can just jump trains like that—one minute no school, the next minute online school, the third minute, American school. My head's dizzy trying to keep up!

"It'll be fine. I emailed your Hong Kong teachers to let

them know you'll be starting regular school here," Mom says. "They all understand."

I gulp. Does that mean if I don't like my new school, there will be nowhere to go back to? My siblings don't seem too bothered. Lea runs off to change, singing "Into the Unknown," excited as ever, as my brother and I clear the table and get our backpacks ready.

We're going into the unknown, all right!

Dad FaceTimes us in the car on the way to our new schools, telling us to take lots of pictures.

"I wish I could be there," he says.

We see Cody in the background. His hair has grown so much—he's starting to look like a giant cotton ball. I can hardly see his eyes.

"Why don't you take Cody to the groomers?" Mom asks.

"I can't. They're all closed," Dad says. "You wouldn't believe it—yesterday the grocery store down the street ran out of toilet paper. No joke!"

"That would *never* happen in America," Mom says, shaking her head. "Even if we had the virus here, people would never panic to the point of stockpiling toilet paper . . . that's ridiculous."

"So what are you going to do?" I ask Dad.

"Try to keep my toilet trips down to a minimum," Dad says. I *hope* Dad's joking. I wouldn't be able to last if I were there; I'm so bad at holding it in.

"You want us to send you some?" I ask Dad.

"No thanks, that'd be the world's most expensive toilet paper!" He chuckles.

Mom tells Dad we need to go as she pulls into the parking lot of Davis Elementary School. It's a school I've been to many times in the summer to play with my sister but have never gone inside. I take a deep breath as Mom parks.

"Here we go," Mom says. "You two excited?"

Lea nods eagerly, like she's going to a carnival. Which school is for my popular sister. For me, on the other hand . . .

"All right, kiddos, good luck! I love you!" Dad says.

"Love you, too, Dad!" I say. "Stay safe!" But the video cuts out before Dad can hear my "stay safe."

Mom turns to Bowen. "You want to come with us or wait in the car?"

"Wait."

The blond woman in the office greets Mom as she walks in. Mom tells her they've been emailing, and the woman's face brightens with recognition. "You're the family that's just moved back from Asia!" she says. "Welcome!"

As Mom and the administrator talk, I gaze out the window, staring at the other kids. There are white kids, Black kids, and Latinx kids, but no one who looks like me.

Mom calls us *hun xuer*, mixed blood. Dad says we're more like boba milk tea—the best of both cultures. Unique in our own way. I start thinking about boba, getting a little distracted. Before I know it, I'm listing all twenty-eight flavors from Cha Long, my favorite boba place in Hong Kong, in my head. Dad and I used to go after he picked me up from soccer. Even though Mom always says no sugary drinks before dinner, Dad and I would sneak trips.

I look around, wishing Dad were here in the office with us.

If he were, he'd tell me not to worry. I'll like my new school. And the other kids will like me. But I worry anyway.

Lea, on the other hand, doesn't seem worried at all. She's too busy signing her name to every flyer and petition on the office bulletin board. I'll bet she'll make five hundred friends by the end of the first week.

"Do you guys have after-school sports?" I ask the secretary. Maybe that's a way I can make some new friends.

"Unfortunately, we don't . . . ," she says. "You can check with the local clubs, though. They might have a team you can join. What's your sport, sweetie?"

"Soccer," I tell her.

Mom cuts in. "And I know we were talking a little bit about learning support on email. . . . Does the school have any occupational therapists?"

I squeeze my eyes shut. Oh, please, *please* let there be a Lily at my new school!

"I'm sorry, but we currently don't have that, either," the school secretary tells her, making copies of our passports and immunization records. "Budget constraints."

"Oh." My face falls.

Mom tries again. "It's just that my son has ADHD. . . ."

I look up. I *do*? *I* thought I had a blurting-things-out problem. ADHD is what Amir's little brother has, and that's *way* worse. He once threw a shoe at me and banged his head on the floor when he tried to fly off the kitchen counter. *I* have it too??

"I assure you, we have lots of students with all sorts of different learning habits," the school secretary says. "And we can handle them *all*."

I yank on Mom's shirt. "What do you mean, ADHD??" I ask. But Mom ignores me.

"All right, you're all set. I'm going to pass everything on to our principal, and hopefully, you and your sister can both start tomorrow! First grade and fifth grade!" the secretary says.

I walk out of my new school that day with the knowledge that my parents have been keeping a secret about me my whole life. If we hadn't come to America because of the virus, would I ever have known?

Chapter 22

- ✈

Yay! We did it!" Mom says, high-fiving Lea, as we walk back to the car. "That was easy!"

Too easy. I can't believe they didn't want us to take any tests or anything. In Hong Kong, I had to do so many screenings and interviews for school. There was even a test on how outgoing you are. Thinking back, I wonder if there might have been a secret test for ADHD that my parents snuck in. How do they *know* I have it??

"What does that tell you about America?" Mom asks, opening the door to the car.

"That they have no standards?" I ask, still sour over her keeping a secret from me.

"No, that they're inclusive! And welcoming of everyone!" Mom says.

We get back in the car, and Bowen immediately grabs Mom.

"I searched the middle school on that website Auntie Jackie said. It's rated three out of ten!" he shrieks. "I can't go there for seventh grade!"

"You haven't even seen it," Mom says, starting the car. "Let's just take a look."

As Mom and Bowen bicker over Bowen's middle school, it takes every ounce of patience for me not to ask Mom more about my ADHD. But I know I can't say it in front of Bowen. He'll never stop teasing me if he knows. I'm sure he thinks ADHD is A Dangerous Horrible Disease. Which it isn't . . . right?

Mom tries to calm Bowen down as she drives by talking about the exciting lunch options in American schools. "They have pizza, tacos, hamburgers—you name it! And they serve it hot!"

That gets my brother's attention.

"Really?" Bowen asks, his reluctance softening at the thought of warm lunches. In Hong Kong, there was no cafeteria at our school and we all brought our lunches from home and ate them in our classroom. I had the same soggy ham-and-cheese sandwich every day.

"Yes! Hot lunch all the time!" Mom says. I look over at her. Her enthusiasm is a little much. I wonder if she's just saying that to try to get us out of her hair.

Soon we arrive at the middle school. We all peer out the window at the sharp fence and campus full of trailers. There's a field and a track, but the track material's worn down practically to dust.

"It looks like something out of *The Shining*!" Bowen says.

Mom taps his arm lightly. "It does *not*," she says. "C'mon, let's go check it out."

She turns off the car and grabs her purse.

My sister and I wait in the hallway while Mom and Bowen go inside the office. We sit on the floor as middle schoolers stroll in and ask for late passes. There sure are a *lot* of late middle schoolers.

"You excited about school?" Lea asks me.

"No."

"Well, I am!" Lea grins.

Mom and Bowen finally come out, and we scramble up.

"How was it?" I ask.

"We're all set," Mom announces with a smile. "They're going to figure out Bowen's schedule, and then he's good to go! Same as you and Lea!"

I glance at Bowen, who bolts straight for the exit door. He doesn't even bother checking out the clubs and activities on the wall. Mom suggests we go to In-N-Out Burger to celebrate our new American schools.

Lea and I smile. In-N-Out is our absolute favorite burger place in the world, and it's so irresistible even Bowen mumbles okay.

"It'll be fun!" Mom says.

We get into the car. Mom tells us she did a case study on the fast-food chain in business school as she starts the engine. "You want to know why it's so successful?"

"Why?"

"Because they kept it in the family," she tells us. "They never sold out."

According to Mom, for more than six decades, the family that started In-N-Out held on to it.

"The founders had two boys who were polar opposites . . . ," Mom says, winking at me and Bowen. "But despite their differences, they stuck together." I look to my brother.

My brother turns around and tells me in no uncertain terms that when we get there, I can't take any of his fries. I roll my eyes. I don't care what Mom says—if I ever start a successful burger joint with Bowen, I'm definitely selling it.

Chapter 23

---✈

I n between bites of juicy burgers and fresh-cut fries, Mom tells us our favorite hamburger story—the story of how she learned English.

"When I first came to the US, I didn't know a single word of English, not even the word 'girl.' Which made it pretty hard to find the bathroom," she says.

Lea giggles. Mom always pauses at the same place in the story, and my siblings and I always ask the same question.

"So what did the teacher do?"

"The teacher didn't do anything. She thought I would never speak. And I thought that too. But I worked really hard, and by the end of the first year, guess what?"

"What?" we ask.

"I spoke!"

"Hooray!!!" Lea cheers, throwing a couple of her fries up in the air.

"The teacher was so thrilled, she got me a hamburger from McDonald's," Mom says, her eyes shining with nostalgia.

"Did the other kids make fun of you because you couldn't speak English?" Lea asks.

Mom nods. "Some," she says, adding quickly, "But it'll

be different for you three. You already know the language, unlike me. You all have mouths!"

I open my mouth wide. *Especially* me.

Afterward, I'm still sipping my chocolate milkshake when Mom turns into Target.

"Let's get you guys some school supplies," she says, parking the car.

All right! I *love* Target. In Hong Kong, we don't have anything like Target. Instead we have little shops for everything—curtains, headphones, plates. I especially loved the stationery store. It was run by a husband and wife, and their cat, Tofu—who sat on the warm printer all day long.

I wonder how Tofu is doing as we get a cart. Dad said all the stores are closed. Did Tofu lose his warm printer bed too? Lea heads straight for the stationery section and loads up on every color of highlighter. Bowen puts a bunch of rulers and protractors and other fancy math stuff on top of Lea's stash. I stare at my siblings shopping like Mom hasn't lost her job. I wonder if I should say something. But I don't want to be the party pooper. And Mom doesn't seem too worried—she's reaching for more Post-its herself—so I tell myself maybe it's okay.

Money is so weird. It's there, like a balloon, but no one talks about it until it pops.

After we stock up on supplies, we head over to the snack section. Talk about a selection! They have Cheddar Jalapeño *and* Flamin' Hot Cheetos as well as eighteen different varieties of Goldfish, including *purple* Goldfish. Lea immediately reaches for them.

"I'm *so* serving this at my birthday party!" she says, hugging the package to her chest. She starts filling the cart up with purple Goldfish.

"That's not for two months!" I remind her. Hopefully, by then Mom will have a new job. Or the virus will be over and we can go back!

"Well, all my future friends have already RSVPed," she informs me matter-of-factly, grabbing more snacks for her party.

Mom comes back from the mask section as Lea's stocking up on Goldfish. "They don't have any face masks here, either . . . ," she says, disappointed.

She looks down at our cart. "You guys need *all* those snacks?" she asks us, picking up a giant package of Ring Pops and putting it back.

Lea makes puppy-dog eyes at Mom. "Please, Mommy, I really need them. . . . I gotta eat my way through my I-miss-Daddy blues!"

Mom sighs.

"Fine, then we'll need to get another cart," she says. "I still need to get toner and paper to print stuff for my interviews."

"On it!" I volunteer, running toward the front of the store. I know *just* the cart to grab.

I get to the front and hop on one of the shopping carts you can drive. I know I'm not supposed to drive them, but they're the best thing about America and they're the fastest option by far! So I get on.

Bowen sees me as I'm driving and waves his hands at me to stop.

"Knox, what are you doing?? You're not supposed to be on that thing!" he calls out.

He chases me, but even his track legs can't keep up with my Batmobile! I slam on the accelerator, giggling.

"Knox! No!" Mom says.

"Stop!" the store manager calls.

Uh-oh. Now the store employees are after me too. It makes me so nervous, having all these people chase me, that I don't look where I'm going and crash into a towering display of Mountain Dew. As the soda cans come tumbling down, sticky soda squirts in every direction!

I jump off the cart, covered in soda.

"I'm sorry . . . ," I start to say. But the store clerks are too livid to even look at me.

Mom bites her lip. "How much for all this?"

I look around. There are like fifty cases of Mountain Dew! It's going to cost a fortune. I can feel Bowen's eyes burrowing into me—*This is all your fault!*

As Mom swallows hard and reaches for her purse, Bowen charges at me. I make a break for it. Bowen chases me throughout the store, and I scramble through the aisles, trying not to break more things. I finally slip into the women's pajamas section and hide under a bathrobe.

It feels safe and cozy in the terry cloth bathrobe. . . . I snuggle up to it, wishing Mom weren't mad at me. Wishing I hadn't wreaked such havoc. Wishing I could come out and everyone would laugh and think it was funny. But most of all, wishing a stop sign had gone up in my head. But it didn't. Lea finds me twenty minutes later.

"We're going now," she says.

I poke my head out from under the bathrobe. "Is Mom still mad?" I ask.

Lea chews her lip. I'm guessing yes.

With a sigh, I get up and follow her to the entrance, not wanting to make Mom any madder.

The staff and manager shake their heads at me as I walk out of the store, their disappointment as loud as if they had screamed, *What's gotten into that kid?* I look down. The pain is almost unbearable. It's a question I've been asking myself my whole life.

Mom and Bowen are sitting in the car when I get in. I glance at the back and see only one small paper bag of school supplies and a single package of purple Goldfish. "Where's all our stuff?" I ask.

"We had to put everything else back because the Mountain Dew you spilled cost a hundred dollars!" Bowen hisses at me.

I put my hands to my mouth. A *hundred* dollars?

I gaze at the pens and Post-its and one small package of Goldfish—all we could afford after my stunt.

"I call dibs on the Goldfish!" Lea says. She's the one person in my family not fuming mad . . . or maybe she just doesn't understand.

I look up slowly at Mom in the rearview mirror.

"I'm sorry, Mom," I say gently. "It won't happen again."

"Of course it will," Bowen says, and leans back, muttering, *"Knot."*

I keep my eyes straight ahead on Mom. She doesn't say anything to me as she starts the car. The silence is so hard. I stare at my feet, feeling the heat of her and Bowen's disappointment. It feels like a Double-Double burger of I-screwed-up.

Ever so quietly, Lea takes a couple of Goldfish out and hands them to me. I look down at them, trying not to think, but thinking anyway, that I'm the purple Goldfish of the family.

I crush the snack in my hand.

My sister looks over. "Don't crush them. They're cool!" She takes one and holds it up to the window. The bright sun illuminates the colorful Goldfish. "I like it because it's different from the pack!"

I smile at my sister, grateful for her words. She's the only person who doesn't make me feel bad about being me.

Chapter 24

--✈

That night, I stay up late looking up ADHD on my iPad
while Bowen snores next to me.

*ADHD stands for attention deficit hyperactivity disorder. It
is a medical condition. A person with ADHD has differences in their
brain development—*

Differences in my brain?! I immediately close my iPad, terri-
fied of reading on.

I try doing the breathing exercises Lily taught me. *Did Lily
know?* Is that why I had to see her? Was she secretly trying to
train me, like Yoda in Star Wars? I close my eyes and imagine
wielding my ADHD like a lightsaber. Bowen's mocking voice
creeps into my head. *It's not a lightsaber, Knot! It's a disability!*

I get so mad, I take Bowen's super-expensive headphones
and bend the leather band hard with my hands. I stop just
before they break. Then I drop them on the table. I glance at
Bowen. Thankfully, he does not stir.

If Bowen knew I even touched them, he would kill me.
They're Bose. My parents got them for him when he scored
a ninety-ninth percentile on a test, which at the time seemed
totally unfair and now makes me wonder, with my ADHD, will
I ever get a good enough score to get headphones?

I tiptoe out of our room and knock on Mom's door.
There are so many questions I want to ask her about my con-

dition . . . like do Lea and Bowen have it too? Or is it just me? Is it something I might be able to grow out of if I just keep putting lotion on it like my eczema?

I push Mom's door open. But she's already asleep.

I go back to my room and crawl into my bed. I turn to my side, hoping tomorrow will go better. Tomorrow I will find the courage to read the rest of the page about ADHD. And start at my new school. And not cost Mom bazillions of dollars in messes.

Mom scrolls through her Spotify the next morning in our sparkling clean car. As punishment for the sodas, I had to get up at the crack of dawn to help her vacuum out the car and wipe down the interior with all-purpose wipes. Which was a lot of work given how many Goldfish my sister and I ate.

As my brother and sister pile in, Mom puts on "Survivor" from Destiny's Child, her favorite song.

"Why do you like this song so much?" Lea asks.

"Because it's all about the ups and downs of life. And how there are challenges, but if you work hard, you can survive anything!"

As the song plays, I sit back and listen to the lyrics. I think to myself, if Mom could survive being the new kid in school without knowing English, maybe I can survive being the new kid in school with ADHD.

"Remember, you don't need to make a lot of friends. You only need to make one," Mom says. "That's all I had when I was a kid."

"Who was your friend?" Lea asks.

"A girl named Lucy," Mom tells us.

"Did she come to your birthday party?" Lea asks.

"Oh, we celebrated lots of birthdays together," Mom tells us with a smile.

I hope I'm so lucky. I still remember sitting in first grade, wanting to disappear. All the other kids already knew each other from playdates their moms arranged before school even started, but my parents were too busy working and my *lao lao* was too old to figure out Facebook groups.

So I would sit by myself at recess, making rocket noises, pretending I was an astronaut. The other kids thought I was *super* weird.

I look down at my backpack full of my fidget and focus toys. I hope the kids in my new school don't think it's weird that I brought them.

Mom turns on the radio as the song finishes playing.

"In the latest coronavirus news, at least twenty-four Americans onboard the *Diamond Princess* cruise ship in Japan are infected with coronavirus. A fierce debate is brewing as to whether to fly the four hundred twenty-eight Americans onboard back, as passengers plead to President Trump, 'Get us off this ship!'"

The other radio host says, "But Tom, you have to understand, allowing the infected people to come back doubles the number of coronavirus cases here in the US. I mean, have you seen the terrifying images and videos from China? All from eating—"

Mom switches the radio off.

Bowen looks at Mom. He hesitates for a second before asking, "You think we should tell people we came from Asia?"

Mom thinks for a minute. "If you want, you can tell them you're new from here. I mean we sort of are."

"Why wouldn't we tell people we're from Asia?" Lea asks, not understanding.

Bowen shakes his head. "Never mind."

Mom parks the car in the elementary school parking lot, and my sister and I get out. We grab our backpacks and I reach for my soccer ball as Bowen mutters "Good luck" to us. Mom takes our hands and walks us to our new classrooms.

Lea gets dropped off first. Her teacher is a tall, cheery woman, Mrs. Hernandez, whose big smile reminds me of Auntie Jackie. As Lea bounces into her new classroom, Mom snaps a picture of her to send to Dad.

Next it's my turn. As we walk into room 16, the other kids stare curiously at me. There are twenty-something other kids spread out all over the classroom—on mats, beanbags, wobble cushions, and chairs. They are Black, white, and Latinx. Only one other Asian boy, as far as I can tell. I smile at him, until Mrs. Turner's dangling earrings jolt my attention.

"Welcome to room sixteen!" she says. "I'm Mrs. Turner!"

I smile at my new teacher, a Black woman holding a mug that says, IT TAKES A BIG HEART ♥ TO TEACH LITTLE MINDS.

"Hi," I say shyly.

Mom asks Mrs. Turner if she can have a word with her in private.

"Of course!"

As Mrs. Turner steps out of the class to talk to my mom, the Asian boy scoots over on the mat on the floor and says, "You can sit here if you want." I walk over and put my huge backpack with all my focus toys down on the floor next to him.

"What's your name?" the other kids turn and ask.

"Knox," I reply.

"Like the beach?" they ask.

A few of the girls start giggling, and I turn red.

"Ignore them," the boy on the mat says. "My name's Christopher."

"Knox." I smile. Oops, I already said that.

Mrs. Turner walks back in and sees me sitting next to Christopher. "Good, Knox, I'm glad to see you're all settled in. Now! Who wants to explain to Knox how our classroom works?"

A hand goes up. A boy named Patrick starts to explain the three corners of the classroom—there's a Calm Down corner, a Tablet Reward corner, and a Focus corner full of focus toys. Mrs. Turner sits in the fourth corner, at her desk. I stare at the Focus corner, fascinated. They *already have* fidget toys!

"What's the Tablet corner?" I ask curiously.

"It's when you've earned time as a reward for staying on task!" Mrs. Turner says, pointing to the tall stack of Chromebooks and tablets. "You can play *Minecraft* or Scratch."

"You can play *Minecraft*??" I all but scream.

Mrs. Turner chuckles. "You certainly can, if you've earned it." She points to the mats and beanbags. "And feel free to get up and move to different stations in the classroom. We have a flexible seating policy."

Wow. They don't even have that on airplanes!

"Now, Knox, why don't you tell us a little bit about yourself?"

I get up nervously and say, "Uh . . . I'm Knox. I'm from . . ." I shift my weight from foot to foot, debating. "Here," I finally say.

The kids look at me funny.

"You're from here? But you're just starting school now?" one of the kids asks.

"Maybe he was homeschooled," another kid answers.

I nod. *Yeah, that's it!*

Mrs. Turner encourages me to keep going.

"I have a brother and sister," I continue. "And I like soccer. A lot."

"Welcome, Knox. We're so glad to have you." Mrs. Turner smiles.

I smile back as I take my seat. That wasn't so bad. As I get my focus toys out from my backpack and line them up on my mat, I look around. No one even bats an eye. Maybe I can do this thing after all, I think to myself as I hum Mom's favorite song in my head.

Chapter 25

--✈

Mrs. Turner teaches us math and reads from *The One and Only Ivan* before recess. It's this story about a gorilla in a mall and people are always looking at him. I sort of feel like a gorilla in the mall today too, but Mrs. Turner makes sure I'm following along and so does Christopher.

Every time I don't understand something or don't know where something is, Christopher writes it down on a Post-it so I don't forget. Luckily, I have a bunch from Mom.

By the time recess rolls around, I've already earned five minutes of free tablet time.

I follow Christopher and the other kids to the playground, hugging my soccer ball in my arms. Mrs. Turner reminds me not to kick the ball over the fence, because there's a creek just beyond the fence. I promise her I won't—I just want to kick it around with Christopher. But before I even have a chance to play soccer with him, one of the kids tags Christopher and says, "You're it!"

Christopher groans. "I don't want to play coronavirus tag with you guys," he says.

What tag??

"Oh, c'mon, you're the virus! You have to play!" the other kids say.

Christopher shakes his head firmly. "No."

Still, the other kids run away from him like he's it. "Christopher has the virus! Christopher has the virus!" they scream. As the other kids run for their lives away from my new friend, shrieking with glee, Christopher kneels down and turns himself into a ball on the ground.

"Here, tag me," I tell him.

Christopher shakes his head. "No, it's okay," he says.

When he doesn't tag me, I bump myself into him. "I'm it," I declare to the other kids.

Christopher looks up at me, puzzled. With my arms outstretched, I run around the playground going, "I'm it! I'm it!"

But no matter how many times I say it, some of the other kids still keep running away from Christopher. Finally, I blurt out, "Hey guys. I'm from Hong Kong! I've actually been right near the virus!"

That gets their attention.

"WHAT??!" they shriek.

Christopher gestures wildly with his hands—*What are you doing??* He probably thinks I'm making it up, but I'm *actually* telling the truth.

"You're *Asian*?" Tyler asks.

I know I don't look it. My brother looks much more like Mom than me and Lea. We look more like caramel-swirl ice cream cones. But it shouldn't matter that I have sandy hair and light skin. I'm still Asian!

The other kids start running like crazy, screaming, "Knox is IT!" as the recess bell goes off.

Walking into the classroom, I look timidly over at

Christopher. Now that he knows I'm from Hong Kong, will he still want to sit next to me? I'll understand if he doesn't. Instead, he walks over, takes a seat, and squeezes my green apple squishy toy. His eyes smile back at mine.

Chapter 26

---✈

Climbing into Mom's car, I hold my arms up triumphantly. My first day was a success! Well, mostly, except for the coronavirus tag thing. And most of my classmates probably think it's weird I lied about Hong Kong. But still, I have a new teacher I like. I got ten minutes of tablet time to play *Minecraft*. But most importantly, I made a friend!

I wave goodbye to Christopher from the back seat.

"How was your first day of school?" Mom asks me.

"Good!" I tell her as Lea climbs inside. "I think I made a friend!"

"Oh my gosh, that's wonderful, honey!" Mom high-fives me. "I'm so happy for you!"

I can't wait to tell Dad about it! A friend on the first day— that's like scoring a goal in the first ten minutes of the game!

Lea sinks her chin into her hands. "Well, that makes one of us," she says. "I had to sit on the friendship bench all by myself."

"The friendship bench?" I ask, squeezing my eyebrows.

"It's this bench you sit on if you don't have anybody to play with. The teacher said if I sat on it, one of the other girls would come by and play with me. But none of them came by. . . ." Lea frowns.

I reach into my backpack for my snack box, but not even

the prospect of purple Goldfish makes her feel better.

"I'm so sorry, bao bao," Mom says. "But it's only the first day . . . it'll get better."

Lea looks at Mom. "What if it doesn't?" she asks. "What if they're all best-friended up? What if by the time my birthday comes around, I'm still sitting on the friendship bench?"

"You won't be," Mom says as she drives over to the middle school to pick up Bowen. "You'll find your pals. It just takes a little time."

"What about the boys? Did you try playing with them?" I suggest.

Lea turns to me and lets me know, "I go to school so I can develop female relationships!"

I put my hands up—*Geez, okay!*

We get to the middle school and Bowen runs up to the car.

"What took you guys so long??" he asks, jumping inside. Before Mom even has a chance to answer, Bowen declares, "I can't stay at that school!"

"Why not?" Mom asks.

"They don't have any foreign languages! All the French and Chinese I've been learning will be completely wasted! They don't have design technology or economics, either." Bowen frowns. "If I stay here, I'm looking at a three-out-of-ten future!"

"You are *not*," Mom says to him. "And since when have you become so obsessed over rankings?"

"Since you told me, 'If you want to get into Berkeley, you gotta be the best of the best!'" Bowen reminds Mom.

"And you still can!"

"Not if I stay at this school," he says. "I have to go to a private school. I looked it up, and Pacifica Prep has seven times the AP offerings!"

"You know we can't afford private school right now," Mom says gently.

"So I'll get a scholarship!"

"Even if you get in, the commute is out of the question for me. I'm only one person. I can't be driving you three for hours all over the place every morning. I'm trying to find a job."

Bowen digs his hands in his hair. I can tell he's super disappointed—academics is his life. I open my mouth to try to offer him words of comfort—I've had *plenty* of not-so-great school experiences. But I close my mouth. Now's probably not a good time to give Bowen advice.

Later that afternoon, Lea comes and finds me in the back-yard while I'm dribbling my soccer ball. I didn't get to play at recess, so I'm making up for lost kicks.

"Where's Mom?" I ask.

Lea sighs. "Upstairs, working on her résumé. Can I watch?" she asks, taking a seat on the grass.

"Sure," I say. I walk my sister through all the steps I'm doing as I play, trying to remember the things my coach in Hong Kong taught me. I wish I had a coach here. I've been itching to ask Mom about signing me up for local clubs, but I'm worried about how much that stuff will cost.

"I miss Dad," Lea says.

"Me too," I say. If Dad were here, he could coach me for free!

"Do you think he'll make it over for my birthday?" she asks.

Nope! Not if flights cost $3,000! But one look at my sister's face and I don't want to dash her hopes. "Maybe," I say instead. "We'd have to come up with a plan."

Lea stands up. "I like plans!"

We look over at Bowen, who overhears us from the screen door. He starts walking over.

"We'd have to come up with three thousand dollars," he says.

"I thought you said it was impossible," I mutter.

"Yeah, well, that was *before.* Now I need him to get over here so he can talk some sense into Mom. I can't stay at that school!" Bowen says.

I clap my hands, glad the three of us are all in agreement for once. Operation Dad Come Over—*let's do this.*

"So how are we gonna get the three thousand dollars?" Lea asks, jumping up and down excitedly on the grass.

I have an idea!

"What if we sell your Bose headphones?" I suggest to my brother.

"No way!" Bowen shouts.

"C'mon." I cross my arms. "Do you want Dad here or not?"

"Why do we have to sell *my* headphones?" Bowen asks. "Why can't we sell your stuff or Lea's?"

"I don't have anything valuable!" I exclaim. "The most expensive thing Mom ever bought me, I spilled all over Target!"

"*Yeah!* And all I have are a bunch of stuffed animals!"

But Bowen shakes his head firmly.

"Well, I'm not selling my headphones," he says. "They were a present from Dad, for getting in the ninety-ninth percentile on a test. Do you know how hard that was? I might *never* be able to pull that off again!"

I kick the grass as Bowen walks away. I can't believe he's picking his headphones over Dad.

Chapter 27

--- ✈

The next morning, I go into Mom's room super early to talk to her. She's in bed working. I notice she's taken over the whole bed. When we first arrived, nearly three weeks ago, she slept on the right side of the bed only, just like she did in Hong Kong. Now she's moved to the middle, which makes me a little worried.

Mom pats the space next to her and I crawl into bed with her.

I remember crawling into bed with Mom whenever it was Hungry Ghost Festival in Hong Kong, the seventh month of the lunar calendar. It's a time for people to burn fake money and other offerings to their ancestors. If I close my eyes, I can still smell the burning incense on the street.

"Mom, are we gonna burn incense in September?" I ask.

Mom looks up from her computer, amused.

"What made you think of that?" she asks.

I shrug. My mind goes in all directions sometimes, like water. . . . Speaking of which . . .

"Why'd you tell the school secretary I have ADHD?" I ask.

Mom puts her computer away.

"It's nothing," she says. "You might not even have it. It's just something we're keeping an eye on."

"So I *don't* have it?" I ask. "And why didn't you tell me any of this?"

"Because there was nothing to tell. You're right on the edge. . . ." Mom tries to put her arm around me, but I wriggle away.

"On which side??"

Mom doesn't say.

Instead, she tries to distract me by recording a voice message to my *lao lao* and *lao ye* together with her on the phone. I drift asleep as Mom talks into the WeChat, the soothing sound of her Chinese drowning out the many questions in my heart . . . about what I may or may not have.

When I wake up, Mom's down in the kitchen. Bowen's munching on cereal like a lawn mower.

I pack up my school bag, taking out some of my focus toys. I don't need so many, now that they have them in my classroom. This gives me so much extra space, I can finally fit my soccer ball inside! I hope I get to play soccer with Christopher at recess instead of coronavirus tag.

"You still need those baby toys for your hand muscles?" Bowen asks, looking up from his cereal bowl.

I scowl at him as milk drips from his spoon. Was that what my parents told him my focus toys were for? So he wouldn't make fun of me?

Mom walks into the kitchen. "Wow. Look at this. There are now sixty thousand cases of the coronavirus, including the first case in London. And they're calling it COVID-19."

I forget the focus toys and go over to look at the article. "So it's spreading??" I ask.

"I wouldn't say it's spreading. There are only a few cases in the US," Mom says. "But just in case . . . I'm packing some hand sanitizer in all your backpacks."

Mom puts her laptop down and goes to get the little bottles of hand sanitizer she ordered online.

"I'm not using that," Bowen declares.

"Why not?"

"You want me to pull that out at school and have everyone stare at me?? Then they'll *really* think I have it. . . ."

I turn to Bowen. Is *that* why he doesn't like his new school?

Mom throws some in his backpack anyway. "It's a matter of your health and safety," she says, reminding him of his own words.

"There's no virus here. You're just overreacting from the news!" Bowen says, taking the hand sanitizer out and tossing it on the table.

Mom lets out a deep and frustrated sigh as Bowen points to her computer.

"How's the job search going?" he asks.

Mom shakes her head. "I've been sending out résumés, but no one's emailed me back yet," she says. "I just don't get it. I have all this incredible job experience from Asia!"

As Mom frets and chews her lip, I think about recess yesterday. I wonder, do grown-ups have coronavirus tag too?

Lea points to Mom's profile picture on her LinkedIn.

"You know what you need?" she asks Mom. "A makeover."

Mom bursts out laughing.

"I'm serious." Lea's eyes widen with wonder. "I can help you!"

"I seriously doubt a better picture will make a difference . . . ," Mom starts to say, then takes in Lea's hurt face. "But if you want, we can try it!"

"Get ready to look *nothing* like yourself!"

Mom chuckles as she grabs the car keys and shuffles us out the door.

I reach for the hand sanitizer on the counter. When Bowen's not looking, I sneak it into my brother's backpack. Just in case.

In the car, we ask Mom what types of jobs she's applying for. She says she's applying all over, in finance, tech, biotech.

"I don't really mind where I work. But I do want to get a job with more flexible hours, so I don't have to be on the road all the time like at my last job."

"That was *brutal*," I tell Mom. Bowen and Lea quickly second my opinion: "The worst!"

Mom glances at us. "Oh, c'mon, it wasn't that bad . . . ," she says.

"I once secretly recorded you saying good night to me so I could play it back when you were on the road," Lea confesses.

"Really??" Mom stops the car at a light and turns to Lea. "Oh, honey, I'm so sorry. I hope you know I missed you guys every second when I was gone. But it was part of my job. Every banker in Hong Kong had to do it." She reaches out a hand to us. "But I'm here now. For good."

I want to believe Mom's words. But so far, we haven't really had much of Summer Mom, even when she doesn't have a job. She's been too busy searching for work.

"You know, Mom, if you need to travel, *I* can deal with these two," Bowen offers.

I burst out laughing—*Yeah right*. Bowen gives me an offended look.

"Um, I don't think so," Lea agrees.

"Thanks for the offer, Bowen, but I think I'm good. I actually want to spend more time with you all," Mom says.

I smile at Mom.

"Oh, by the way, I made some calls and guess what? The soccer tryouts for the local league are coming up in March!"

"YES!" I thrust my fist in the air, hitting my knuckles on the roof of the car. *Ow*.

"Be careful! Remember, until I find a new job, we don't have any health insurance."

"What about Dad's job?" I ask.

"That doesn't cover us in the United States," Mom says.

"So how do people here get insurance?" I ask.

Mom explains that in America, most people get it through their employers, because insurance is so expensive. Unlike in Hong Kong, they don't have universal healthcare.

"But what about the people without a job . . . what happens if they get sick?" I ask.

Mom bites her lip and doesn't say anything for so long that I look down. *Oh*. I promise her I won't head the ball or do anything dangerous.

"How about track?" Bowen asks.

"I finally got in touch with your school's track coach last night, and he says you can come by practice in a couple of weeks!"

A smile stretches across Bowen's face—the truest smile I've seen on his face since we landed.

"How about me?" Lea asks. "Anything for art after school?"

"I put your name down on the waiting list for this work-shop at the Lawrence Hall of Science at Berkeley!" Mom tells Lea.

Lea grins. "Thanks, Mom!" She taps my arm lightly with her elbow. "See? Things are getting better. We're surviving this."

"We certainly are!" Mom laughs as she pulls up in front of our elementary school. Before she lets us out, she reminds Lea that if none of the other kids want to play with her today, she can go to the library.

"That's what I did when I was a kid."

"But I thought you said you had a best friend," Lea says to Mom.

"Not always. I only told you about the good years."

I furrow my eyebrows as I get out of the car. If Mom only told us about the good years, what happened in the bad years?

Chapter 28

I stare at the cracks in the pavement on the way to my classroom, wondering why Mom didn't tell us the whole story and what else she's keeping from us. Christopher runs up to me and asks if I've seen the Netflix special on pandemics. He has to return a book at the library drop box, so I walk with him.

"Oh yeah! I've seen it like five times!" I give him a tip. "Don't watch that and *Contagion* back to back. I did that in Hong Kong. Trust me, I didn't sleep for a week!"

I shudder at the memory.

"What was it like? Being in Hong Kong when the virus hit?" Christopher asks me.

I smile at him. The nice thing about letting it slip on where I'm from is I can actually talk about it. I tell Christopher about the masks and pressing the elevator buttons with toothpicks.

"With *toothpicks*?" he asks. "And people actually do it?"

"Oh yeah, everyone does it. We've all been through SARS," I say proudly, feeling like a virus expert. I actually haven't been through SARS, but my dad has. So I basically have.

"Wow, that's pretty cool," Christopher says. "Maybe we should have that at the restaurant—give everyone toothpicks when they sign their credit card on the iPad."

My eyes widen. "You have a restaurant?"

"My parents do," Christopher says.

"Is it close by? Can I visit?" I ask as we walk toward our classroom together, excited by the prospect of some homemade food.

"Sure! It's called Uncle Chang's Sichuan Garden," Christopher says. He tells me it's by Lucky's. "My mom makes the *best* honey walnut prawns!"

"I'd love some honey walnut prawns!" I close my eyes and think of my *lao lao*'s back home. She used to make them for us whenever she came down. And Bowen would polish off a whole dish!

I take a piece of paper from my backpack and jot it down: *Uncle Chang's Sichuan Garden—Christopher's restaurant!* I got the idea of writing notes to myself from Christopher. He's always writing things down on Post-its. It's kind of cool. Like Old Me talking to Future Me.

He tells me that lately, fewer people have been coming into his parents' restaurant. "They think they might get the virus or something."

For real?

"I know . . . ," Christopher says to my shocked face. "Hey, thanks for standing up for me yesterday at recess."

"Of course," I say. In a small voice, I ask gently, "Are they always like that?"

My friend looks down. "It started ever since we got a couple cases in San Francisco."

At the mention of cases, I pull out my hand sanitizer. I squirt some into my hands and offer some to Christopher. He takes a few squirts.

"I'm sorry," I say. "That's so mean."

"It's okay," Christopher replies. "Hopefully, it'll be over soon. And I can go back to not being *it*!"

We both shake our heads at the ridiculousness.

"Tell me more about Hong Kong," he says.

I smile and tell him all the things I miss about it, like my dog and the man at the cheese store who always gave me a free piece of cheddar. Most of all my dad.

"I wish he didn't have to live in Hong Kong. . . ."

As we're walking, Christopher pulls out a little bottle from his backpack.

"I forgot to take my ADHD medication," Christopher says when he notices me staring at his hand holding the bottle.

"Did you say ADHD??" I ask, my eyes widening.

I watch, fascinated, as Christopher takes out an orange pill and pops it into his mouth. He washes it down with some water from his water bottle. I get so excited, I squirt some of my hand sanitizer into the air.

"I have ADHD too!" I tell him. "At least I think I do. . . . I don't know. . . ."

"Trust me, you'd know if you had it. You blurt things out and you touch stuff you're not supposed to, like a bald man's head. You feel like you're either in trouble or you're *about* to be in trouble all the time."

I grab Christopher by the arms. "That is *exactly* how I feel! Constantly!"

Christopher laughs. "Congratulations!" he diagnoses me. It's both thrilling and terrifying hearing the confirmation. I fall a little quiet. Christopher says gently, "Hey . . . it's nothing to be ashamed of. *Despite* what Tyler says."

I look up at Christopher. "He teases you about that, too?"

Christopher nods and quickly puts the pill bottle away.

I reach out an arm to stop him. "Can I have one of those?" I ask Christopher. I wonder why Mom never got me any pills. Maybe they aren't available in Hong Kong, like the purple Goldfish and the Cheddar Jalapeño Flamin' Hot Cheetos they have here.

"Sorry," Christopher says, zipping up his backpack. "My doctor says I can't give these away. They don't work the same for everyone."

"Why not?"

"Because everyone's different," Christopher says. "You should go and see my doctor. You want his number? I can get it from my mom."

I start nodding, then remember we don't have health insurance yet. My face falls.

"What's wrong?" Christopher asks.

"My mom lost her job. We don't have health insurance right now . . . ," I tell him. I brace for his reaction. Is he going to judge me? In Hong Kong, the other kids would definitely judge me for that.

But Christopher just says, "Well, when she does, I'll give it to you."

I smile. It feels good to know I have options. That I'm not the only kid in the world going through this. And that I finally have a friend who gets it.

Chapter 29

--✈

"**M**akeover time!" Lea announces when Mom comes to pick us up.

Mom asks us how school was as we climb into the car. I tell her I learned factors and multiples today.

"And I actually *learned* it because Mrs. Turner let us watch a video on how to do it," I say. "Mrs. Turner says some kids learn better watching videos."

That's when I had a EUREKA moment in my head: that's totally how I trained Cody to fetch my slippers—from YouTube! Which just goes to show. Dogs learn in different ways too.

"That's wonderful!" Mom says. "How about you, Lea? Did you have to sit on the friendship bench today?"

"No, I went to the library today like you said," Lea says, grabbing a book out of her backpack and presenting it to us—*A Complete Guide to Special Effects Makeup*.

I point at the words "special effects." "Uhh, you realize that's for the movies. . . ."

"It's gonna be so lit!" she squeals.

I lean over and look at my sister's other books—*102 Cookie Recipes*, *Sisters* by Raina Telgemeier, and *How to Start a YouTube Channel and Become an Online Star*. "Really?" I ask, picking the YouTube book up.

"What? It can happen!" she insists. "You gotta think big, Knox!"

I roll my eyes as Mom pulls up to the middle school and Bowen gets into the car.

"Mom! I've been researching and there's this Chinese American International School in San Francisco!" Bowen says breathlessly when he gets into the car. "If I apply now—"

"In San Francisco?" Mom asks. "No, that's out of the question."

"I can take BART!"

"You're not taking BART every day," Mom says as she pulls out of the parking lot. "Look, if you really want to take Chinese, you can take it at the community college over the summer, or online."

"I don't want to take it *that* bad . . . ," he says.

Mom looks at him and pulls over to the side of the road.

"Then . . . why do you want to go to CAIS?"

"Never mind," Bowen mumbles.

Mom shifts the car into park and we sit for a second under a leafy elm tree. "You know, I remember when I was growing up, I was the only Chinese kid in an all-white school," she says gently.

Bowen looks up. "Really?"

"We were living in San Clemente," Mom says. "My parents were working in a small restaurant."

Wait, I never heard about this. "I thought Lao Lao and Lao Ye were doctors!"

"They were . . . in China," Mom says. "But when we got to America, they worked as a cook and waitress."

I try picturing my *lao lao* and *lao ye* serving people in a restaurant. They both move like turtles now. Maybe if they wore roller skates, it could work.

"My friend Christopher's family runs a Chinese restaurant," I announce. "Can we go there for dinner sometime? His mom makes the best honey walnut shrimp!"

"Honey walnut shrimp?" Lea asks eagerly. She pats her stomach. "Get in my tummy!!!"

Mom glances hesitantly down at her purse. "Maybe we can swing it . . . if we don't order a lot."

"YES!!!" Lea and I squeal.

"You were *saying*," Bowen reminds Mom. "About being the only Chinese kid in your school?"

"Oh yeah," Mom continues her story. "It was hard at first, but I ended up really liking it. I remember I had my first crush. This boy Thomas—"

"Ew, Mom, no!" Bowen protests, putting a stop to that story. Which is too bad because I really want to hear more.

"Anyway, my point is you just have to give it time. It'll turn around, you'll see," Mom says.

When I get home, I go up to my room, grab my iPad, and lock myself in the bathroom. I take a deep breath and open up the ADHD page again. This time, I don't stop at "differences in their brain development"—I make myself read on.

According to KidsHealth, people with ADHD are inattentive, hyperactive, and impulsive. It says kids with ADHD might "interrupt, push, grab, and find it hard to wait. They may have emotional reactions that seem too intense for the situation."

I scrunch my face at the webpage. *Oh please.* Like my reactions are any more intense than Bowen's!

I scroll down to treatments. As soon as I click on the ADHD medication chart, a million different medications pop up, including Concerta. I don't want to go to a concert!

My iPad starts ringing. It's my grandparents.

"Hi, didi!" they greet me in Chinese. "We got you and your mom's voice message. How's America? Are you getting along with gege? We miss you so much!"

"Miss you too, Lao Lao!" I say, leaving the bathroom and going to sit down on my bunk. I don't think my grandparents want a visual of the toilet. "Hey, how come you never told me you and Lao Ye worked in a restaurant?"

"Oh, that was a long time ago," Lao Lao says. "Your mom told you about that?"

I nod.

"A lot of Chinese people worked in restaurants back then," Lao Lao says. "It was the only way to survive."

"Was it hard?" I ask.

"Oh yeah, very hard," my *lao ye* says, walking over to the computer. "We had to cook and clean, get up at the crack of dawn."

I wonder if those were the bad years Mom was referring to. They don't seem so bad. I'd love to make dumplings with Lao Lao. She always lets me dip my finger in the water to seal the *pi-er*.

"Did Mom help?"

"Oh, she helped a lot!" Lao Ye nods. "Your mom translated for us and helped us with the customers. Where do you think she learned how to do business?"

"Now she's a proper banker!" Lao Lao says proudly.

I bite my lip. I take it Mom hasn't exactly told Lao Lao and Lao Ye about losing her job. I want to tell them, but then I remember the time I got a really bad score on my math test and Bowen beat me to telling my parents. And I hated him more than the test score.

So instead, I tell my grandparents about Christopher's parents' restaurant.

"He's my new best friend," I announce proudly.

"You're lucky you get to go to school," Lao Lao says. "Everything in Beijing is shut. They're doing temperature checks in all the apartment blocks. If you have even a slight temperature, they put you in automatic quarantine!"

"Wow!" I tell Lao Ye. "You guys should come here!"

"Oh no, I'm not getting on a flight in a pandemic. Not at my age!" Lao Lao says.

My mom calls my name.

"I gotta go," I tell Lao Lao and Lao Ye. "I miss you guys."

"Miss you, too," Lao Lao says. "Be careful. Remember, this virus knows no borders. . . ."

Chapter 30

H ow do I look?" Mom asks, spinning around in the chair in the living room to show me the new makeover that Lea gave her. Lea *way* overdid it with the eye shadow.

"Um . . . are you trying to get a job as the Joker?" I ask Mom.

Mom jumps up and goes to the mirror. She screams at her raccoon-like reflection.

"I was just following the book!" Lea says.

Mom starts dabbing her face with makeup remover as Dad video-calls her on WhatsApp.

"Whoa!" Dad says when Mom answers the phone. "Is this a new look?"

Mom glances at my sister. "Lea and I were just . . . trying something out."

"Lea did that?" Dad asks, impressed.

Lea takes the phone from Mom.

"Hi, Daddy, I miss you," she says.

"Miss you, too, smoochie," he says. "Two smoochies don't make a mochi!"

Lea smiles at the inside joke between her and Dad.

"So what are you guys up to?" Dad asks.

"I gotta get dinner started," Mom says, and hollers up to Bowen in our room to help her in the kitchen.

"I thought we were going to Christopher's!" I protest.

"Not tonight," Mom says. "We just went to In-N-Out the other day. . . ."

"But can't we go and just get one little thing??" I ask, putting my hands together. "His restaurant's not doing well! We gotta support him!"

Mom hesitates for a long time. "Okay . . . ," she finally relents. "But just *one* thing. I still don't have a job and Dad's salary just got cut—"

"Julie!" Dad calls out.

Mom puts a hand over her mouth. Our heads flip to Dad. What salary cut? What's Mom talking about?

Dad sighs. "Don't worry, you two. It's not a big deal. . . . We'll get through it. A lot of people I know—"

"Like Dad said, nothing for you guys to worry about." Mom abruptly ends the call.

As she walks up the stairs to wipe off the charcoal makeup, I scramble after her, *very* worried.

Chapter 31

--✈

What happened to Dad's salary?" I ask in the car.

"*Nothing,*" Mom says. There she goes again, trying to ignore the money balloon. She continues talking to Bowen about his upcoming math test and quizzes him on ratios and proportions as she drives.

"Just *tell* us," I say to her, thrusting my body forward from the back. I look to Bowen to back me up, but he's too busy reciting math answers like a parrot. I don't know who he's trying to impress—the window? The armrest? The money balloon is clearly popping right before our eyes! Why won't anybody talk about it? "How much did they cut his salary??"

"It's none of your concern," Mom says, pumping the brakes.

"Of course it is!" I look to Lea for backup, and she nods and lunges forward.

"Does that mean I can't go to my after-school art thing?" she asks.

Mom doesn't answer. Instead, she pulls into a gas station to fill up the tank. The whole time she's getting gas, my eyes are glued to the ticker, watching it go up and up and up. I don't realize I'm holding my breath until the pump finally stops.

Mom pulls out her credit card and gets back in the car.

She sits there for a second. "These are tough times in

Asia," she tells us. "Your dad is fine. He's hanging in there. It could be a lot worse—a lot of his coworkers got furloughed."

"Fur what?" I ask. I picture a furry loaf of bread. *That's* a weird thing to give people.

"Furloughed. It's when your employer temporarily lets you go home because they don't need you to work, and you're not paid," Mom says, starting the car.

Oh.

"That's why I'm working so hard to find a new job. Which I *will*," Mom insists. Her phone dings with a text right on cue. "This could be it!" We all hold our breath as Mom asks Siri to read the message.

Please, please, please . . . let this be Mom's new boss. So we can fill up the money balloon again and not have to worry about eating furry bread.

But it's just Comcast texting Mom to say our internet bill is overdue.

Christopher runs out to greet us when we get to the restaurant.

"You guys came!"

"Of course." Mom smiles, shaking Christopher's hand. "I'm Julie, and this is Bowen and Lea."

"Is this restaurant all yours?" Lea asks.

"Yup!" Christopher says proudly, leading us inside. The delicious smells of sizzling prawns and crispy spring rolls swirl up my nose. "It belonged to my great-grandfather. It's been in my family for three generations!"

"Wow, that's amazing," Mom says. "Do you ever help out at the restaurant?"

"Sometimes, but my mom never lets me in the kitchen. She says I run around too much," Christopher says, leading us over to a table with a bright red tablecloth and a big glass lazy Susan. "Once I broke twenty-five jars of soy sauce."

"Sounds like someone I know," Mom says, winking at me. I turn a little red.

Christopher's mom, Mrs. Leung, walks over and greets us warmly. She gives us big thick menus, even though we're ordering dinner to go. The menus have gorgeous pictures of each dish. As Mom looks over the choices, I gaze around at all the empty tables in the restaurant.

There are only three customers eating. The chairs look so lonely, just waiting for people.

"You should have seen this place before the virus," Christopher leans over and whispers. "Completely packed."

"Really?" I whisper back.

Christopher nods. "We even got an award for Best Small Business for the Community," he tells me, pointing to a plaque on the wall as a man comes in for his take-out order.

"Everything on the menu looks delicious," Mom says, admiring the pictures of the beautiful dishes. "We're so homesick for Chinese food."

"Then you must try our delicious *moo shu* pancakes. We make them by hand," Mrs. Leung says, ringing the take-out customer up over the counter.

As Christopher's mom describes the handmade *moo shu* pancakes, the take-out guy looks up in alarm. He's a young white guy with earbuds and perfectly white sneakers.

"You make these pancakes by hand?" he asks, gazing down at his large order.

Mrs. Leung nods. "Yes. First, we make the dough, then we roll it and steam it," she says to him.

"Well then, I don't want it . . . ," he says, putting the bag down. "You can take it all back."

"What??" Mrs. Leung asks, looking down at all the food he's ordered. There are about ten boxes. "What about your dinner party?"

"I just . . . I'd feel more comfortable ordering pizza," he says. "I hope you understand . . . we can't be too careful these days."

Christopher looks absolutely blue as the customer walks out without paying. "What are we going to do?" he asks his mom.

Christopher's dad comes out of the kitchen. The look on his face when he sees his cooked food just sitting there in the plastic bag, unwanted, is heartbreaking. "Take it away," Mrs. Leung tells him in Mandarin.

"Actually, no, we'll take it!" Mom calls out. I look over at her. Is she sure? That's a *lot* of food! And she said we're only getting one thing.

Before anyone can object, Mom slides her credit card across the counter and pays for all the food the other customer ordered. "We'd be honored to eat your homemade pancakes," she says to Mrs. Leung, who puts a hand over her heart.

"Thank you," Mrs. Leung says. "But are you sure you can eat all this?"

"Oh, we'll eat every last *moo* and *shu*! Don't worry about that!" Bowen says, patting his tummy.

As Mrs. Leung charges Mom's credit card, Bowen, Lea, and I help take all the food out to the car. Mom gets inside a few minutes later, her eyes misty.

"What's wrong?" I ask her.

Mom shakes her head and tries to brush away the tears with her fingers as she sits in the driver's seat, holding the receipt. "Nothing."

Lea reaches for her from her booster seat. "Are you sad because it was too expensive?" she asks. "We'll eat it all, *promise.*"

"No, it's not that," Mom says. "I'm just sad because of the way that man treated Christopher's mom. . . . It made me think of when I was a kid and customers would always give my parents a hard time. I really thought that times had changed . . . but now, it's happening all over again." She lets out a soft cry.

I hold out a hand and Mom squeezes it tight.

"It makes me worried about what's going to happen . . . ," Mom confesses, her chin quivering. "And whether I can find a job . . ."

I unbuckle my seat belt and lean over so I can give Mom a hug. As Lea and I cling to Mom, she holds us. "Mostly I just really miss your dad. . . ."

"Oh Mommy," Lea whispers.

All this time, my siblings and I have been quietly missing Dad, but we never thought about how Mom's feeling. He's her best friend.

"At least you got us," I say in a small voice.

Mom smiles through her tears. "Yes, I do." She turns to us, all serious. "You must promise you'll always do your best to right wrongs, okay, guys?"

Lea, Bowen, and I nod. "Promise."

Mom sets the receipt down as she puts her seat belt on. Bowen and I both glance at the receipt. Wow. Mom paid $218 to right that wrong.

"Hope you like *moo shu* pork!" Mom calls.

"We *love moo shu* pork!" the three of us answer.

Lea comes into our room late that night and wakes me and Bowen up.

"Geges?" Lea asks, turning the lights on.

"What do you want?" Bowen growls, sitting up.

"We *have* to get Dad to come over here," Lea says. "You saw how sad Mom was."

I've been thinking about it too, the way Mom burst into tears like that. I've never seen her do that before. She's usually so in control and as cool as a cucumber.

"I knew this would happen. She can't handle us," I say, shaking my head. "We're too much."

"Especially *you*," Bowen adds.

"Hey! I'm not the one constantly whining about going to private school," I shoot right back.

"I would only *go* if I got a scholarship," Bowen says.

"You guys stop!" Lea whisper-yells.

I fluff my pillow and lie on my stomach.

"Maybe if Mom finds a new job, things will get better," I say.

"If Mom does find a new job here, they'll be separated forever," Lea wails. "Her and Dad—they'll grow apart!"

Tears brim in her eyes as she tucks her face into her pj's

and I recognize the worry. It's the same worry I get when I see Mom's pillow in the middle of her bed. But it's even scarier when my sister says it like that.

"And then we'll have to be divided up," my sister mutters from behind her shirt. "Mom will get me, Dad will get Bowen. And Knox will be split right down the middle, one arm each."

"Hey!" I exclaim, feeling my arms to make sure they're intact.

Bowen throws his cover off—now he's wide awake. "Okay, okay, if we were going to get Dad over here, how would we do it?" He snaps at me, "Don't even think about touching my headphones!"

"We'd have to come up with three thousand dollars," Lea says.

I ask the obvious question that's been weighing on my mind. "Would Dad come over just to visit or to live?"

"To live, definitely," Bowen says. I smile, relieved to hear him say that, now that I've finally found a good teacher and a good friend! Phew!

"If Dad lived here, he could take me to BART in the mornings!" Bowen says.

"And tell me funny stories. That's how I made so many friends at my old school, recycling his stories!" Lea says. "And it's just not the same on Zoom. The connection is so choppy and I always miss the punch line."

"So it's agreed." I glance at my siblings. "Operation Dad Come Over starts now!"

The three of us shake on it. I make a rocket-blasting-off noise.

"We should *probably* find him a job here too," Bowen says.

"How on earth are we going to do *that*?"

I hold up a finger. My siblings watch as I hop down from my bunk and load up the website that Mom's been glued to every day. "LinkedIn, baby!"

Chapter 32

The next day it's Valentine's Day, and Mom comes running into our room at dawn with amazing news. "Guess what?! A recruiter got back to me—I have an interview on Monday!!"

"Woo-hoo!!!" Bowen and I cheer. I get down from my bunk and reach for a notebook to take notes.

"So Mom, what company is it??" I ask.

"It's this tech company, Focu$. They have an app that deducts your money if you procrastinate on the things you're supposed to do."

"There's an app for that?" Bowen asks.

"There's an app for *everything* these days," Mom tells us.

I wish there were an app for getting Dad over here. On that note, I ask Mom, "So how does this LinkedIn thing work? Do you just apply?"

Mom shakes her head. "First you must get over five hundred connections."

"Why five hundred?"

"That's the magic number that makes people take you seriously."

I write *500 TO LOOK LEGIT* in my notebook. Now the key question . . .

"Do you know if Dad's on LinkedIn?" I ask, holding my breath.

Mom laughs. "You know how Dad is. I've been telling him to make a profile for years, but . . . ," she sighs.

I grin at Bowen. YESSSSS!!! Dad's procrastination is our opportunity!

At school, I try to pull up LinkedIn while my classmates are busy exchanging Valentines, but unfortunately, it's blocked. I frown and gaze over at the many little red and pink envelopes scattered all over our classroom. I'm not expecting anything, since I'm new. But my teacher, Mrs. Turner, surprises me with a big Trader Joe's bag.

"Happy Valentine's Day, sweetie," she says.

Mrs. Turner chuckles at my shocked face.

"What, you thought we were going to let you go home empty-handed?"

Speechless, I dump the Trader Joe's bag on my table. It's filled with pink and red and purple cards. I immediately start opening them up.

Half of the Valentines say, *To New Kid*, and the other half say, *Dear Knocks*. Still, I smile so hard, my face hurts. I've never gotten a Valentine before from anyone at school in Hong Kong, not even Amir!

I peer up at Mrs. Turner at her desk—this must have been her idea. Frantically, I search for my pad of Post-its and write her a Valentine.

Dear Mrs. Turner,
Happy Valentine's Day. Thanks for making me feel welcomed.

Love, Your student,
Knox

I cross out "Love" even though I really do love Mrs.
Turner and write "Your student" because it sounds more official. While I'm at it, I make one for Mom, one for my sister,
and one for Christopher. I don't make one for Bowen because
he'll probably think it's too babyish. But I secretly hope he got
a Trader Joe's bag too.

Chapter 33

--✈

Bowen did not get a Trader Joe's bag of Valentines, unfortunately, and when he sees me with my giant stash of cards when Mom picks him up, he barks, "Who cares about Valentines? I'll bet half those cards were written by your teacher."

Which makes me really angry.

"You're just saying that because you didn't get squat!" I tell Bowen.

Mom scolds me for my "mean outburst," even though Bowen's the one who started it. Bowen and I sit in silence the rest of the way home, while I quietly slip Lea her Valentine's Post-it. Lea grins and takes out a coloring pencil and her notebook and draws me a flower. She adds it to my Trader Joe's bag. When we get home, there's a *real* vase of flowers waiting for Mom outside our door.

Mom runs out before even turning off the car. They're from Dad!

The smile on Mom's face—even wider than when she received her interview news—goes a long way toward melting my pillow worries.

That night, while I cut the stems of Mom's flowers and Lea puts them in a vase, Bowen helps Mom prep for her big interview.

"Feed me some more interview questions," Mom says to Bowen, popping a breath mint in her mouth.

"Okay, try this one: Why are manhole covers round?" Bowen asks. I give him a funny look. Where did he *get* these interview questions?

"What? Google apparently asked this question!" he says, pointing to his computer.

"Because it's easier to remove the lid?" Mom asks.

Bowen shakes his head. "So the cover can't fall in," he tells her.

"Oh."

"Okay, here's another one. You've been given an elephant. You can't give it away or sell it. What will you do with it?"

Mom nearly chokes on her breath mint. "Are you serious?"

"Hey! I didn't make it up. These are the kind of questions tech companies like to ask!" Bowen says, nodding to the website.

"Okay, okay," Mom says, putting two fingers to her temples and thinking hard. "I would probably take it on a trip to 'visit' its homeland and lose it there. Can I do that?"

Bowen makes the *errrr* wrong-answer buzzer sound. "I don't think so. . . ."

Mom covers her face with her hands. "I'm never going to pass this interview. Who am I kidding? I'm not cool enough to work at a tech start-up. I don't have enough black turtlenecks! I drive a Honda minivan, for *crying out loud*!"

We all rush to comfort her.

"You're the coolest mom I know!" Lea says.

"Yeah. You may not have an elephant, but you have the

three of us," I add. "And you haven't given any of us away or sold us."

"Yet," Bowen adds jokingly.

Mom gives us a half smile.

"Thanks, guys . . . ," she says.

I turn to Bowen. "Here, let me." I sit up and try to look like a job applicant. I gesture to Bowen to hit me with the same questions.

"If you were a tree, what would you be?" he asks.

"Oak—definitely!"

"How do you test an elevator?" Bowen asks.

"With your finger, or a toothpick if you live in Hong Kong!"

"Explain the internet."

"Information on pages ranked by machines. Some of them are fake."

Mom laughs. "Whoa, you're really good at this!" she exclaims.

"You just gotta go with the first thing that pops into your head! Don't think!" I tell Mom.

"Maybe *you* should get a job working in tech."

I grin at Mom.

"Okay, my turn!" Bowen says. "Ask me a question!"

I don't have special tech questions like he does, so I just shoot him regular ones.

"Why are you so competitive all the time?" I ask.

"Because I like to win," Bowen answers.

"What do you miss about Hong Kong?"

Bowen thinks for a minute. I expect him to say dim sum or the world's longest outdoor escalator, which was right by our apartment, but instead, he answers, "Being able to fit in."

Mom looks over when he says that. "Oh, sweetie," she says, reaching out a hand. She tries to give Bowen a hug, but he wriggles away.

"Whatever, it's just an answer," Bowen mutters, closing his laptop and going to the kitchen.

I sit there, thinking about my brother's response . . . and feeling bad I rubbed it in that he didn't get squat Valentines.

Chapter 34

On Saturday morning, my siblings and I gather in my room for another secret Operation Dad Come Over club meeting. I'm excited to show them my progress with Dad's LinkedIn, but there's something I have to ask first. It's stuck in my head like gum.

"Hey, Bowen, what did you mean by not fitting in here?" I ask him gently.

"Nothing," he insists. "It was just an answer! Now where's Dad's LinkedIn??"

I quickly open up my laptop.

"All right," I say to my siblings. "I set up Dad's LinkedIn page using Bowen's email."

"Nice," Bowen says.

I give him an appreciative smile.

"We just have to fill it out. Does anyone know all the places where he's worked? I know he's at Simden and Cadwell now."

"I think he's worked at a bunch of law firms," Bowen says.

"What are the names?"

"I don't think it really matters. They're all the same."

I shrug and google "law firms" and enter the first ten that come up under employment history. And just to mix it up, I give Dad a bunch of different jobs at each one—partner, summer associate, legal secretary, office manager. I look them over. That sounds about right. Moving on to education.

"Dad went to school with Mom, right?" I ask Bowen. I enter *UC Berkeley* under education. I look up. "Did he graduate with honors?"

"No, Mom's the one who graduated with honors. *She's* the academic superstar. That's why the chancellor gave her that special glass in the kitchen!"

"What's a chancellor?" Lea asks, confused.

"I think it's someone who takes a lot of chances," Bowen responds.

"So no honors for Dad?" I ask, making sure.

"No honors. He was just okay. I don't think he got any glasses."

I don't see an option for "just okay." So I type in: *Tried my hardest*, which is what my teachers are always putting on my report cards.

When I'm finished, I show the profile to my siblings. We scroll through Bowen's phone, looking for a good pic of Dad. We finally settle on one of him barbecuing last summer, holding up a hot dog. Who doesn't like a hot dog?

"Looks great!" Lea says, giving an excited squeal. "What job should we apply for first?" she asks.

"Not so fast," I remind my siblings. "Remember what Mom said about five hundred connections to look legit?"

I point to Dad's big fat zero connections.

"How are we going to get to five hundred? We can't make five hundred fake LinkedIn accounts. That would take five hundred fake email addresses!" Bowen shakes his head. "I don't have enough phones for that!"

Lea's eyes brighten. "I have an idea."

Chapter 35

--✈

Lea's great idea is to hold a garage sale next weekend—both as a way to start raising the $3,000 we need for the flight ticket *and* to get people to add Dad on LinkedIn.

I have to admit, it's pretty genius. I think about all the boxes in the garage. And the garage sale where we bought our wet suits. We could make a killing!

"We do have a lot of junk lying around the house," Bowen agrees, looking around our room. There's so much we can sell, including the baby strollers crammed in our closet.

"We'd have to get Mom on board," I say.

That Sunday, as we head over to TJ Maxx to buy an interview outfit for Mom, we ask her if we can have a garage sale.

"Sure!" Mom says in the car. "We used to have garage sales all the time when I was a kid. You'll have to research each item when you set the prices and keep track of the money, of course."

"I'll be in charge of that!" I volunteer.

"And I'll make the posters!!" Lea exclaims.

Mom smiles as she drives. In her hurry to pack, she forgot to bring any of her work clothes. Hopefully, we'll find something at TJ Maxx. Mom says everything in TJ Maxx is cheaper than at the mall.

I crack my knuckles, getting ready for some serious bargain hunting as Mom pulls into the lot. Inside the store, Lea and I bounce from aisle to aisle, trying to be the first to find the winning outfit for Mom. I pick out a nice green dress with little giraffes on it—it only costs $15.99!

But Mom says no.

"It's a tech company," she says. "I have to look serious, but not like a square."

"A square?"

"You know, excited but not over the top."

Circular and sad. Got it.

Lea pops over while I continue searching through the racks, holding up a pair of jeans with so many holes, I can't believe they're for sale.

"She's *not* wearing that," I say to Lea.

"This is the style!" she cries. "It costs *more* with holes."

I glance down at the price tag. *Sixty dollars?!* "That's like ten dollars a hole!" I protest. "That's insane. You can just rip them up yourself for free. Here, watch—"

But before I can start ripping, Mom pulls the jeans out of my hand.

"Stop it!" she says. "Calm down!"

She orders me to the suitcase section, where I'm less likely to "destroy stuff."

I sigh.

As I walk to the corner and watch my family shop from the other side of the store, I think back to what Christopher said about having ADHD and feeling like I'm always in trouble or about to be in trouble. I wish Mom would know that I'm not *trying* to destroy stuff. I just can't help but react sometimes . . . and no amount of "calm downs" will change that.

Chapter 36

--- ✈

In the end, Mom goes with a pair of boring black pants, a white shirt, and leather pumps. She looks like someone trying to get you to sign a hundred-year contract at T-Mobile, but what do I know? The total comes to $112.

At the sales counter, the credit card machine belches a loud error sound, which makes Mom jump.

"I'm sorry, ma'am, do you have another credit card? This one is not going through," the cashier says.

Mom's face turns red. "What? How's that possible? It's auto-paid from our bank account."

The cashier looks at Mom awkwardly. "Well, it's been declined. Do you have any cash?"

As Mom fumbles through her purse for cash, my siblings and I avoid the stares and eye rolls from the people waiting behind us in line. What's happening? *Was it all the* moo shu *pancakes from the other day?*

Mom finally produces six crumpled-up twenty-dollar bills and we get out of there.

"What happened?" my siblings and I ask in the parking lot. Mom and Dad's credit card *always* goes through—even that time Dad went to Nike in Hong Kong and bought me and Bowen a bunch of track and soccer stuff, *full price!*

"We must have emptied our checking account . . . though

I don't see how!" Mom says, frantically texting Dad as she unlocks the car.

"Was it the other day at Christopher's restaurant?" I ask, suddenly worried. It was all my idea that we go.

Mom shakes her head. "No, honey, that wasn't it."

"Then was it Target?" Bowen asks, his eyes cutting into mine. I shrivel in my seat.

Mom video-calls Dad on the car speakerphone as she turns on the engine. "I don't know, but I'm going to find out."

Dad answers on the third ring. It's six in the morning for him, and he smiles sleepily into the camera.

"Hey, guys!"

"Hi, Daddy!" We wave.

Cody barks excitedly behind him, his tail so fluffy, it looks like a feather duster.

"Hey, we were just shopping at TJ Maxx and . . ." Mom pauses, trying to figure out how to tell him. "My credit card was declined."

Dad lets out a deep sigh. "I was hoping this wouldn't happen . . . ," he says. His eyes dodge the camera as he tells us he's been having a hard time paying for all the expenses on his reduced salary.

I glance distractedly at Dad's background, not recognizing the room he's in. "Dad, where are you?" I ask.

"I . . . I had to move into a smaller apartment," he confesses.

"What?" Lea and I ask. "You moved??"

"When were you going to tell us?" Bowen asks, his face in complete shock.

"We didn't want to worry you guys," Mom starts to explain.

We turn to Mom, our eyes piercing into her. "You knew about this?!"

"I'm so sorry." Mom glances at Dad on the video call. "We just figured, you guys have been through so much lately. We didn't want you to be scared. . . ."

"So you were just going to hide the fact that Dad lives in a totally different home now?!" Bowen erupts. I nod, sharing in his fury.

"Believe me, if there was any way we could have kept the apartment, I would have done it," Dad tells us. "But we just couldn't afford it. And plus, you four aren't living here anymore. Cody and I don't need all that space."

In that moment, I realize how permanent this is. Even if we wanted to go back to Hong Kong now, we couldn't. Our home's gone.

"What about all our stuff?" Bowen asks.

Lea lets out a sharp cry. "My stuffed animals!"

"My lockbox!" I add, covering my mouth. There are about twenty ancient Chinese coins in there that my *lao lao* and *lao ye* gave me—they're completely *irreplaceable*!

"Don't worry, I shipped all of your stuff over to you in California," Dad assures us. I wonder how much *that* cost. "It's on its way right now."

"But did you explain to them what was happening?! April the panda and Carl the hippo, did you talk to them??" Lea asks. She puts a hand to her chest, like a worried mama. "They'll be so scared!"

Dad promises Lea that he talked to each and every one of them. Still, tears pool in our eyes.

"We didn't even get to say goodbye," Lea says in a small voice.

"I'm sorry," Dad says, his voice breaking. We gaze up at him and see that he also has tears in his eyes. This must be hard on him, too. I ask him to show us his new apartment.

As he walks us through his new one-bedroom apartment, I see the familiar things that make my heart ache for home. The big armchair where I'd curl up by the sunny window and Dad would read to me when I struggled with reading back in third grade. The cast-iron skillet that Dad would make us steak on and always feed a bite to Cody, even though Mom told him not to.

The tall wooden giraffe Dad got from Africa. The framed poster of Wayne Wong, Bowen's favorite skier. A lump forms in my throat as we reach out a hand to the screen to all the pieces of our past that make up our memories.

As Dad takes us into his kitchen, we stare at the bare walls.

"Where's the height wall?" I ask Dad.

The height wall was where Mom measured our heights every April and drew a line on the wall in Sharpie. Every year we'd wait excitedly for April, to see and compare how much we'd each grown. When Dad doesn't answer back, I feel a sadness ripple through me all the way to Hong Kong.

"I guess there were some things I couldn't ship . . . ," Dad says softly.

Mom reaches out a hand to us. "Bao baos," she says gently, looking into our eyes. "Sometimes grown-ups have to make hard decisions, but it's always for the best. You have to trust us."

I search Mom's eyes for a long time, wondering why I should trust her. When there's so much she hasn't told us.

"Things are going to turn around for us, I promise."

Chapter 37

--✈

That night, I mourn for the loss of our home in Hong Kong, and all the memories that came with it. I cry silently into my pillow, holding my breath, hoping my brother won't hear me. But he does anyway.

"Are you *crying*?" he asks.

"No!" I insist.

I squeeze my eyes shut, trying not to think about it. The worry that we might lose Dad, too, that one day we'll wake up and something'll happen to him. And Mom'll just be like, *Oh yeah, I didn't feel like telling you. . . .*

"It's just an apartment," Bowen says. "Remember the grumpy guy downstairs?"

He reminds me of our mean downstairs neighbor by way of a thunderous stomp of his foot under my mattress, and my butt cheeks jump. I tell him to stop it.

"Don't you care?" I ask him. "What about all the Nerf gun wars we had? All the times we built forts when we were little." One by one, I list all the things we used to do as kids in that apartment. *Before you started calling me Knot,* I want to add.

Bowen chuckles. "Oh yeah."

"Remember the time we built that long train, all the way from your room to mine?" I ask.

"And it passed through the kitchen?" Bowen adds.

"Yeah! And Lea put little packets of ketchup on it!" I sit up and smile. It's fun walking down memory lane with Bowen.

"And the massive pillow fights!" Bowen calls out. "Mom would always yell at us to stop, but we'd hide under the pillows and she'd have to remove each one to look for us?"

"Then we'd bury her inside?" I start laughing uncontrollably.

Bowen laughs too.

"I miss that place . . . ," I say out loud.

"Me too," Bowen says with a sigh. "I miss not being the only Asian kid in my class."

I turn around on my tummy to try to look at Bowen's face in the dark. Could it be that he's finally opening up to me? That we're finally having a real conversation? I want so badly to say something smart and grown-up. But I don't respond, for fear of ruining the moment.

"But I'm *not* going to miss having to silence Lao Lao's calls on the bus because I don't want my friends to hear and think I'm a mainlander," Bowen says.

Whoa.

"Did they say something to you . . . ?" I ask softly. I know I'm treading on dangerous little-brother territory, but I can't help it. It's so rare that Bowen opens up to me like this. I may never get another opportunity again.

"They didn't have to . . . ," he says, letting out a heavy sigh. "I just wish people would realize we're not the Chinese government. We're the people."

I thrust up an arm—dang straight we are!

I gaze down at Bowen, trying to make out his eyes in the

moonlight, but it's too dark and all I can see is the shadow of his nose.

"Anyway, it's not like we've lost them," Bowen says, rolling onto his side.

"What?"

"The memories. We still have 'em."

"True." I yawn sleepily, nodding from the top bunk. "And as long as we can get Dad over here, we can make new ones."

"Hopefully, Mom will get her new job tomorrow," Bowen says, yawning too.

"Hopefully," I say, closing my eyes. I feel much better having had a heart-to-heart with my brother. "Hey, gege?"

"What?"

I open my mouth to tell him—I hope he knows he does fit in here. And if anyone ever says anything mean to him, he should know, I've got his back. Always. But I don't want him to get mad and snap at me that *I* should be the one to talk about fitting in, so I just say, "Don't fart tonight."

And we go to sleep.

Chapter 38

K NOX!!!" Mom holds up her new shirt from TJ Maxx the next morning. "There's a giant stain across the front. Who did this??"

Bowen pounds with his fist from the bottom bunk, like, *What'd you do now?!*

"I couldn't sleep last night!" I start to explain. In the middle of the night, I was worried about Mom riding BART. I kept thinking, *What if Lao Lao's right and the virus really is here?* "So I got up and sprayed Lysol on your shirt."

"You sprayed *Lysol* on my new shirt?!" Mom shrieks.

Bowen jumps out of bed and grabs the shirt to examine it. "You just WASTED seventy dollars, you know that?"

"Maybe we can get it out," I say, running to the bathroom. I come back with a spray bottle of water. "Here! Let me have it."

But Mom refuses to give the shirt to me. "You've done quite enough. My interview's in an hour and a half. I just have to wear it like this!"

Bowen takes my spray bottle from my hand and squirts me with it instead, while Mom goes to change.

"Nice job!" he says. "If Mom doesn't pass this interview, it's all your fault."

I slump my shoulders forward as I drag myself down the stairs. Seemed like a great idea at the time.

"Just trying to keep us alive," I mutter.

I watch the news in the kitchen as I pour myself some cereal. The number of cases on that cruise ship in Japan keeps climbing higher and higher! I point to the TV, but Mom's too busy trying to figure out how to cover the stain on her shirt with one of Lea's pins. The only person who looks over is Bowen, who rolls his eyes and says with his mouth half-full, "It's a *cruise ship*. We're not on a cruise ship."

I turn the TV off.

"There, I think that covers it!" Mom says, showing us her shirt. She somehow managed to hide the stain with one of Lea's flower pins.

"You look great!" Lea announces.

"Really?" Mom asks, peering down at her leafy pin. "You sure I don't look like I'm applying for the Girl Scouts?"

"Hey! What's wrong with the Girl Scouts?" Lea asks, putting a hand to her hip. "I'm thinking of applying myself."

"You should!" Mom encourages her as she grabs her keys.

We take turns wishing Mom luck when she drops us off at school.

"You've got this!" Lea says to her.

"And remember, if they throw a curveball at you, just do what I do!" I remind Mom.

"I'll spray them full of Lysol," she teases, winking at me.

As Mom drives off, I spot Christopher on the playground.

"Hey! How was your weekend?" I ask Christopher, running up to him.

"Pretty good. I folded about two hundred menus. How about you?"

That sounds so fun! "My mom's got an interview for a new job today!" I tell Christopher. "And we're having a garage sale this weekend!"

"That's awesome!" Christopher says. "Can I come?"

"Yeah! Absolutely!" I say, jotting down our address. I pull out my homework and ask Christopher a question I had about the math. I *was* gonna ask Bowen, but seeing how mean he was to me this morning—so much for thinking things were better after our talk last night—I decided not to.

Christopher explains how to do it a couple of times, but it still doesn't sink in. "Here, give me a blank piece of paper," he says. "I'll draw it for you."

I pull out a piece of paper.

I watch, fascinated, as Christopher *draws* out the math. He sketches a bunch of take-out containers and shades some of them in. And just like that, everything clicks! I know what the answer is!

"Thanks!" I exclaim.

"No problem." He smiles. "Sometimes you just need to look at a problem a different way to solve it."

I put my homework away, glad I have a friend I can ask for help. And not feel bad about it. As we walk over to our classroom together, I ask Christopher if business picked up at the restaurant over the weekend.

Christopher makes the so-so sign with his hand.

"Have you guys thought about doing Uber Eats?"

Christopher shakes his head. "People are barely coming in as it is. You really think they'd order from us if we deliver?"

I nod enthusiastically, thinking back to the first few nights when we got here and how we relied on Uber Eats—

before Mom insisted on cooking. "It doesn't hurt to try!"

Christopher takes his organizer out and jots it down at the top. "Thanks, I'll look into it."

"No problem." I smile.

At recess, we kick my soccer ball back and forth, but Tyler and his friends still try to tag us.

"You're it!" Tyler yells at Christopher.

"Don't think so," Christopher replies.

"It's coronavirus tag! You don't have a choice!" Tyler's friend Conrad says, getting mad.

"He doesn't have to be it just because you tagged him!" I say to Conrad. "And besides, it's a stupid game!"

Tyler turns to me, his face boiling red. "What did you say?"

"I said it's a stupid game," I say, standing as tall as I can. I keep my foot steady on my soccer ball, but I can feel my heart racing. "And it's offensive!"

"It's not offensive!" Tyler makes a face at me. He turns to his friends, who all shake their heads, like it's totally ridiculous.

"Yes, it is!" Christopher agrees.

"Well, we're playing it anyway. And Christopher, you're it," Tyler insists.

He starts reaching for my friend, but I push his hand away. "Stop!"

"Stay out of it, *Beach*," Tyler says to me.

My face burns. "What'd you call me?" I ask him.

He repeats it, so embarrassingly loud that I lose it and I kick the soccer ball *hard*. It flies straight up in the air and over the ten-foot-tall chain-link fence, and lands with a thud in the creek behind.

"Haha! Now you've lost your ball!" Tyler laughs.

NOOO! That's my best ball, hand carried from Hong Kong. Dad got it for me for my ninth birthday!

I run instinctively over to the fence and start climbing it. I refuse to lose my soccer ball. For all I know, it's the only thing Dad got me that's left and everything else of mine that he shipped might be lost at sea!

I grab the fence with both hands and kick with my feet. Christopher and the other kids shout as I climb.

"Knox, what are you doing? Get down, you're not supposed to climb that fence!"

"It's too high!"

"*Please*, Knox! I'll buy you another ball! Just come down," Christopher cries.

I shake my head in the powerful East Bay wind. The wind is so strong, my T-shirt is like a kite. Still, I refuse to come down. Dad told me to take good care of the ball, and I'm not letting him down. I have to get it back, so we can play together again. If I don't, we may never play again! With each step, I climb higher and higher, until my T-shirt turns into a pillow and I can feel the entire fence swaying. *Whooaaaa!*

I look down to see Mrs. Turner running over. She's practically a dot from up here!

"Knox, get down!!" she orders. "You're going to get hurt!"

But I'm already at the top! All I have to do is climb over. As I put one leg over, followed by the other, there's a collective gasp.

"Be careful!!!" Christopher shouts.

"I'm almost there!" I call back.

Tyler runs up close to the fence and peers up, while I hang on tight.

Quickly, I scurry down the fence on the other side, one foot under another. When I get down far enough, I jump onto the grass . . . and land in a puddle of mud.

The other kids shriek and giggle as I look over to see Tyler, covered head to toe in mud. I press my lips together to keep from laughing too—though I have to admit, it's pretty funny.

A deafening whistle wipes away my smile. I lift my eyes to see the principal's face.

Uh-oh.

Chapter 39

P rincipal Murphy gets so mad at me after my fence-climbing stunt that she threatens to call my mom. I beg her not to.

"Please don't call my mom!" I hug my soccer ball to my chest—which thankfully they let me keep—as I sit in her office. "She's at a very important interview!"

"Not anymore, she's not," Principal Murphy says, frowning at me. "Do you know what could have happened?"

"I was just trying to get my ball!" I tell her. I point to my arms and legs—not a scratch, just a couple of mud stains. "I'm not even hurt."

"But you could have been. That's the point."

In the end, no amount of begging or promising never to climb the fence again gets me off the hook. As Principal Murphy makes the call, I bury my face in my hands. I glance at the clock—barely ten thirty a.m. Mom's interview's just starting! She is going to *kill me*.

"What were you thinking?!" Mom asks, walking into the principal's office to get me.

I bite the inside of my cheeks so hard, the fleshy part is like a soccer ball in my mouth.

"Did you miss your interview?" I ask in a tiny voice, sneaking a peek at her.

Mom doesn't even have to answer. I can tell just from her eyes.

"Never mind about my interview—you put yourself in danger!" Mom says, taking a seat beside me. She gives me a once-over, checking for bruises. "You *know* our situation."

I swallow hard and look down. Our lack of health insurance didn't exactly register into my decision to climb that fence. Why hadn't it? I plunge my head into my hands.

"Don't worry. We already checked him. He's fine," Principal Murphy says to Mom. "But the other student was *covered* in mud—"

"You should have seen Tyler!" I blurt out proudly. One look at my mom's thundering face and I go back to biting my cheeks again.

Mom turns to Principal Murphy. "I'm so sorry. I'm going to have a strong word with him when we get home."

"Do," Principal Murphy says, nodding. "That kind of behavior is not okay here at Davis Elementary. We don't want our students putting themselves or others in danger. Is that clear, Knox?"

Principal Murphy's eyes linger on me as I promise it'll never happen again. She tells me she's going to give me the rest of the day to go home and reflect on my behavior. I walk out of the office with my mom, muttering "Sorry" once again.

"Can I stop by the classroom and tell Tyler I'm sorry?" I ask Principal Murphy as I'm walking out.

"That would be nice," she says.

Mom waits outside my classroom while I go in and apologize to Tyler. Most of the mud's been cleaned off his face, though I can still see some in his ear. I guess I must have splashed him pretty bad.

Tyler doesn't react when I say sorry. I don't know if it's because of the mud in his ear or because he really can't hear me. Still, I'm glad I said the words. It feels good to be the bigger person.

Christopher whispers to me as I get my backpack, "Are you okay?"

I whisper back, "Yeah, but I think I screwed up my mom's interview."

"Oh no! Is she mad?"

I shake my head. "Not yet, but I'm sure once we get home, I'm gonna get it."

Christopher gulps. "Let me know if you need some comfort food. I'll Uber Eats some over to you, once we sign up!"

I smile at my friend. "Thanks."

Walking out of the class, I see Mom shaking her head—almost in tears—as she apologizes to Mrs. Turner. My teacher puts a hand over Mom's shoulder and tells her it's all right.

"Really, I get it," Mrs. Turner says. "Boys at this age."

"No, it's not just boys at this age. I have an older one, Bowen. And he would *never*."

The disappointment on Mom's face as she compares me to Bowen is so overwhelming, I'm almost tempted to run across the field and climb over the fence again. But I don't.

"C'mon, Knox, let's go home."

I hang my head low as I follow my mom to the car.

"I just wanted to get my ball back . . . ," I mutter when we get to the parking lot.

"I know what you wanted!" Mom snaps, turning to me

when we're in the car. "It's always about what *you* want! Not what anybody else wants or what makes the most sense! You never stop and think!"

Whenever Mom gets like this, I make myself a T-shirt cave and go inside. Today, I put my arms and head inside my shirt, hunkering down for Mom's mad-storm.

"You're lucky Principal Murphy did not suspend you," she says. "This could have gone on your permanent record."

I poke my head out from my T-shirt cave.

"What's a permanent record?" I ask.

"It's a report card that follows you in America, keeping track of all the good and bad things you've done—"

"Like on LinkedIn?" I ask Mom. America sure has a lot of report cards.

"Yes, but it starts even earlier," Mom says. "And once you have something on your permanent record, that's it—it's on there forever. You can't get a good job—forget about LinkedIn, you won't even be able to go to college. That's why so many people end up in jail."

My eyes go wide. *In jail???*

Tears start building in my eyes inside my T-shirt cave. It's not true. Mom's lying. I'm not going to end up in jail just because of some dumb fence. People don't end up in jail because they went to get their soccer ball . . . do they?

I mutter from inside the cave, "What did the people at the procrastination company say when you had to come get me?"

I peek outside when Mom doesn't answer.

"Did they get mad?"

Mom starts the car. "No . . . but I don't think they'll be inviting me back," she finally says.

I go back inside my cave.

Mom's long fingers reach inside my cave and I jump. "Hey," she says, her voice softening. "I'll find something else."

I hope so. Slowly, I move my hand and our fingertips touch.

Chapter 40

--✈

fold laundry and eat the rest of Christopher's *moo shu* pork—it really is the best *moo shu* pork I've ever had—while Mom sends out more résumés. She took away my iPad as punishment, which stinks because I really want to ask Dad about what Mom said about jail. Was she *serious*?

Finally, at three p.m., Mom comes out of her room, stuffs a CLIF bar into her mouth, and grabs her keys. It's time to go pick up Bowen and Lea.

"C'mon, let's go," she says.

Swallowing hard, I get up and follow Mom to the car. I'm really dreading picking my brother up—once he hears what happened, I'm dumpling meat. But Mom says I have to come. She lets me sit in the front for once, which is nice, considering. We listen to "Today's Hits and Yesterday's Favorites" in the car—KOIT 96.5. I'm thinking I'm definitely a yesterday's favorite. Mom tells me a funny story about how there's a dentist in Hong Kong who always plays KOIT in his office. And even though he overcharges, Dad goes to see him anyway because KOIT reminds him of home.

I smile. "Well, he can listen to KOIT all the time when he comes here," I tell Mom.

Mom smiles back and doesn't comment about the coming-here part.

We pick up Lea first. My sister's too preoccupied telling Mom about the new rainbow trout they got in her class to notice I'm already in the car. As soon as we get to the middle school, the first thing Bowen asks about when he swings the door open is Mom's new job. I start putting my arms inside my T-shirt again.

"So did you get it?!" He leans forward to Mom excitedly.

"Not exactly . . . ," Mom says.

Bowen's super bummed. "Was it the interview questions?"

"No—we didn't get to that." Mom glances at me. "I had to leave early."

"Why??"

Bowen turns to me. I can see the steam coming out of his ears and shrink my head into my T-shirt cave. "What did you do?" he demands.

"Nothing!" I cry, putting my arms over my head.

"Leave him alone, Bowen," Mom commands. "It's *fine.* I'll find something else."

"So it *was* you!"

I can't take the guilt any longer, so I blurt out, "I didn't know they were gonna call her, okay? All I was trying to do was get my soccer ball!"

"You screwed up Mom's interview over a soccer ball?"

My head throbs. "I have ADHD, okay?!" I scream into my cave.

The words leave my mouth before I can stop them, and I instantly put my fingers to my lips. Oh *nooo.* What have I done? I squint through the thin fabric wall of my T-shirt cave, trying to make out my brother's face.

Bowen puts a hand over his mouth. "Of course you do!

The Target crash! The Lysol! It all makes so much sense!"

It makes me so angry that my condition totally fits into his puzzle piece of me. How long has he been suspecting it? Did my parents tell *him* before they told me?

"What's ADHD?" Lea asks.

"Nothing," Mom says, pulling the car over. She turns around to the back seat. "Stop it, Bowen. Or we'll sit here all day. I've got time."

Bowen doesn't make another peep the rest of the ride home, though I know he's saving it for later when we're alone. I can already hear the thoughts swirling in his head—they whir even louder than my own.

I put my hands over my ears, wishing I had never told him, never confirmed what he's been thinking for years.

As soon as we get home, I race up to our room and lock the door behind me.

Bowen charges up the stairs after me.

"Open up!" he demands.

I shake my head, sliding my body down to the floor, looking at the poster Bowen put up by his desk. It's a poster of a lion with the words EXCELLENCE IS A COMMITMENT. IT WILL ENABLE YOU TO ACHIEVE GREATNESS. ORDINARY IS NOT AN OPTION. I stare at the poster, wondering where ADHD fits into that. Can I still achieve greatness with ADHD, or is that not an option?

Bowen continues knocking and trying to jiggle the doorknob.

"C'mon, some of us have homework to do and tests to study for! We can't all get extra time on the SATs, like you!" my brother shouts.

I stare at the door. What extra time?! Why would I need

extra time? It dawns on me that he's making fun of me.

I kick Bowen through the door with my shoe. *How dare he?* I run to his desk and grab his expensive headphones—and hide them deep in my backpack, where he'll never find them. *I'll show him!* First thing tomorrow, I'm gonna pawn them. And then I'll use the money to get Dad over here. That's the only way I can live with my ADHD *and* Bowen.

Chapter 41

-- ✈

I finally get Mom to give me back my iPad that night after I tell her I need it to do my homework. I'm texting Christopher about pawnshops when Dad calls me on Skype. I glance over at Bowen at his desk—he still hasn't figured out his headphones are missing. Maybe he'll just forget about them and Dad will already be over here by the time he figures it out. I get up to go somewhere more private to talk to Dad. Once again, I walk into Mom's closet. She's downstairs making dinner with Lea.

Squished between Mom's new work clothes and big chunky heels she brought over from Hong Kong (I don't know when she'll ever wear them here), I talk to Dad.

"How was school today?" he asks, feeding Cody. I reach out my hand to the screen to try to touch my dog. I could sure use a furry friend right now.

"Pretty good," I say, picking up Mom's leather boots and play-fighting with them. I don't want to tell Dad about the fence.

"You might want to take it easy on your mom's shoes . . . or she's going to make you play a new game called Clean Up Her Closet."

I put Mom's shoes down.

"So what'd you do at school?"

"Nothing."

My sadness must have traveled through the Wi-Fi, because Dad asks me, "Just nothing?"

I shrug. "I hung out with my friend Christopher."

"It's great you're making new friends at school," Dad says.

I look into the camera. Something about the quiet cocoon of the closet gives me the courage to ask, "Hey, Dad, did you know I have ADHD?"

Dad studies my face. "Did Mom tell you?"

I nod slowly.

"I'm sorry we didn't tell you sooner, bud. How do you feel?"

I mutter to Mom's clunky boots, "I always knew I was a little different." Then I peer at Dad. "But how bad is it? ADHD?"

"It's not bad at all," Dad insists. He stops feeding Cody and looks into the camera. "Think of it as a"—he searches for the right word—"superpower."

"A superpower?" I ask, looking up hesitantly.

I wonder if this is just something Dad's saying to make me feel better, like the time I tried to make oatmeal raisin cookies and accidentally used paprika instead of cinnamon. Dad insisted they tasted *way* better, even though they kind of tasted like barbecue cookies.

"A lot of very successful people have ADHD. Here's the thing about it that you might not know: while you may have problems focusing on certain tasks, you can also *hyper*-focus on other tasks . . . the ones you really like."

"Like soccer?" I ask hopefully.

"Exactly," Dad says. "You have a superpower, my friend."

I smile, propping the iPad against Mom's shoeboxes and lying back on her sweaters.

"Tell me more about hyper-focusing," I say to Dad, putting my hands behind my neck. I like the sound of that. A *lot.*

Dad talks animatedly with his hands. "When you hyper-focus, you can accomplish anything. You can stay fixated on something way longer than everyone else can."

That explains my obsession over rockets and the time I researched snakes for an entire summer. And the time I figured out that fancy shampoo Mom was buying? It had the *exact* same ingredients as regular shampoo!

"Wait, but how come it's hard for me to stay focused in school?" I ask Dad. *I never get any As . . . unlike Bowen.*

"Well, because not everything makes you want to hyper-focus," Dad says. "The stuff that you think is boring, for instance."

"Yeah, like spelling," I chime in.

"Exactly. Why's there a *p* in 'receipt'?" Dad asks.

I chuckle. "Don't even get me started on 'zucchini'!"

As we take turns listing the *many* weird spelling words in the English language, I roll around in Mom's closet, laughing. I wish Dad were right here next to me.

Dad's smile lights up the tiny closet. "The sky's the limit for you, buddy. You just need to find things you're passionate about and then . . ."

I make a sound effect like a rocket taking off, and Cody woofs. I smile, glad he still recognizes me, that I haven't disappeared in his doggie mind like a squirrel he may or may not have chased in a dream.

"All you have to do is work on controlling your impulses," Dad says. He hesitates for a second. "Like on the fence today."

My rocket crash-lands. "Mom told you?"

I pick up one of Mom's tall boots and hide behind it. *Why did Mom have to tell Dad???* Now he thinks I'm failing at school, when really I'm doing good—honest!

I tell Dad I was just trying to save my soccer ball.

"*Our* soccer ball," I add, crouching lower. "Mom says I might end up in jail."

"Wait, *what?*"

Reluctantly, I tell Dad about the whole permanent-record thing. No college. No job. And possible jail time. I don't realize how much it's been bothering me until I get it off my chest. Then stare, petrified, into the screen.

"You're not going to end up in jail," Dad reassures me. "I'm sorry Mom said that. She's been dealing with a lot right now. . . ."

"I know. I made her miss her interview . . . ," I confess. I step on my forehead with Mom's boot. No one's madder at me than myself.

"It's okay—she'll get another one. Your mom is a fighter, you hear? It's not your job to worry about your parents."

I look into the camera. *But I do worry. I worry about you guys every day,* I want to say.

Instead I give Dad a weak smile and say, "Thanks, Dad."

"I'm very, very proud of you."

I nod and try to screenshot the words in my mind as I snuggle against Mom's fuzzy bathrobe, pretending it's Dad's warm arms.

Chapter 42

--✈

Bowen wakes me up on Tuesday at six o'clock with a shove. "Where are my headphones?" he whisper-yells in my ear.

Uh-oh. He caught on! I bury my head deep under the covers, pretending to be asleep.

Bowen throws my covers back. "I need them for school!"

"Are you sure you didn't leave them at TJ Maxx?" I ask innocently. Bowen searches through our room like a tornado, throwing papers, pens, candy, and gadgets onto the floor, including my iPad. "Hey!" I protest, jumping down from my bunk and hugging my lifeline to Dad.

"You better not have taken them," Bowen yells. He points a threatening finger at me. "If I find out you took them, you're dead!"

I gulp hard.

Lea walks sleepily into our room with her stuffed unicorn. "What's with all the noise?" she asks, rubbing her eyes. "I'm trying to sleep!"

"Knox took my headphones," Bowen tells her.

"I did not!" I cry in mock outrage. "You probably left them at school. Maybe they're in your locker."

Our bickering is temporarily muted by the sound of our parents' loud voices. We've heard our parents fighting before in Hong Kong, of course, but they rarely ever raised their voices at each other—especially not on the phone. Cautiously, we walk over to Mom's room and lean on the door, trying to listen in.

"Are they screaming at each other . . . on the phone?" Lea asks.

I put a finger to my mouth, *Shhhh.* I overhear Mom saying, "I was just warning him what could happen if he doesn't control his impulses. Look, you're not here every day. *I am.*"

I suck in a sharp breath when I realize who they're screaming about. Lea looks at me and my brother with frightened eyes.

"It's starting," she says to her stuffed unicorn, sliding down onto the floor. "They're falling apart."

"They're not falling apart!" Bowen cries, taking Lea's hand and leading us back to our room. "They're just arguing on the phone."

"We have to get Dad over here quick! Before they completely hate each other and Dad has to dress up like an old cleaning lady to get us back!" Lea says, climbing onto my bunk.

Bowen gives her an odd look.

"I'm watching *Mrs. Doubtfire* on Hulu," Lea explains.

"Do we even have Hulu?" Bowen asks.

"I signed up for a free trial with my school email." Lea shrugs.

"You guys, you're getting distracted!" I say. And here I thought I was the one with the focusing problem. "Lea's right—we need to get Dad over here. Where are we on the garage sale posters?"

After Bowen's terrifying outburst about his headphones, I'm thinking maybe pawning them isn't such a great idea. Lea climbs down and runs back to her room. She returns with four big garage sale posters, all decorated in glitter. Leave it to my sister to design something explosively eye-catching!

"Good work. I'll bike around after school and put them up in the neighborhood," Bowen says.

"You have time to do that?" I ask, surprised. Bowen usually never had time to do anything with me and Lea back in Hong Kong. "Don't you have homework?"

"That's one good thing about my new school—not a ton of homework."

"Great!" I say to Bowen's back as he turns and heads toward the bathroom.

"Wait, what about what we're going to sell?" Lea asks.

I think of all the shoes in Mom's closet. Those clunky heels? She'll *never* wear them. "Let's go through Mom's closet tonight when she's making dinner," I suggest to my sister. "There's tons of good stuff in there!"

Chapter 43

That night, while Bowen helps Mom make dinner, Lea and I raid Mom's closet.

We find a big bag of clothes labeled *College clothes— SAVE FOR LEA*. Lea is deliriously happy when she sees her name and starts taking all the stuff out. There are tie-dyed dresses, fuzzy hats, strappy heels, baggy jeans, and fringe leather jackets. It looks like a museum for bad fashion choices.

But Lea wraps her arms around all of it anyway and declares, "MINE!"

I hold up a giant belt that looks more like a road divider.

"You're really going to wear this?" I ask.

"I might!" Lea insists, grabbing the belt and putting it on. It's so big, it wraps around her three times and looks like she's being choked by a plastic fettucine.

Lea looks down. "Fine," she says reluctantly, and uncoils the belt from around her waist. "But we're not selling *everything*. We have to keep some of it."

"Of course we're going to keep some of it," I say.

We dig through the clothes and find a bunch of Berkeley shirts—we decide to keep those. My sister generously divides them between us. For everything else, we try to come up with prices.

"Hey, look!" Lea says, holding up a thick pack of blank

address labels underneath an old stack of Christmas cards. "We can use these stickers for price tags!"

We start slapping the stickers on Mom's shoes and clothes.

Lea holds up a pair of patent leather black pumps with heels so high, they look like weapons.

"How much for these?" she asks, pretending to stab me with them.

"Five dollars!" I say. "And I think we need to put some sort of warning on them."

Lea scribbles a note, *Dangerous shoes. Discount—$4.50.*

I reach for Mom's fringe leather jacket and try it on. I look awesome, like a heavy metal rock star! I'm keeping this one. I glance over at my sister, trying on Mom's Spanx—it goes all the way down to her ankles. And kind of makes her look like an eraser.

"Hey, look at this!" Lea says, picking up some stapled papers buried deep in the bag of clothes.

"What is it?" I walk over and examine the title page. I see the words "Political Science 158, UC Berkeley" on the top right corner. "It's one of Mom's old college papers!"

My eyes do a double take when I flip to the back and see the grade—a C–. That's a grade I would get, but *Mom*??

"I thought Mom got straight As at Berkeley!" I say to Lea. We look down and read the comments.

Will,
I think your thesis is entirely inaccurate. There is no way China will ever emerge as a major economic player—it is simply inconceivable that a nation that had 90 percent of its people in poverty in 1980 can truly ever fully transform

itself. I know you're from China. But as a Chinese student, you must always be cautious of letting your personal biases on China influence your judgment, if you wish to be taken seriously in America. Should you wish to rewrite this, I would be open to looking over it again. But as it stands, this is a C– effort.

Professor Grandin

Lea and I look at each other. "Who's Will?" we ask at the same time.

After dinner, Bowen, Lea, and I gather in my room. I ask Bowen how the garage sale poster route went. He said he put them up at all the stop signs by our house. We study the mysterious paper with one of Grandma Francine's old magnifying glasses. Unfortunately, the thing is typed, so we can't compare it with Mom's handwriting.

"Maybe Will was Mom's old boyfriend," Lea suggests.

I jerk my head up, nearly knocking my teeth with the magnifying glass.

"What?? No!" I tell her.

"Mom met Dad in college!" Bowen reminds her.

"That's what *we* think," Lea says, her eyes going wide. "What's Mom doing with this Will guy's paper? And why did she keep it for so long? Maybe she was madly in love with—"

I reach over and cover Lea's mouth before she can finish the sentence. I do not like this old boyfriend talk. I do not like it one bit.

"Or *maybe* it's just Mom's friend," I suggest, a far more likely scenario.

173

Lea makes a face. "Girls can't be friends with boys!"

"Of course they can," Bowen and I blurt out at the same time. I think about my Trader Joe's bag full of Valentines under our bunk—at least half of them were from girls. And they're nice—they're not part of Tyler's posse. And their hair always smells like Pop-Tarts when I stand behind them in line.

"No, it'd be too weird," Lea says. "It'd be like having an additional brother."

Bowen and I both cross our arms.

"And what's so wrong with that?" we ask.

Lea wriggles in her eraser Spanx—I can't believe she wore it underneath her *Frozen* cape all through dinner and Mom didn't even notice. "No offense, but the two of you are already a *lot*."

I frown and put the college paper down. Then I slap a sticker on my sister—*$1.00*.

"Hey!" Lea protests.

Chapter 44

--- ✈

The next day at school, I tell everyone about our garage sale. Well, everyone except Tyler, that is. He's still not talking to me. But at least he and his friends have stopped playing coronavirus tag at recess!

"So what are you going to do with your brother's headphones?" Christopher asks me, kicking my soccer ball back and forth. "You still going to sell them?"

We stop and take a break under the tree. Christopher pulls out his Rubik's Cube.

"Nah," I say. "Too risky."

"So you gonna give them back?" Christopher asks, twisting the cube.

"That's too risky too. Knowing Bowen, he'll probably have them dusted for fingerprints." I shudder. "I'll just have to hide them in the garage until he forgets, I guess."

"That works," Christopher agrees.

I gaze over at his Rubik's Cube. He's *really* good. I wonder if that's his superpower. Excitedly, I tell him what Dad said about hyper-focusing.

Christopher stops turning the cube and smiles. "I've heard that before," he says. "I definitely have it when I'm playing video games."

"And when I'm playing soccer!" I shout out.

"But *not* when I'm folding take-out containers," Christopher says.

I ask him how the restaurant is going. "Did you sign up for Uber Eats?"

"Yeah, but did you know? They charge a thirty percent fee for delivery!"

My eyebrows shoot up. "Whoa!" My math isn't as good as Bowen's, but even I know that's way too much! "You guys should just deliver the food yourselves. . . ."

"I wish," Christopher sighs. "It's just my mom and dad and me in the restaurant now. And I don't exactly know how to drive."

Oh yeah.

"Can you guys hire someone?" I suggest.

"Too expensive," he says. "We can't even afford an additional waiter right now. . . ."

The recess bell rings. I put my hand on my friend's shoulder, sad that he's going through a hard time. "Don't worry," I tell him as we walk back to class. "I'm sure if we put our heads together, we can hyper-focus on a solution."

Christopher gives me a lopsided smile.

Chapter 45

-- ✈

On the day of the big garage sale, Mom gets thrilling news!
"I got another interview!" she says, walking into the
garage.

"WOO-HOO!!! Go Mom!!!" I clap my hands together. I
knew she could do it!

"It's for an edu-tech company. Unfortunately, I don't
know too much about the industry, so I need to prepare for it.
Do you kids think you can do the garage sale on your own?"

"Totally!" I say, glancing at my siblings.

"What kind of stuff are you selling?" Mom asks, looking
curiously at the boxes on the tables we're setting up outside.

"Just a bunch of old stuff we found lying around!" Lea
quickly tells her.

Mom hesitates before heading back inside. "Am I going
to miss any of it?"

I try to imagine Mom now in her old fuzzy newspaper cap
and plaid skirt and platform shoes. I scrunch my face—she
would look like a meme. "Nope!"

After Mom goes back to prep for her interview, Lea, Bowen,
and I set up for the sale. We have a short driveway, like all
the other houses on our street. But unlike our neighbors who
like to park their cars in the driveway, Mom always parks our

Honda inside the garage, leaving us plenty of space to set up tables.

Bowen looks down at the many colorful shirts and scarves we got from Mom's closet, along with a few other knickknacks, like this red velvet box I found stuck way in the back of her clothes. "You sure Mom's gonna be okay with us selling all her old clothes?"

"It literally said 'save for Lea' on it," Lea tells him. "So it's basically all mine!"

"What about us? She didn't save anything for us??" Bowen asks, upset.

"Relax. I saved her leather jacket for us," I tell him.

We finish setting up Mom's old college clothes, but the tables still look kind of bare. So I grab an old lamp from a dusty bin in the garage and add it to the table. There's so much of Grandma Francine's things stuffed in the garage that we'll never use—old tea sets, candleholders, and mirrors. We might as well trade them for something we'll *actually* use— Dad. I slap one-dollar stickers on everything and add them to our table.

When all the items have been marked, we take our places at our stations—Lea is sales, Bowen is security (in case anyone tries to steal anything), and I'm the cashier.

"Remember—we can't let anyone leave without adding Dad on LinkedIn," Bowen says. Lea and I nod.

Before too long, neighbors stop by, drawn by Lea's glittery signs.

"That'll be five dollars," I say to our first customer, a lady who hugs my mom's Tory Burch strappy sandals like they're made of solid gold.

"Here you go!" the woman says happily, handing me a crisp five-dollar bill. "What a find!"

"Oh, and you gotta add my dad on LinkedIn," I say to her, showing her Dad's profile on my iPad.

"Huh?" she asks.

"We're helping my dad find a job. But he doesn't have enough connections. My mom says you need at least five hundred connections to look legit."

The woman raises an eyebrow at me as she taps in her email on my iPad. "Your dad know you're up to this?"

"No, it's a surprise!" I tell her.

"A surprise? I think you kids better tell your dad about this," she says.

The man behind her, holding Mom's silk bathrobe, calls out to her impatiently, "Who cares? Just add him already! I want to go home and try this on!"

"All right!" the woman says, quickly adding Dad. "There. I added him."

Lea walks over with a plate of homemade cucumber spa slices. "Thanks!" she says, smiling at the lady. "And while you're at it, if you could give him an endorsement, we'll throw in a free cucumber eye mask!"

"Ooooohh!" the woman squeals with delight.

Chapter 46

---✈

The garage sale was a hit! Grandma Francine's dusty old lamps and saucers were especially popular! By the end of the day, we've made $180 and raked in a whopping seventy-two connections, with endorsements like *Good negotiation!*, *Excellent sales skills!*, and *Good strategic thinking!*

Bowen, Lea, and I high-five each other after my friend Christopher and the last customers of the day leave.

"THAT. WAS. AWESOME," I say, counting the crisp cash bills.

"At this rate, we'll get to five hundred connections in no time!" Bowen says.

"Let's hold another one next weekend!" Lea suggests excitedly.

Our enthusiasm wanes when Mom steps into the garage. She takes one look at the empty bins in the garage and asks, "Where are all of Grandma Francine's old antiques?"

I gulp loudly.

It takes Mom one hour and twelve minutes to finish yelling at us. The whole time, my siblings and I are sitting on the couch, drowned in guilt, our sweaty palms soaking the cold, hard cash in our hands.

"I can't believe you sold our family heirlooms!" Mom says.

"Some of that stuff has been in your dad's family for generations! All those lovely tea sets and silver candleholders!"

"Those were *silver*??" I ask, my eyes bulging. They looked so rusty!

Mom nods. "How much did you sell them for?"

My siblings look to me, and my eyes plunge to the ground. "A dollar," I tell Mom.

"A dollar?!" Mom grabs a sofa arm.

"I thought it was like your rag dresses from college!" I say in my defense.

"*Rag* dresses??" Mom exclaims. "I'll have you know those were very much the *style*. And I saved every penny to buy those dresses . . . which was why I kept them all these years, so I can give them to Lea."

"Awww," Lea says, putting a hand over her heart.

"And now I can't . . . ," Mom mutters. "Whose idea was this anyway?"

I turn to see both my siblings pointing at me. *Thanks a lot, guys!*

"I'm sorry, Mom, but I really thought you didn't want them anymore," I say. "You're always telling us to donate the toys that we don't play with. . . ."

Mom's face softens a little. She sighs. "I just wish you had asked me first. . . ."

I nod with regret.

"Was it just my clothes and some candleholders?" Mom asks. "You didn't take anything else out of my closet?"

I shake my head. "Nope!"

"No brooches or earrings that were in the special velvet box in my closet?"

At the mention of a velvet box, I freeze. "What earrings? We didn't sell any earrings." I think back to all the stuff on the table . . . then remember the velvet box. The one that couldn't open. Oh no. I glance at my siblings. "I thought that box was empty!"

Mom puts a horrified hand to her face.

"Tell me you didn't sell it! There were earrings inside— real rubies! They were an anniversary present from your father!" Mom shrieks.

My brother and sister stare at me.

"I didn't know!" I say. "I thought it was empty. Honest! I even tried opening the box, but it wouldn't open! That's why I wrote a quarter."

"You sold it for a quarter??" Mom says, feeling her forehead with her hand like she's about to pass out. "They're worth like a thousand dollars!"

Lea jumps up from the couch. "We have to get it back!"

"Do you remember who paid for it??" Bowen asks.

I shake my head. "I don't remember! There were so many people!"

"Think, Knox, *think*!!" my siblings urge.

I squeeze my eyes shut, trying to remember. A blur of faces swirl through my mind, but honestly, I was too hyper-focused on getting them all to add Dad on LinkedIn, I can't remember what any of them looked like. At the thought of LinkedIn, it suddenly hits me. "We have everyone's emails! We could send them an email!"

"And say what? We accidentally sold you thousand-dollar earrings for a quarter, please email us back?!" Bowen asks, shaking his head. "They'll never respond!"

"You have so little faith in people!" I shout.

Bowen points his finger at me. "You're the one giving away family treasures for a quarter! They're probably already on some old lady's ears by now. . . ."

Lea bursts into tears at the heartbreaking possibility that our mother's precious anniversary earrings from Dad are on another woman's ears.

"It's okay . . . ," Mom says, trying to calm us down. "Not like Dad and I are going on a date anytime soon. . . ." She feels her bare earlobes with her fingertips.

"I'm so sorry, Mommy," I say.

Mom puts her hand over mine. "I know you are. And I'm happy you guys took the initiative to start a garage sale." She looks into our eyes. "But next time, please be more careful."

"I promise I'll get you back your earrings," I say to Mom.

I stand up and walk to my room. Even though I try so hard, I keep messing things up.

Chapter 47

--- ✈

Lea shuffles into our room later that night in her fuzzy slippers with a heavy look on her face. "I just talked to Mom," she says to me. "I told her it wasn't *all* your idea to sell her stuff. It was mine, too."

I climb down from my bunk, surprised. She didn't have to do that. Still, I appreciate it.

"What are we going to do?" Lea asks, plopping down on the floor.

I sit down next to her with my computer on my lap and load up LinkedIn. One by one, I sort through Dad's new connections, trying to see who could have possibly bought the earrings. But all of Dad's new adds look like they could rock a pair of rubies!

"We *have* to find Mom's ruby earrings," Lea says. "We can't just let some stranger walk off with them!"

"Agreed," I say.

"Okay, so mei mei," Bowen says, using the Chinese term for "sister" as he joins us on the floor. "You were sales. Do you remember seeing anyone holding the box?"

Lea closes her eyes. "I think I saw a couple with a spotted poodle standing by the box."

Bowen frowns. "A spotted poodle??" he asks Lea. "There's no such thing!"

Before I know it, Lea and Bowen start arguing about whether or not poodles can be spotted.

"Maybe it was a mix between a Dalmatian and a poodle!"

"They don't exist!"

"You want to bet?" Lea asks.

I wave my hands in the air to put a stop to the puppy debate. "So what did they look like? The couple?"

"I don't remember," Lea says.

We all think for a long, hard minute. Then Lea's eyes brighten and she runs across the room to the window.

Our eyes follow our sister's finger as she points to our neighbor across the street. There, up on the beam of his roof, is a video camera, pointed right at our garage!

Chapter 48

It's too late to go over to the neighbor's house that night. Mom has a rule about not going out at night ever since Dad's luggage got stolen from the garage. I was only two when it happened, but Bowen said it was super scary. Mom tried all day long to call the cops, but because nobody got hurt, the cops didn't even come by.

So we wait till morning.

Bright and early the next day, we head across the street. We've never gone to talk to our neighbors before, except when Mom went around and let everyone know about the luggage theft, and that's when folks started putting up security cameras. I gaze up at the camera as we wait for our neighbor to answer the door.

"Hello?" we ask. "Anyone home?"

We hear slow, faint shuffling coming from inside. Finally, an old man opens the door.

"Hi! We're from the yellow house." I smile at him, pointing to our home. "We were wondering if we could check out the footage from your security camera. Something happened at our house this weekend. . . ."

"Oh, I don't know how that thing works. But if you wanna check it out, go right ahead." He opens his door wider to let us in.

"Thanks!" we say.

"Name's Cliff Brady," he tells us. We shake his hand as we walk inside. I peer around his spacious living room.

Mr. Brady shows Bowen the den—he tells us that's where he keeps all his Wi-Fi and home surveillance stuff. As Bowen disappears into the den to check it out, Lea and I wait in the living room, marveling at all the pictures and memorabilia on Mr. Brady's walls. He sure has lots of stuff! I'd *love* to have a garage sale with it, then immediately kick myself for thinking that. What did Mom just say about selling off other people's stuff?

I point to an old picture of a major soccer match.

"Wow . . . you were in the World Cup?" I ask him. I peer enviously at the uniforms of England versus Argentina.

Mr. Brady chuckles. "No, I covered the World Cup," he says. "I was a journalist for many years. Now I just sit by the telephone, waiting for my grandkids to call me." I glance at his phone. It's one of those old telephones with the round dial.

"Cool!" Lea says, sitting down and playing with it. "I wish we had one of these!"

"It's so old-school!" I say, reaching for it too.

"You like it?" Mr. Brady chuckles. "I got it for three dollars at a garage sale!"

"We had a garage sale this weekend!" I tell him. My face falls. "That's kind of why we're here. We accidentally sold our mom's anniversary earrings."

"Oh, well, you gotta get those back," Mr. Brady says. "They're irreplaceable! I still remember every anniversary with my lovely Dorothy as though it were yesterday. . . ." Mr.

Brady walks over and, with a trembling hand, picks up a faded old black-and-white wedding picture of him with his wife.

Lea and I walk over to look at it.

"She passed, unfortunately," Mr. Brady says, shaking his head. "It's just me now, in this big old house all by myself." His eyes get misty for a second. "I miss her every day."

My sister and I tell Mr. Brady that we miss our dad too. That's why we had the garage sale—to raise enough money to get Dad a plane ticket so we can be a family again.

"Well, here, let me help with that," Mr. Brady says, taking out his wallet. With his shaky hand, he starts pulling out bills, but I push them back. It wouldn't be right to accept his money. Mom wouldn't like it if she knew.

"Thanks, but we need to earn it," I say to Mr. Brady.

"Good for you!" he says. "I like that."

"So if you ever need someone to cut your grass or give you a cucumber facial . . . ," Lea says.

"Well, I already have a gardener. But I like the sound of a cucumber facial," Mr. Brady says.

Lea grins and holds up a finger. "Be right back!"

Twenty minutes later, my sister is in the middle of slathering Mr. Brady's face with homemade cucumber gel—her facial keeps getting more and more professional—when Bowen walks back in from the den.

"Got the footage!" he says, holding up a USB. He adds with a smile to Mr. Brady, "Oh, and I fixed your Wi-Fi!"

"You did?" Mr. Brady asks, face beaming and glistening with thick, gooey cucumber aloe vera. "I've been trying to get that thing fixed for months!" He reaches for his wallet and stuffs twenty dollars into our hands. "Here, kids, you've earned it."

"Thanks!" We grin as we race back to our house with the USB!

Chapter 49

-- ✈

We squeeze in front of Bowen's computer, clamoring to look at the footage. The bright noon sun streams through the window.

"There's the spotted poodle right there!" Lea points to a little dog at the garage sale.

"That's not a spotted poodle," Bowen corrects her. "That's a Boston terrier."

"Really?" Lea asks, looking closely at the dog. He seems to be wearing a special collar. It glistens in the light every time he runs up to his owners and licks their hands.

"Oh, and there's the box!" I point to it in the hand he's licking.

Bowen pauses the footage and zooms in on the owners' faces. They are two guys. The box is in the hand of the guy holding the leash. I pull up LinkedIn and we start searching through profiles of the people who added Dad, but unfortunately, none of the profile pictures look like the guys in the screen.

Either they changed their profile pictures or they somehow slipped by without adding Dad—those sneaky rascals!

"Now what? How do we find them?" Lea asks.

My mind races a mile a minute. "We know they have a dog!" I say. "Let's go to the—"

"Dog park!" Lea finishes the thought, jumping up.

I grin.

Bowen takes a screenshot of the Boston terrier couple and prints it out with his printer. We run downstairs and grab our bikes, hollering to Mom, who's on the phone talking to Auntie Jackie, that we'll be back by dinner.

"Okay, if we see them, *I'll* do the talking," Bowen says when we get to the parking lot of the local dog park. I look over at him. It's nice he's helping us with this, but why should *he* do all the talking?

"Why you?" I ask Bowen.

"Because I'm the oldest!" We can hear the friendly barks of curious pups, and it makes me miss Cody so much.

"Fine," I reply.

Lea points to a little Boston terrier that looks just like the dog in our picture, trotting ahead off leash.

We immediately start running after it.

"Here, little guy, wait up!" Lea says. But when we get close, we see that unfortunately, it's not the same dog. He doesn't have a sparkling collar on his neck, like the dog in the picture.

The owner, a woman with pink hair and a Team Herbivore shirt, pulls out her AirPods and asks us, "What's going on?"

"We're trying to find a dog that looks just like yours," I tell her, holding up the picture.

She glances at the picture. "I'm sorry," she says, shaking her head. "I don't know those two guys."

Putting her AirPods back in, she starts jogging away, then stops. "Wait, but I think I've seen that dog before, at puppy socialization class!"

"Really?" we ask.

"Yeah, now I remember the collar. Here, I can give you the number of the instructor," she says, jogging back.

"That'd be great!" we say. Bowen pulls out his phone and the woman adds the number into it.

"Thanks!" we say to her.

As the woman jogs away, I leap into the air. "We caught a scent in the trail! We're gonna get Mom's earrings back!"

Lea and I hold our breath as Bowen calls. Unfortunately, the dog trainer doesn't answer. We leave a message. As Bowen puts his phone away, a labradoodle runs over to us. For a second I think it's Cody, and my heart leaps to my throat! But then I realize there's no way Cody could be here, and the collar on him says *CHARLIE*.

We bend down to pet Charlie the labradoodle.

"Awww, you're so cute," Bowen says, while Charlie licks Bowen's ear, making him laugh. "You're a good boy, aren't you?"

The next thing I know, a loud and cranky voice snaps sharply at us, "Get away from my dog!"

We turn around and come face-to-face with a furious-looking white man in a fisherman's hat and glasses. "Did I say you can touch my dog?" he barks at Bowen.

Bowen scrambles up and shakes his head, looking down. "No, sir."

"Then why are you touching my dog, you oriental??" the man demands.

Bowen freezes. I furrow my eyebrows, confused, wondering why he's calling my gege by the term used to refer to rugs. Obviously, Bowen's not a rug.

"You can't just go up to people's dogs and touch them, it's unhygienic!" the man continues to rant.

Lea and I take a step backward, away from the angry man and his dog. We're both scared. But the man turns to us and mutters, "You two are okay."

I look up at him, confused. "But you just said—"

"I'm only worried about this one," the man says, pointing to Bowen. "People like him are the reason we now have this virus in the world. Go back to where you came from! If your people weren't so filthy—"

Bowen immediately turns and sprints away, hiding his hot face with the sleeve of his hoodie.

"'Your people'??" I say to the man. "That's our brother!"

"Yeah!" Lea cries out. "You can't speak to him that way!"

"He's your brother?" The man frowns at his dog. "C'mon, Charlie, let's get away from these crazy mutts," he says as he gives his dog's collar a hard yank and pulls him away from my sister and me, eyeing us with disgust.

We find Bowen on a bench on the outskirts of the park and sit down next to him. I try to talk to him, but every time I say something, he snaps, "Stop. I'm *fine.*" I know he's not really fine because he's clutching the paper with the Boston terrier's picture so hard it's practically soggy.

My mind can't stop thinking about what that man said, and it makes me want to scream. How could he say that to Bowen? To us? My hands ball into fists as I replay his words— *these crazy mutts.* It fills me up with so much pain. And yet I know the pain I'm feeling is nowhere near what Bowen must be feeling. I gaze over at my brother, wishing he'd let it out. Even a trickle . . .

But all he says is, "Don't tell Mom about this."

"Why not?" I ask him. "It's not right! She needs to know!"

Quietly, my sister whispers to me, "Why'd that man say, 'Go back to where you came from'?" she asks. "Does he mean our house three blocks away?" She doesn't get it. She's too little to understand.

"No, that's not what he meant," Bowen says as he gets up and walks over to his bike. He kicks the metal kickstand hard as he reminds me, "Don't tell Mom."

I wish I could tell my brother he shouldn't be embarrassed by what happened. *That man* should be embarrassed. We did nothing wrong. As I pedal furiously, following my gege home, I hope the pain will slowly dry up like the slobber on my hands where the dog licked me.

Chapter 50

---✈

Bowen doesn't say anything at dinner about what happened at the dog park. When Mom asks us how our afternoon was, he gives me a *don't you dare* look, then stuffs a bunch of instant dinner rolls into his mouth. Mom is too busy trying to get Lea to eat her vegetables to notice anything is wrong.

I google the term "oriental" on my computer after dinner. Bowen walks in as I'm searching and immediately slaps my laptop shut.

"Don't google that," he hisses at me, like I'm looking up something R-rated. "EVER!"

"Okay, okay," I promise him. Instead, I pick up the posters Lea made for the garage sale. We took them down around the neighborhood after the sale. I start rolling them up.

"What are you doing?" Bowen asks.

"I'm saving these. You know, in case we have another garage sale."

"We're *not* having another garage sale," Bowen says, reaching for the scissors. "I'm cutting these up."

I look up at him in alarm and hold the posters close to my chest protectively. "But what about Dad?" I ask. "What about our plan to get him here?"

Bowen doesn't say anything.

I sink to the floor and peer up at him, trying to read his

face. As gently as I can, I bring up what happened at the park. "You can't let that guy get to you. Forget about him. . . ."

"I can't just forget, okay?" Bowen says. "You don't understand, it's different for you!"

I search my brother's eyes, struggling to understand.

"People look at you and they see a white kid. They look at me, and they see . . ." Bowen covers his face with his hands. "A virus carrier."

"Well, they're wrong!" I jump up in fury. I walk over to my brother and gaze between the cracks in his fingers. I take a deep breath and tell him the real reason why I kicked the soccer ball way over the fence. It wasn't because of my ADHD. It was because of the mean things Tyler was saying about Christopher and me.

"Why didn't you tell me?" Bowen asks, putting his hands down.

I shrug. Because some things are easier to carry inside, I guess. Even if they poke into you like the sharp wires of fences.

"Who is this Tyler kid?" Bowen says.

"He's nobody, just a kid in my class."

"Ignore him. Put your headphones on. That's what I did at school before I lost them." Bowen looks around. "I can lend you mine when I find them again."

I look up at him, surprised. Wow. Maybe I shouldn't have hidden them.

"Hopefully, Mom will get a good job soon and we can both go back to private school," Bowen says.

I nod, even though I actually like where I am—I like my friend Christopher. And I like my teacher. But I don't argue with Bowen. Instead, I give my brother a hug. It's an impulsive thing, and it only lasts a second.

We both stand awkwardly afterward, looking at the floor, pretending it never happened. Thankfully, my computer dings with a notification.

"It's Dad's LinkedIn," I tell my brother, walking over to my computer. *Whoa.* "He got thirty more connections!"

"From who?" Bowen asks, sitting down next to me.

I click on one of the new profiles. They're all connected to Dad by someone who came by. "They must be friends of the people from the garage sale!" I beam at my brother. *It's working!*

I click on Dad's smiling profile picture and zoom in so his face is real big. "We can't give up now! Dad needs us!"

Ever so quietly, Bowen goes over and picks up the posters. Instead of throwing them out, he rolls them up.

I feel the glow of pride build inside me as I close my laptop and crawl up on our bunk. It feels good knowing that I could make my brother feel a tiny bit better tonight. . . .

Maybe it's not the end of the world that I share a room with him.

Chapter 51

B owen's phone rings before school the next morning, while he's in the bathroom brushing his teeth. I look up from my computer. I have found that the secret to getting more connections on LinkedIn is to ADD EVERYONE, so I add jugglers, pet groomers, tour guides, and professional cuddlers. I didn't even know you could be a professional cuddler! America really is the land of opportunity!

"Bowen! Your phone!" I say, taking it over to the bathroom. I glance at the caller ID. "It's the dog trainer calling us back! What do I do?"

Bowen mumbles something I can't make out.

"Answer it!" Lea says, bursting out of her room in a pair of freshly ripped jeans—with the scissors still in her hand. Told ya you could do it for free!

I click accept call.

"Hello?" I say.

"Hey, is this Bowen? I got your message about the Taradippins' dog."

"The Taradippins?" I ask, signaling my sister with my hand—*Quick! Grab me a piece of paper!*

Lea dashes into her room, gets her Wonder Woman notepad, and flips to a new page.

"Yeah, they live over at—" she starts telling me, then stops.

"Actually, I'm not supposed to give out anyone's address. . . ."

"Oh, please?" I beg. Quickly I tell her all about the garage sale and the ruby earrings mix-up and how mad our mom is. Seeing the urgency of the situation, the dog trainer gives me the address: Maximillian Taradippin and his brother Pax, 1459 El Camino Road. But she tells me they can't know it came from her. I scribble it down in Lea's notepad.

"They won't!" I say to the dog trainer. "Thanks!"

"Glad to help. Hope you find your earrings!"

Bowen comes out of the bathroom.

"I got it—1459 El Camino Road! That's where the earrings are!" I tell my brother.

"That's not too far from here!" Bowen says.

"Really? Maybe we can go after school!" Lea says, jumping in her ripped jeans.

"Go where?" Mom asks, walking up the stairs.

"Nowhere," we blurt out.

I glance at Bowen and Lea and I can tell they're thinking the same thing. *Let's not get Mom's hopes up.*

"Don't forget you have track tomorrow," Mom reminds Bowen. "First training!"

"I'm psyched!" he says.

Bowen tells Mom about all the YouTube track videos he's been watching as we pile into the car for school, listing off a million facts about Usain Bolt. Mom reminds us, "Speaking of fast, make sure you three get to the parking lot on time at pickup today. I've got my Zoom interview."

"Got it!" we promise.

"Also, you guys need to be real quiet downstairs while I'm talking to these people, please?" Mom puts her hands together.

"No prob! We'll go biking around the neighborhood!" Bowen tells Mom.

"Perfect!" Mom smiles. "I like this new Bowen, spending time with his siblings."

"Me too." Lea smiles.

That afternoon, while Mom has her interview on Zoom, we bike over to El Camino Road. Bowen and I bike faster than Lea, zipping down Fitzgerald, dodging cars and pedestrians. Bowen and I pause at a corner and wait for Lea to catch up.

There are a couple of homeless people hanging out by the corner. I look down at my Ziploc bag of coins and dollars from the garage sale. I brought it along so I could return the money to the Taradippin brothers.

"Should we give them some money?" I ask Bowen.

Bowen immediately shakes his head. "No! If you give them money, they're gonna want the whole thing! Put that bag away—quick, before they see you!"

I frown at Bowen. Leave it to him to always think the worst about people. I ignore him, walk over, and give the nice homeless woman a dollar.

"Thank you, bless you, child," she says to me, putting the dollar in the pocket of her thin sweater. She hugs the sweater tight around her.

"No problem." I smile. I glance down at the shopping cart she's pushing. It's from Lucky's, and inside it's filled with books, an old violin, and a dusty leather purse. The leather purse looks just like Mom's. I wonder if she used to carry it to work.

I wish I could ask her what happened. How did she get

here? But I know there are some questions you're not supposed to ask people. It's something I learned from school last year when I asked Rosie Huang why she took two different school buses—one on Mondays, Wednesdays, and Fridays, and the other on Tuesdays and Thursdays. Turned out, her parents were separated. I hope we get Dad over here soon, so I don't have to take two different planes.

Bowen calls me back with a sharp holler.

I wave goodbye to the nice lady and walk over to my brother.

"So what'd she say? Did she want more?" Bowen asks.

"No," I say. "She just said thanks."

I glance over at her again, shivering in the bay breeze in her thin sweater. It gets cold out at night in El Tercera. Is her thin sweater going to be enough? I wish I hadn't sold all of Mom's old college sweaters. As the woman pushes her Lucky's cart down the road, I ask my brother in a small voice, "You think that's ever going to be us? If Mom doesn't get a job . . ."

It's a thought I haven't said out loud before, and now that I said it, it seems as big and terrifying as a boa constrictor.

"No! That'll never happen to us," Bowen insists.

I absorb his definitive answer. So unwavering and strong, just like Bowen. Still, I wonder, *How can he be sure?*

"We have a house," Bowen reminds me.

I wave at the woman as I get on my bike. "So . . . maybe she did too."

Bowen shakes his head like it's too childish of a conversation for him to continue. "Our parents went to good schools. They're successful people."

I grip my handlebars, trying to believe it. Trying to

understand the meaning of "success." Is it being able to answer every interview question? Even the ones about lost elephants? Or never having to hold your breath every time Mom gets gas?

"I see Lea. Finally! We can go!" Bowen says, pushing away on his bike. He flies ahead of me and the homeless woman, and I chase after him, wishing I had his legs. His confidence. His sureness that no matter what happens, we'll always be okay.

But I don't.

Chapter 52

--✈

By the time we finally get to the Taradippin brothers' house, we're all out of breath. I gaze up at the enormous ranch-style home as we walk across the huge, lush lawn.

"When I grow up, I'm going to have a house just like this," Bowen says. "It'll be so sick."

"Can I come over and play soccer on your lawn?" I ask.

"We'll see," Bowen says.

I cross my arms at my brother. "What do you mean?"

"I mean, by that time, I'll be older and have actual friends," he says, which makes me roll my eyes. But before we can get into it, Lea skips ahead and rings the doorbell.

We all wait for the owner to emerge. A white man in square-framed glasses and a baseball hat opens the door. He looks like he's just out of college. I recognize him from the garage sale.

"Good afternoon. We're looking for Maximillian and Pax Taradippin," I say.

"I'm Max. Can I help you?" he asks.

A puppy runs up behind him, barking. No sooner do my eyes adjust to the puppy than I see what's behind him. There, in Max's large mansion, is an avalanche of face masks and hand sanitizer, piled from floor to ceiling!

I point to all the boxes of single-use surgical face masks—

the ones we've been trying to buy for Dad. They're sold out literally everywhere! "Why do you guys have so many face masks?"

Max stiffens and moves the door slightly. "What do you care?"

"Who's that?" a voice behind him calls. A guy who looks to be Max's brother walks over. He picks up his puppy and scratches the dog's belly. "If you guys are here to sell stuff, unless it's sanitizer, we're not interested."

Bowen studies them. "Are you guys . . . doomsday preppers or something?"

The brothers burst out laughing. "No, we're businessmen," Max says, beaming.

His brother puts an arm around Max's shoulder proudly. "We're in the virus business."

"The *virus* business?" My jaw drops. "Wait, you're gonna sell *all* those face masks?" I point to the colossal stash—it's enough to protect an entire city!

"We already have!" the brothers say.

As it turns out, the Taradippin brothers have been quietly buying up all the face masks and hand sanitizer around town and selling them for ten times the price on Amazon and eBay. They gladly let us into their house to show off their loot.

"As soon as the news of the virus hit Asia, BOOM! We were on the road," Max brags. "You'd be amazed how much people will pay for this stuff. As much as ten dollars a mask!"

"We thought we'd have to ship them to desperate Asians, but nah," his brother says. "Turns out there are desperate folks right here!"

"We can't *wait* till the virus actually comes here. We'll

make a fortune!" Max adds. The brothers high-five each other while we gawk at them.

"So you're just ripping people off basically," I blurt out. Bowen shoots me a look.

"Hey! We give people what they want!" Max protests, stomping his foot on the hardwood floor. One of the boxes of face masks falls to the ground. "For a small finder's fee, of course."

"Speaking of selling things"—Bowen clears his throat—"we're actually here for a velvet box we accidentally sold you. At our garage sale this weekend?"

"Oh yeah, the ruby earrings, I remember," Max says.

"Tell me you didn't sell them on eBay," I say, scrunching my face.

"Not yet," he says.

PHEW!

"They're our mother's. An anniversary present from our dad . . . Would it be possible to get them back?" Bowen asks.

Max exchanges a look with his brother.

"Please!" Lea cries. "They're the only thing holding them together!"

Max tells us to wait a minute. He squeezes by the pyramid of bottles of hand sanitizer glistening in the light and goes into another room.

"You mean these?" he asks when he returns, holding out his hand.

There, in his palm, lie our mother's sparkling ruby earrings. Our eyes turn the size of saucers.

Chapter 53

---✈

S orry," Max says, closing his hand before we have a chance to even touch the earrings. "A deal's a deal."

"But it was an accident!" I say. "They weren't supposed to be in the garage sale!" I dig out our Ziploc bag full of quarters and dollars. "Can we buy them back from you?? Here's two dollars."

The brothers laugh in my face.

"Fine! Here, take all of it!" I offer, holding out our entire bag of garage sale money.

"Knox!" Bowen cries.

"There's like twenty-five dollars there!" Max balks.

"More like two hundred dollars!" I tell them.

"But you said these were anniversary earrings," Max says, opening his hand and holding the rubies up to the sunlight. "That means they're real! And if they're real, they're worth a whole lot more than two hundred dollars!"

"They're not!" I glance at my siblings. "Our dad is . . . er . . . real cheap."

"That's why our mom left him!" Lea adds. We all nod solemnly, trying our best to look like the spawn of a miserable cheapskate.

Max slips the earrings into his pocket. "Well, I'm still keeping them," he says. And with that, he pushes us out the door.

. . .

Bowen, Lea, and I sit on the curb outside Max's house, a gorgeous home wasted on well-sanitized pirates.

"Maybe we should go to the police . . . ," I say.

"And say what? We accidentally sold something valuable and we want it back? They're not going to do anything," Bowen says. "They didn't even come to our house that time Dad's luggage got stolen. And that was a theft!"

"Well, we *have* to do something," Lea says. "We can't just let him keep Mom's earrings!"

Bowen's phone beeps. It's Mom calling.

"Hey, where are you guys?" she asks on speakerphone. "Come home! I just passed my first interview!"

As soon as Mom tells us her good news, the three of us forget all about the earrings and jump and whoop. Lea does a happy dance.

"Hear that?" I shout back at the Taradippins. "We'll be back, suckers!"

Chapter 54

-- ✈

I t's five thirty p.m. by the time we bike all the way back to our house. Mom's in the kitchen making chicken soup. As she scoops up the soup into four bowls, I ask her about her interview. "What'd they say? Did you get the job? Does this mean we finally have health insurance?"

Mom chuckles. "Not yet, but I passed the first hurdle! There'll be one more web interview and then I might have to go to New York for the in-person interview."

"To New York?!" Lea cries.

"That's where the company headquarters are. Relax, it would only be for one night. And it's not even a definite yet," Mom says.

"Can Dad come over and take care of us while you're in New York?" I ask, thinking out loud. I could show him my new school! We could go to my beach! He could finally meet Christopher! But Mom nixes the idea with a regretful shake of her head.

"I'm sorry, guys," she says. "We can't afford that right now."

I gaze down at the Ziploc bag of coins by my feet as Mom cuts up little pieces of bread and puts them in Lea's chicken soup. We're still a long way away from $3,000.

"So who will take care of us when you go to New York?" Lea asks.

"Maybe you guys can stay at Auntie Jackie's?" Mom suggests.

I look down at my reflection in the soup, trying to decide if the juicy pork chops were worth the jealousy. I don't know if I can handle seeing Uncle Joe tuck in Maggie and Noah at night.

Mom asks us how our afternoon bike ride was as we eat. The broth tastes delicious, but there's hardly any chicken in my bowl. Mom says she forgot to go to the grocery store. I gaze over at Bowen to see if he got more chicken than me—he didn't.

"It was okay," Bowen says. "We just biked around the block."

"Yeah. And we saw some *interesting* people." Lea glances at me.

"Like who?"

I kick Lea under the table. "Like a homeless woman," I say instead. "I gave her a dollar."

"Mom, don't you think it's bad giving homeless people money?" Bowen asks. I roll my eyes as he continues. "I told Knox not to, but he did it anyway."

"I don't think it's bad. They're just trying to get back on their feet, same as us." Mom puts her spoon down. "Let me tell you a story."

I break off a piece of bread and lean in for another one of Mom's stories. Except this one's different. Tonight, she tells us about the summer when Lao Lao and Lao Ye lost their jobs at the restaurant.

"We had to sleep in our car that summer. I'll never forget—it was ninety-eight degrees outside, and the heat in that cramped car . . ." Mom starts fanning herself, like even now the memory burns hot. "It felt like we were being baked alive."

We gasp. Suddenly the thin soup before me feels thick and plentiful.

"You're telling us *we* used to be homeless?" Bowen asks, leaning so far in, he knocks over the salt and pepper shakers.

Mom nods slowly.

"Why didn't Lao Lao ever tell us this?" Bowen asks.

Mom picks the salt and pepper shakers back up. "She didn't want to scare you. And she was probably embarrassed," she says. "I know I was at the time. But I'm starting to realize it's important to tell you kids these things. So you understand. A *lot* of people have been down that path, including our own family."

"Wow," I say to Mom. I don't know what to say. But I'd like to hear more. Like how did they lose their jobs? And what happened after the summer in the car?

Mom doesn't tell us.

Instead, she scoops up the rest of the chicken broth from the pot and tells us to eat up. There's not much left, and she gives all of it to me and my siblings. I take one of my pieces of chicken and put it in Mom's bowl.

Afterward, we help Mom with the dishes. When the dishwasher's all loaded up, we ask her if there's anything else we can help with.

Back in Hong Kong, we had a wonderful lady named Wong Tai Tai who came by on the weekends and helped us clean the apartment. But here, Mom's all on her own. She smiles.

"It has been a while since I vacuumed," she says.

Bowen, Lea, and I pick up a mop, a rag, and a vacuum each.

Lea runs upstairs to clean the bathroom, while Bowen mops the kitchen floor and I vacuum all the carpets. It's hard work at first, until Lea comes up with the brilliant idea to make a dance party out of it.

Lea puts on the song "We Are Family" and cranks up the volume as we sing our hearts out with our Clorox sprays. Mom puts a gloved hand to her heart as she watches us—her new helpers. I suddenly get an idea.

"Hey! Let's FaceTime Dad!!!" I say.

"Great idea!" Mom says.

Dad answers on the first ring and laughs when he sees us. To our great surprise, he gets up from his mountain of legal contracts and starts cleaning with us. It's a *clean-off*! Lea and I sweep and wipe as Dad does silly dance moves. Bowen jumps in front of the camera and does air guitar with the vacuum extension hose. My sides hurt from laughing. It makes the time go by *so fast*. Before you know it, the house is spotless.

Mom takes a picture of us virtual cleaning with Dad and warns him, "This may become a weekly tradition!"

"Oh, it's on!" Dad grins.

I smile too. I'm glad they made up. It makes me feel all warm and toasty inside that we can still have fun as a family, even if Dad can't be here.

(Though I hope he can. Really soon.)

Chapter 55

--- ✈

can't believe we were homeless once," Bowen mutters in the dark from the bottom bunk.

I know! I roll onto my tummy. "Mom's stories are so different from Lao Lao and Lao Ye's. . . ." All my grandparents ever talk about is how big the yards are in America and how they got free samples of guacamole at Trader Joe's. I thought they had a really nice life here when they used to live here.

I close my eyes and try imagining living in a car with my siblings. We'd have to put up some dividers. And curtains. Before long, I am full-on redecorating our car in my mind and am wide awake.

I think about the tents under the freeways in Berkeley. I ask my brother, "Hey. How come there aren't a lot of homeless people in Hong Kong?" I don't think I've ever seen cars with curtains or people living in tents in Hong Kong. . . .

Bowen replies it's because families in Asia are always taking care of each other, even extended relatives. "That's why they all live together."

I smile, strangely comforted by this. I think of my *lao lao* and *lao ye* living with us when we were babies in Hong Kong. That was so fun. "Will you take care of me if I'm down on my luck?"

Bowen thinks for a long while before replying, "I guess you

can live in my guesthouse. But you'd have to clean the pool."

"You're going to have a *pool* when you grow up?"

"'Course!" he says. "When I grow up, I'll be super successful."

I see the gleam of Bowen's smiling teeth in the moonlight. To each his own, I guess. I just hope Bowen knows it's okay even if he ends up living in a hut.

"What about you . . . ?" he asks back quietly.

I turn my head and glance down, amazed he's even asking. Of course I'd take care of him. And not just because I'm Asian.

"Only if you don't hog the remote," I reply.

Bowen yawns.

I close my eyes and drift off to sleep, imagining our future life together, hanging out by the pool, having cookouts, and *all* the video games we'd play. It feels nice to know that one day, we'll be friends, even if we can't be right now.

At school the next day I tell Christopher I can't believe it's been a whole month since we've been in America. He grins and asks how we celebrated. I tell him by having a dance cleaning party with my dad!

"My sister and I forgot to rinse the soapy floor with water," I laugh. "It was so slippery, you could go sock skating on it!"

"I love sock skating!!!" Christopher says. "I did it once in the kitchen at the restaurant!"

Tyler overhears us talking and makes a face. "Who still cleans their house themselves?"

"Um, everyone I know?" Christopher replies. I mouth, *Thank you.*

"Well, *we* have a cleaning lady," Tyler brags.

I look at his smug face. It makes my insides bubble the way he says it, like we're not as good as his family. I want to tell him that not everyone has a hundred dollars to hire someone else to make their bed. We used to in Hong Kong, but now, even if we did have the money, we'd put it into our Dad fund.

But then he'd probably make fun of *that*.

So instead I say, "You know what you don't have? Virtual sock-skating dance parties!"

Tyler rolls his eyes as Christopher and I giggle on the walk toward our classroom.

My eyes bug out in class when Bowen forwards me an email from LinkedIn—Dad's up to 520 connections now! Holy mackerel! All the strangers added him back, *especially* the professional cuddlers!

I tell Christopher about my dad's LinkedIn. "That's great! So now you can start applying for jobs! What kind of jobs are you thinking?" he asks.

I rattle off a list of all my favorite businesses. "I'm thinking Jamba Juice, Best Buy, Hershey's, and Six Flags." I grin. "It'd be *so* cool working at Jamba Juice. Think of all the free smoothies he'd get!"

"Totally!" Christopher agrees. "Six Flags, too."

We pretend to go on one of those upside-down roller coasters together at our mat, until Mrs. Turner gives us a funny look. And reminds us gently to get back to our reading.

"So how'd you do it?" Christopher whispers, getting his book out. We're both reading graphic novels.

I whisper back my strategy of adding strangers.

"You're really a whiz at that thing," he chuckles. "I wish I could connect with five hundred strangers. We sure could use more customers."

"You totally can!" I say. "You can make a page—maybe not on LinkedIn, but . . ."

Christopher thinks for a minute. "What about Nextdoor?"

I ask Christopher, "What's Nextdoor?"

He says it's an app for people in the neighborhood to talk about what's going on.

"Have you been on it?" I ask.

"Yeah. All everyone talked about was how good Zachary's Pizza was," Christopher sighs. "I always want to say something about our restaurant, but I'm afraid people will tell me I'm biased because I'm the owner's son."

"Well, I'm not! I can be your online publicist!" I volunteer.

"Really?"

"Sure, I'm already managing my dad's LinkedIn. And look how well that's doing! I've got this!" I grin at my friend. "We're gonna get your parents' restaurant back on track in no time."

Christopher grins as Mrs. Turner walks by and passes back my math test. I gaze down wearily at my paper, as I do whenever I get a test back. I give myself my usual pep talk—D is for Done and Over With. C is for Cool, and anything B and above is just a Bonus! Still, I can hear the crickets in my ear as I turn around my first official test from my American school.

To my surprise, it's an A– staring back at me, along with the words, *Great job, Knox. Keep it up!*

I grab the paper to my chest. All this time, I thought A was for Are You Kidding, Never Gonna Happen! Turns out, it can happen!!!

Chapter 56

-- ✈

"Mom!!!" I cry, running toward her in the parking lot. I hold up my test—my very first A!!!

"That's incredible!" Mom says, smiling at my paper.

"Yay!" Lea says.

"I'm so proud of you." Mom smiles, pulling out of the lot and continuing on to the middle school. "It's a huge accomplishment."

She points to a black bag in the back and tells me to get it ready for Bowen. "That's his track stuff. He forgot it this morning."

As soon as I see Bowen waiting in the middle school parking lot, I flash my test to him.

"Look, Bowen, I got an A!" I cry out.

Bowen glances at it, then frowns. "Still an A minus," he mutters.

Here I thought we could both celebrate Dad's new LinkedIn connections together, but he had to pour ice on my good news.

"Bowen!" Mom scolds him. She looks me right in the eye. "Don't listen to your brother."

Mom hands Bowen his track bag. "You ready for your track tryout?" she asks him.

Bowen nods, gazing over at the track. I notice there's a soccer pitch on the side. I grab my soccer ball.

"Can I come watch? And kick my ball around?" I ask. It's been so long since I've played on Astroturf. "Please???"

"Sure!" Mom says.

Bowen rolls his eyes. "Fine. But Mom, you have to make sure he stays away from me and my new teammates. He can't embarrass me!"

"He won't," Mom says, letting us off. "I'll be back as soon as I drop this off."

She points to a stack of papers on the passenger-side seat. "I've got to get these to New York. They're for my interview."

Speaking of interviews . . . I crane my neck. "Hey, Mom, how do you apply for jobs on LinkedIn?" I ask.

Mom tells us it's pretty simple. All you have to do is search and click apply on the job listing page. Then if the company wants more information, they'll contact you.

"Can I come to FedEx with you?" Lea asks Mom.

"You're going *now*?" Bowen asks Mom. "You promised you'd make sure Knox doesn't embarrass me!" He holds the door open as he frowns at Mom.

"It'll only take a few minutes—it's important. I'll be back before you know it," she promises. Bowen slams the door. I slide the back door open, but before I can scramble after my brother, Mom reaches out an arm and catches me. She holds me back.

"Hey, kiddo. Promise me you'll take it easy—remember, we still don't have health insurance."

I nod. I remember every day.

"I'll be careful," I tell Mom.

"No heading," she instructs me sternly, pointing her index finger at me as I reach for my stuff.

"Fine . . . ," I say to her, flying out of the car with my soccer ball.

I run toward the soccer pitch and the track. "Bowen! Wait for me!!!"

Chapter 57

Stepping onto the soccer pitch for the first time in a month, I kick the ball high into the wind. Though the turf is patchy and worn at Bowen's middle school, it still feels like greeting an old friend.

"Oh, Astroturf, how I've missed you!" I say to the turf.

I run toward the goal, breathing in the fresh air as I dribble the ball. I was worried for a second that all the quarantine and time away from soccer meant I'd somehow lost it, but as my feet tap the ball along the grass, I feel the adrenaline soaring through me. I still got it!

SCORE!

I close my eyes and picture Dad at the goal. Then I throw my arms up high and run around the field. I see my brother on the track. I stop for a sec to watch him run. *Whoa.* The other kids are *really* fast. They zip by him as they run the two hundred. Bowen comes in last. He gasps for air, with his hands on his knees, shaking his head.

I look around for Mom, but she's still not back from FedEx.

I dribble my ball over to him, practicing my inside touch, like my old coach in Hong Kong taught me. When I get close to Bowen, I see the other kids looking at him funny as he struggles to catch his breath.

"Hey, are you okay?" I ask.

"Get OUT of here!" he shouts at me.

"Is that your little brother?" the other kids ask Bowen. My brother starts coughing.

"Oh my God, he's coughing!" one kid says. They hurry away from Bowen. He sits down on the bench, mortified, and glares at me like it's all my fault.

The track coach walks over. He's a tall African American man with a visor and clipboard.

"Are you okay?" he asks Bowen.

Bowen nods and says, "Yeah . . . I'm fine. Just catching my breath."

"Here, have some water," the coach says. I notice it says COACH CARTER on the back of his sweatshirt. He hands Bowen a water bottle.

Bowen takes big gulps from the bottle, the water dripping down his neck.

"They're probably just cramps," the coach says as Bowen drinks. "You're not used to training this hard, are you, son?"

Bowen shakes his head.

"I think I'm out of practice," he says. "I haven't exactly been training these past few weeks. . . ."

None of us have. We've been stuffing ourselves with *moo shu* pork and frozen pizza.

"Don't worry about it. We'll get you in top form in no time." Coach Carter smiles at Bowen, putting a hand on his back.

Bowen looks up, surprised. "Are you sure?"

Coach Carter nods. "I'm positive. Welcome to the team."

Bowen smiles as he gets up and follows Coach Carter back to the starting line. He drinks the last of the water and gets into position. When Coach Carter says, "GO," Bowen bolts toward the finish. Even though he's still the slowest, there's mad determination in his eyes.

Mom finally comes to pick us up after most of Bowen's teammates have already gone home.

"What took you so long?" Bowen says to Mom when she pulls up. "You said you were only going to be a couple of minutes!"

"I'm sorry, there was traffic," Mom explains. Lea shows me the stack of free envelopes she picked up at FedEx as we get in the car. "We can use one of these to mail Daddy his plane ticket," she whispers.

"So? Did you make the team??" Mom asks Bowen.

"Yeah," he says. He doesn't say it with a lot of confidence, so I add, "The coach said he's going to get Bowen in top form in no time!"

"I knew he'd see potential in you!" Mom says to Bowen. "How were the other kids?"

"Fast."

"Faster than you?" Mom asks.

"*Much* faster."

"I'm sure you'll catch up to them, gege," Mom says as she turns onto the freeway to go home.

Bowen doesn't respond. He just gazes out the window. The Bay Area traffic is so slow, it's like waiting for a GIF to load. Next to me, Lea doodles on her iPad.

"You should change lanes," Bowen instructs Mom.

"But if I change lanes, I'll have to cut right back in!" Mom hates changing lanes on the freeway, especially when things are slow. She's not the most confident driver in the world. That's because in Hong Kong, she never needed to drive. We always took minibuses everywhere.

"Ugh! If Dad were here, we'd be home already," Bowen fumes in frustration.

Mom turns and stares at him, shocked by the outburst. "What's gotten into you?"

She waits until we're finally off the freeway before pulling the car over and turning to face Bowen. "Is this about me going to FedEx? I couldn't help it. I'm sorry I wasn't at your practice, but you don't get to take it out on me."

I reach to tap Mom's shoulder. I want to tell her that's not why Bowen's mad. He's mad because the other kids weren't very nice to him. And he came in last. It has nothing to do with FedEx.

"Not now, Knox," Mom says.

As she restarts the car, she tells us, "Life is hard enough already. But if we're not kind to each other, it's a double whammy of hard."

I look to my brother, hoping Mom's words sink in.

Bowen stomps up to our room when we get home. I follow him up. He drops to the floor and starts doing sit-ups.

"Didn't you have enough training today?" I ask Bowen, climbing onto the top bunk and taping my A– test up on the wall next to my bed. Most of my other tests are like toilet paper: I look at them and then I throw them away. But this one I'm keeping forever.

"No," Bowen says. With every sit-up, he huffs, "I. Have. To. Outrun. The. Other. Kids."

I raise an eyebrow. Slowly, I climb down from my bunk and sit next to him on the floor. While Bowen does sit-ups, I get out my computer and pull up LinkedIn. "Now that Dad has over five hundred connections, we can start applying for jobs."

Bowen stops doing sit-ups and peers over at my computer. We scroll through the job bank together, clicking through all the various available lawyer jobs that we see. Plus a few other ones.

"How about this one? Virtual game show host." I point to an ad.

"That sounds cool!" Bowen says, and whips up a simple cover letter.

I marvel at my brother's lightning-fast typing speed. I read over his shoulder as my brother writes:

Dear ~~people in charge~~ recruiting managers,

My name is Andrew Evans, and I'm interested in applying for the job available. As you can see from my résumé, I have ~~TONS~~ a great deal of experience and ~~you should hire me because I'm the best!!!~~ I think I would make an excellent addition to your team.

Please contact me by phone or email if you would like to speak further.

Sincerely,

Andrew Evans

Nice! I give Bowen a thumbs-up sign. And just like that, we click and apply. Mom was totally right—applying for jobs is super easy! Within ten minutes, we apply Dad for five lawyer jobs, plus a weather reporter opening, a wine club manager, and a country club supervisor job.

Just as we're about to close the tabs, I spot something *amazing*. "Oh my God, look at this! Undercover shopper at Six Flags!!!"

Bowen frowns.

"Dad's not gonna be an undercover shopper," he says.

"Why not?" The job description sounds *beyond*. "You get to go around Six Flags buying stuff with special marked money!"

"Because! It's not a serious job!" Bowen says. "Dad's not changing his career from being a lawyer to being an undercover shopper!"

"Oh, and being a country club supervisor is so out of this world?"

"At least it says *supervisor*," Bowen says, pointing to the word on the screen.

I frown. "You're so obsessed with what sounds good," I mutter. "We should pick out something Dad actually likes. . . ."

"I'm pretty sure he's not going to like walking around a theme park all day with fake money."

I close my computer. *I* think it sure beats sitting in an office all day. I shudder at the thought. When I grow up, I am going to get a job that involves walking around. I don't care what it is. I am going to be a professional walker.

Curious, I ask my brother, "What do you want to be when you grow up?"

"A CEO," he replies.

"Of what?" I ask.

He shrugs. "Anything."

I cross my arms and look at him. "You can't just want to be a CEO of anything. You have to want to be a CEO of *something.*"

"Fine. I want to be a CEO of a Fortune 500 company. And make lots of money so Mom and Dad will never have to worry about losing their jobs again. There, I said it."

Ohhhhh. I guess it makes more sense now, why Bowen wants to be a CEO.

"And when I make it big, everyone in my school will wish they knew me better." Bowen plops down to do a few more sit-ups as I open my laptop back up and get on Nextdoor.

I gaze over at Bowen, wondering. Why don't his friends want to get to know him better now? I remember back in Hong Kong, he had two good friends—Oscar and Simon Mitchell. They were the only other Americans at Bowen's secondary school, and they were twins. The three of them did everything together, until one day Oscar got mad at Bowen because Bowen wouldn't let him copy from his math test. And Simon took Oscar's side, leaving my brother alone in the dust with his math test.

Bowen was pretty devastated that his friends picked a score over him. I was proud of him, though. I hope the people at his new school are nicer to him.

But I don't dare ask.

Bowen gets up from the floor and announces that he's going downstairs for a snack. He walks to the door. "You coming?" he asks, holding the door for me.

"Not yet. I need to post this thing for Christopher," I tell him, typing away.

"What thing?" Bowen asks.

I read him my first official post as Christopher's online publicist.

Honey walnut prawns—get in my belly.
The other day I had the most delicious honey walnut prawns at Uncle Chang's Sichuan Garden, next to Lucky's. They were big and juicy. I'm talking JUMBO. You could actually chew them for MINUTES in your mouth. I counted. They also had the best barbecue fried rice I've ever tasted. And I've had a lot! So head over to Uncle Chang's if you want some authentic Chinese food!

"What do you think?" I ask.

"I'd take out the part about chewing for minutes. That sounds weird. Which you are," Bowen adds. "Why are you doing this anyway?"

"Because he's my best friend," I tell Bowen. I glance up and ask, "Do you have a good friend at school?"

Bowen thinks for a long while. He starts to close the door as he mumbles, "I'm in middle school. It's different."

Chapter 58

---✈

Christopher skips over to me at school on Wednesday.

"I saw the post on Nextdoor! Thanks so much! We've been getting more phone calls ever since!" he says.

"What are best friends for?" I smile. Christopher bumps fists with me. "And hey, guess what? We officially started applying for jobs for my dad, and this morning, someone responded! Bay Area Legal Aid wants to interview him tomorrow!"

"That's *great*! Was your dad surprised when you told him?" Christopher asks.

"Errr . . . not exactly." I confess to Christopher that my dad doesn't know about his LinkedIn body double yet.

"WHAT???"

"We just don't want him to get mad and tell us to stop! We're going to tell him when we have five job offers in hand. Then he can't say no to moving here."

"But . . . how? Who will pass the interviews?" Christopher asks.

I hold up a finger. Bowen and I have a plan.

When I tell Christopher, his jaw drops. "Your *brother's* gonna pretend to be your dad??"

Okay, so maybe it's not the perfect plan.

"It'll be on the phone anyway, and we've seen our mom

do it a bunch of times! All you do is say 'that sounds fascinating' and 'I'm very collaborative!' How hard can it be?"

After school, I walk to the parking lot and see Lea talking to a boy outside her classroom. Once my sister says goodbye to him, I ask her, "Who's that?"

"That's Stuart," she says. "I played with him at recess today."

"See, boys aren't so bad!" I smile at her. I'm glad she's no longer sitting on the friendship bench.

"He'll do for now," Lea says, gazing over at the girls in her class huddled together with their colorful bracelets. "I'm still holding out for the girls, though. . . ."

"What's Stuart into?" I ask.

"Soccer!" Lea tells me. "Hey, do you think you can teach me some skills?"

"Could I ever!" I grin.

We hop into Mom's waiting car. The radio is on and we listen as we take off our backpacks. "This just in—CDC is saying that the first possible community spread of the coronavirus might have happened here in the Bay Area."

My sister and I look at each other. "Oh no!" we both call out.

Mom shushes us as she turns up the volume on the radio. "Reports are saying a person in California who reportedly did not have relevant travel history or exposure has contracted the coronavirus. Officials are not quite sure how the patient contracted COVID-19, and experts are fearing that, in fact, community spread may be happening."

Lea looks at Mom in alarm. "But we just got here . . . and I *just* made a friend!"

"Nothing's been confirmed yet," Mom says. "It's one case. Let's not panic."

But I am panicking. I don't want to have to buy overpriced masks from the Taradippin brothers! As Mom drives over to the middle school to pick up Bowen, I take the hand sanitizer out of my backpack and squirt two pumps out. I give some to my sister, and she rubs it all over her hands and even her legs.

If the virus really is here . . . can Dad still come?

I try calling Dad as soon as we get home, but he doesn't pick up. Mom says he's probably on a work call. So I call Christopher instead.

"Did you hear about the local case?" Christopher asks.

"What does this mean?" I ask, and clutch the landline phone cord. I tell my friend about the Taradippin brothers and how those earring hoarders have bought up all the masks!

"It ought to be illegal, ripping people off like that," Christopher says. "We never raise our prices, not even on Christmas, when we're the only restaurant open!"

I shake my head in dismay.

"I gotta go. I'm helping my mom sanitize all the tables in the restaurant," Christopher says.

"Are people calling in?" I ask.

"Yeah! Most people want takeout, though," he says.

"Hey, whatever works!" I smile, glad that my ad is gaining traction.

That night, I toss and turn in my bed, thinking about the virus and how if it does explode in America, would we have to move back? But that would mean leaving Christopher and a teacher who, for the first time in my life, sees something in me.

The crickets chirp loudly outside our room. It's an unusually hot night for late February, and we have the windows open to save on air con. With every chirp, I wonder if Dad's reading the news too. *What if he makes us come back?* He won't do that, will he?

Bowen barks at me from the bottom bunk, "Stop rustling around! I need to sleep if I'm going to do well on my interview tomorrow as a fake lawyer."

"Sorry . . . ," I say, freezing my body.

I lie as still as I can, trying to hold my breath. According to YouTube, if you don't have the virus, you should be able to hold your breath and count to ten. I can count all the way up to twenty, no problem. Then I count again, worried I might have counted too fast.

"Will you stop?" Bowen asks. "I can hear you counting!"

"Aren't you worried? If the virus spreads here and we have to go back to Hong Kong?"

Bowen tosses in his bottom bunk. "It's not gonna spread here, and even if it does, America has the best healthcare system in the world. Mom said."

"Yeah, and we can't use it!"

I hear Bowen pull his covers up. "Well, she's close to getting a new job. And if she gets it—"

"But what if she doesn't?"

"She *will*," he insists. "Besides, we already gave up the apartment. We can't go back. *This* is our home."

I breathe a sigh of relief.

"And actually, the teachers at my new school aren't bad. They said I might be able to test out of the seventh-grade math I'm in now and go straight to algebra," Bowen adds in the darkness.

"That's great!" I say to him, plopping onto my stomach. "So you don't want to go to private school anymore?"

"Well, I still want to go . . . ," Bowen says, his voice lingering. "But . . ."

Quietly I voice another worry that's been keeping me up. "What if Dad can't come, even after we've raised the three thousand dollars?" I close my eyes, imagining a month from now, planes flying with giant masks over their plane noses.

"He will. We're his family. Family beats virus, any day."

I smile in the dark and flex my arm, just like Dad, even though my brother can't see me. I yawn and drift off to sleep, listening to the chirping crickets and replaying my brother's reassuring words.

"Good night, gege."

Chapter 59

A t school, there's an eerie sense of worry in the air as teachers scramble to put hand sanitizers in every classroom. Unfortunately, there's not enough for each individual class, so we have to share with the kids next door. Mrs. Turner puts out a table between our two rooms.

"Please, everyone, squirt a dollop on your hands," Mrs. Turner urges. We all line up.

Tyler stands ahead of me in line. Instead of a dollop, he squirts almost a full *cup* into his hands, pouring the stuff like it's whipped cream.

"Tyler! That's way too much!" Mrs. Turner says.

"But I want to be extra safe!" Tyler says. "I don't want to catch the disease!" He glares at me and Christopher when he says "disease."

"You're not *more* safe if you drench yourself in hand sanitizer," Mrs. Turner says. "That's not how it works!"

"She's right," I say. "All you need is about the size of a quarter. But you have to rub it over your entire hand, so you get every surface, including in between the fingers and under your fingernails, for twenty seconds."

I show my classmates, remembering all those YouTube videos Mom made me watch back in Hong Kong. I feel proud, like a pandemic expert!

"Brilliant hand sanitizing!" Mrs. Turner praises me.

My classmates immediately start copying me, and we sing "Happy Birthday" as a class, until we reach the full twenty seconds. Christopher turns and is about to give me a high five when he stops. We bump elbows instead.

After school, I stay behind for a few extra minutes to help Mrs. Turner wipe up the goop that's solidified on the table outside from so many kids squirting hand sanitizer.

"Thanks for helping me clean up," she says. "I hope you're liking your new school."

"I am!"

"I'm so glad. You're doing super," she tells me.

I smile, soaking in her words. I look up into Mrs. Turner's big brown eyes and see my promise reflected back in them. It fills my whole heart.

"Thanks," I say. "You're a great teacher!"

"Awww, I appreciate that," Mrs. Turner says. "I do love teaching. I was telling the district superintendent this morning, I'd be so sad if we had to close."

"Why would we have to close?"

"Well, you know, in case the virus spreads," she says.

The possibility of schools shutting down here didn't even cross my mind! I start panicking, thinking about my siblings and me trapped at home, trying to figure out online school—*again!*

"You know the part about it that makes me the most sad?" Mrs. Turner asks. "All the children who rely on free lunches going hungry. Twenty-two *million* kids depend on free school lunches in the US, did you know that? Many of them children of color . . ." She sighs.

I furrow my eyebrows at the free-lunch part. Am *I* on free lunch? The cafeteria lady almost never asks me for money; she usually goes "You're good, hon" whenever I go up to her. I *assume* Mom's been paying. . . .

"Well, hopefully, it won't come to that," Mrs. Turner says. Her eyes gaze down at the almost empty bottle of hand sanitizer. "Just wish we could get some more sanitizer."

Chapter 60

--✈

Bowen jiggles his leg anxiously on the way home.

"Will you stop?" Mom asks. "You're making me nervous. I have my second interview later today!"

Unbeknownst to Mom, Bowen also has a big interview. In exactly twenty-eight minutes.

"Sorry. But seriously, drive faster."

Mom turns and asks Bowen, "Why are you always in a rush these days??"

I clear my throat, trying to change the subject. "Did you know twenty-two million kids depend on free school lunch?" I ask Mom, thinking about what Mrs. Turner said. Biting my lip, I wonder out loud, "Am I on free school lunch?"

"No," she says, glancing in the rearview mirror. "But I was when I was a kid."

As she drives, Mom tells us that after the awful summer living in their car, she and Lao Lao and Lao Ye finally managed to get a small one-bedroom apartment in San Diego.

"Still, it wasn't easy. I'd save my chocolate chip cookie from school every day for Lao Lao and Lao Ye," she says. "I remember I'd put it in my pocket, and all day long, I'd worry about it getting squished. And I couldn't play sports, either, because I had no health insurance."

"Like us!"

"Well, *no*, not like you guys," Mom says, slightly embarrassed. "Our situation is temporary. I'm going to get a new job—that's why I have my second interview."

"Was it embarrassing, having free lunch?" Lea asks.

Mom shakes her head. "To be honest, I was more embarrassed about my name."

"Julie?" we ask.

"I wasn't always called Julie. I used to be called Wei Wei."

"That's your Chinese name," Bowen says. He chuckles and asks, "Remember the time at the San Francisco airport, the guy looked at your passport and he mispronounced it 'Why Why'? He was like, 'Your mom and dad must have been *really* surprised when they had you!'"

Bowen stops chuckling when he sees the look on Mom's face.

"Imagine getting that as a kid. All the time." She looks away, like the pain of the experience hasn't quite left. "Sometimes, even the *teacher* made fun of me."

"The teacher??" I lean forward. I can never imagine Mrs. Turner doing that—she's the kindest, most patient teacher on the planet. Whenever one of us mispronounces a word during class read-aloud, she always winks and says, "Hey, tomato, tom*ah*to!"

"Is that the reason you changed your name to Julie?" Bowen asks.

Mom nods.

"I finally decided enough, after I had a professor in college who refused to call me Wei Wei."

"He *refused* to call you by your name?" Lea asks, her chin dropping to her booster seat.

"Yeah. He said my Chinese name was a joke and he renamed me Will," Mom says, shaking her fist.

"Is *that* who Will is?" Bowen asks. "Knox and Lea found the essay in your closet!"

Mom is so surprised, she drives right over a large pothole.

I immediately add, "We didn't sell that, I promise! We put it right back!"

Mom sighs at the traffic light. "That was me. Will," she says, holding up a hand. "He couldn't even be bothered to give me a girl's name."

"I'm so sorry, Mommy," Lea says, reaching for the back of Mom's seat.

"The guy sounds like a jerk," Bowen says. "Is he still teaching at Berkeley?"

"Luckily, no. You know why?" Mom asks. "I fought back. I told the department head about his behavior. And a year later, he was removed."

We cheer in the car.

"The point is, there are going to be people in life who try and make you feel bad for being different. Don't let them," Mom says as she pulls into our driveway. "I wish I'd embraced my name growing up, but it took me a long time. It wasn't until much later in life that I finally found pride in my roots. . . ."

She smiles at us in the rearview mirror. "That's why I gave you each such unique names. So you'll always remember and be proud of where you're from."

I catch my brother's reflection as he mouths his name under his breath: *Bo-wen*.

Chapter 61

✈

"All right, let's do this!" Bowen says, dialing the number for Bay Area Legal Aid when the three of us get upstairs. I've got Dad's LinkedIn résumé open and the number on my notepad.

"You know what to say?" I ask him as he dials. "Are you ready?"

Bowen nods. "I was born ready!"

My brother puts the phone on speakerphone when the guy answers.

"Hi, this is Andrew Evans," Bowen says, clearing his throat and putting on his deepest, most official-sounding tone. I recognize the voice from when we used to play Special Agents Rescue when we were little.

"Thanks so much for calling, Andrew. I'm Kyle Jones, the senior supervising attorney here," the guy says. "So I'm looking at your résumé. Very impressive! Tell me, what kind of law were you practicing at Simden and Cadwell?"

Uh-oh. Bowen glances at me. I shrug—I didn't know there were *kinds* of law!

"Uhhh . . . the international kind," Bowen says. I give him a thumbs-up—good answer!

"Transactional, I assume?" Mr. Jones asks. "Or tax? Or governmental?"

"Yes. All of the above."

There's a long silence on the other end of the line.

"O . . . kay," Mr. Jones says. "So tell me, why are you thinking of leaving?"

"I want to be closer to my family," Bowen says, glancing at me and Lea. Another great answer! *Wow. Bowen's really good at this!* "And I want to expand my horizons as a lawyer."

"Oh, really? In what aspect?"

"Pretty much all aspects," Bowen answers. "I'd love more . . ."

He scratches his head, trying to come up with an answer.

"More time off?" I whisper.

"More pens??" Lea tosses out.

"More choices," Bowen finally goes with. "I'd love to get to decide what cases I'm taking on."

"Just so you know, this is more of a junior position," Mr. Jones says. "It's fairly entry level, and you don't get a lot of autonomy."

"I can do entry level! I love entries!" Bowen says.

But it's too late. Mr. Jones does not believe him. "Thanks for your time, Mr. Evans. Best of luck in your job hunt."

With that, Bowen hangs up.

Chapter 62

---✈

Bowen's so bummed he messed up his first job interview for Dad, not even the good news that Mom passed her second interview lifts his spirits.

"It's okay . . . ," I try and console him later in our room. "You'll get something else."

Bowen mutters from behind his computer screen. "No, it's not okay. I'm not like you. *I* can't screw things up. Now, thanks to me, Dad will have to be a random undercover shopper. . . ."

He rests his face on his laptop keys with such grief, I want to hand him one of my T-shirts so he can go inside a T-shirt cave. At the same time, I'm stuck on one thing he said.

"What do you mean, 'I'm not like you'?" I ask him.

"I mean I need to be good at things," he says. He thinks for a long while before adding, "It's my way of getting Mom and Dad's attention, okay?"

I scrunch my face. Now I'm really confused.

Bowen closes his computer. "Ever since you were born, Mom and Dad have been so preoccupied with you. It's always—we must find someone to help Knox with this. Or we have to take Knox to that specialist. I get that you needed it for your eczema and your . . ."

Bowen stops and looks at me.

"My ADHD. You can say it," I tell him.

"Your ADHD. I get that now. But it was kind of like . . . I disappeared into the background."

WOW. All this time, I thought *I* was the one who always disappeared into the background. The one my *lao lao* was least likely to brag about to relatives. Or whose shoe size my parents were most likely to forget.

"What about all the times Mom raves about your grades?" I ask Bowen.

"Yeah, because they're *good*!" he says. "But the minute I stop achieving . . . I'll be yesterday's news."

In that moment, I finally understand my brother's pressure on himself. It's crushing him like a tire.

He opens his computer and starts tapping madly on the keys. *Tap-tap-tap.*

"What are you doing?" I ask him.

"Sending Dad's résumé to every law firm in the Bay Area, even the ones that haven't advertised on LinkedIn," Bowen says. "One way or another, I *will* get him a job."

I walk over and take a seat next to him, reaching for my own laptop. If he's going to do this, we're hyper-focusing together.

As we look up law firms and email their hiring departments, I stare at Bowen and admire his intense concentration skills. The way he's able to scroll through pages and pages of confusing text on each law firm's "Careers" page. Wade through the gobbledygook of corporate-speak. I would have pulled up at least five YouTube videos and bounced around from tab to tab, but he just stays on one page. It's amazing.

"What?" he asks, glancing at me.

"Nothing," I say. Then ask, "How can you just read that stuff?"

Bowen shrugs. "I just make myself do it," he says. "Same as in school. I try to find something interesting about it. . . ." He points at one law firm's website, on the "Benefits and Work Balance" page, where it says *Flexible Time-Off Policy.*

"There's usually one neat thing in everything," he tells me.

Which makes me sit up. "What about me?" I ask.

Bowen looks over and studies me for a long while.

"You're not boring," he concludes.

My face breaks into a smile. "Thanks!" I'll take that. I want to lock away the compliment in my lockbox, but it's currently floating in the Pacific somewhere. It's the highest praise my brother's ever paid me.

I gaze out at the crescent moon and take a breath. "I'm also starting to get good at school," I tell him shyly. "I finally have a shot. . . . I have a teacher who *cares.*"

"You always had a shot, you just never took it," he says.

I frown. That's not true. My teachers in Hong Kong, they looked at me and decided I was no good at school, I tell Bowen. "Have you ever had that happen, someone *decides* what you are before you even do anything?"

Bowen turns back to his computer and continues tap-tap-tapping. For a second, I think the conversation is over and I feel bad revealing this part of me, until he says, "We just gotta prove them wrong. . . ."

And I feel myself soaring, high, high in the velvet sky, even more than if Dad had gotten the job today.

Chapter 63

--✈

Inspired by Bowen's refusal to take no for an answer when it comes to finding Dad a job, on Friday I rummage through the garage before school. Mom's taken a couple of carry-on suitcases down—probably for her trip to New York. Now that she's passed her second interview, she'll be going to the Big Apple soon. I climb on top of the suitcases and crane my neck. There must be something of Grandma Francine's we can trade to get Mom's earrings back from the Taradippin brothers—maybe another pair of earrings? That *look* expensive but aren't quite rubies?

I don't find any earrings, but I find something even better! Dad's sealed box of old face masks Mom was looking for—he had written on the box with a Sharpie: *Extra Face Masks from SARS.*

Boy, are the Taradippins going to lose it when they see this! I hold the virus relics to my chest and holler for my siblings.

"Bowen! Lea! Come quick!!!"

"Are you sure this is going to work?" Lea asks after school, holding up the box of masks and blowing the dust off it. She glances behind at the wildflowers in her bike basket. I can tell she wants to get back to Mom. We told her we were going hiking up the hill by our house.

"Just follow my lead." I walk up and ring the Taradippins'

doorbell. It makes a loud cowbell sound inside. Even their doorbell's obnoxious.

This time, Max's brother answers the door, holding a glass full of beer. There's music playing in the background, like they're having a party. Max is standing on top of a table throwing confetti while his dog barks. He's got a mask under his chin and another mask around his forehead as the TV behind him blasts the second confirmed case of local community spread.

"Are you guys . . . celebrating??" I ask.

"Our sales have been through the roof!" Max says, pushing his forehead mask up like a hairband as he hops down from the table.

I shake my head at these two sad, pathetic creatures cheering on a virus.

"You back with more earrings?" they ask.

"No, actually, we've got something else," I say. Nervously, I pull out the box of SARS masks. "These are from Hong Kong. They protected my dad during SARS." To prove it, Bowen holds up his phone with a picture of Dad during SARS that he AirDropped from Mom's phone.

Max gazes down at my box of masks, fascinated. I can almost see the dollar signs going off in his head.

"Dude, you know what we can sell this for on eBay?" Max asks his brother.

"Survivors' masks! Two hundred dollars!"

"Naw, way more—five hundred," Max says. He turns to us and asks, "How much you want for 'em?"

"We just want our mom's earrings back," I say. I point to the other two boxes Lea's got in her bike basket—we found three boxes total in the garage. We were tempted to save a box for ourselves, but were worried two boxes weren't going to be enough for the greedy brothers. "You can have all of them."

Max and his brother go to discuss in another room. I wait nervously, while their terrier stands guard, barking and running around us in circles at their doormat. My eyes travel to the glistening bottles of hand sanitizer stacked along the wall. *If only I can have one bottle for my classroom.*

But as I reach for a bottle, Max comes out of the room. "We'll take 'em." He hands me back the velvet box.

"Yes!!!" we cheer. Bowen opens the box up to make sure the earrings are in there. They sparkle in the sun!

As my brother clutches the earring box tight in his hands—I still can't believe my plan worked!—my sister hands Max the masks. I point at the hand sanitizers, finding the courage to make one last request. "Hey, you think I can get some hand sanitizer from you guys? It's for my teacher at school."

"Sorry, no can do," Max replies, smacking my hand away. "These babies sell for seventy-five dollars a pop online."

"Seventy-five dollars??? Who can afford *that*?"

"Rich people!" Max answers, closing the door.

Chapter 64

--- ✈

Well, at least we got the earrings back!" Bowen says.

I nod. It would have been nice, though, to get a bottle of hand sanitizer for Mrs. Turner, too.

"Mom's gonna be so relieved. Can I be the one to give them back to her?" Lea asks, putting her hands together.

"No way! I was the one who got them back from the Taradippin brothers!" I protest.

"We wouldn't even have *found* the Taradippin brothers if it weren't for me fixing Mr. Brady's Wi-Fi!" Bowen reminds me.

"Hey! *I* was the one who remembered the poodle!" Lea says.

"Okay, okay, let's *all* give them to her," I say, waving my hands in the air and trying to get my siblings to focus on the bigger picture. "We did it! We actually got Mom's earrings back. Remember how impossible that seemed?"

My siblings and I marvel at each other. It's amazing what we can accomplish when we don't fight.

"It was actually kind of fun." Lea smiles.

It really was.

Bowen glances at his phone. "Hey, look, the country club supervisor position got back to us." He holds up the email invitation to connect by phone.

"I call dibs on that interview!" I blurt out.

• • •

That night, Lea stands behind Mom, covering her eyes with her small hands. When Lea moves her hands away, I unveil Mom's earrings with a silk handkerchief.

"My earrings!" Mom cries as Bowen shines a flashlight on the glistening stones.

She reaches for them gingerly.

"We worked together, Mommy," I say to her. Lea encourages Mom to try them on as Bowen hands her the wildflowers.

"I bet you did! Thank you so much, my bao baos." Mom leans over and kisses the tops of our heads. "I don't even know what to say."

She holds the earrings up to the light. "I still remember when your dad got me these. It was the year we decided to move to Hong Kong together."

Lea climbs into Mom's lap as Mom sets the flowers down and tells the story. "Your dad thought it would be an adventure, seeing Asia. And I wanted to see what it would be like to live in a place where . . . well, where I stood out less."

"Did you feel like a purple goldfish too?" I ask Mom.

She chuckles and tells us about her old job. "Back in those days, there was a lot of blatant discrimination. I remember trying to get more customers for the bank I was working for in San Francisco, and my boss said, 'Why are you wasting your time? Chinese people all hide their money under the mattress,'" Mom says, shaking her head.

We all stare at her. No one is more stunned than my brother.

"They said that to you?" Bowen asks.

Mom nods. "I was worried that if I stayed, I'd eventually hit a ceiling."

I look up at the ceiling in Mom's room, imagining Mom bumping her head against it. Ouch!

"How about now?" I ask.

"Now things are a little better, but discrimination and racism still exist. The more we speak up about it, the less it spreads. It's like a virus." She smiles at us. "You know what the vaccine for racism is?"

I shake my head.

"Love," she says, holding out a hand to us. We walk into her arms, even Bowen, who doesn't try to wriggle away this time.

Chapter 65

I wake up the next morning smiling, thinking about what Mom said. I like this other side to Summer Mom, telling us stories. Even though some of her stories are sad, they're real. And I like real. I might even like it better than going out for frozen yogurt and to the movies.

I find Mom downstairs mixing boxed pancake batter and talking to Auntie Jackie about the details of her flight to New York. It's the last day of February, and I kick a soccer ball around in the backyard with Lea, showing her my moves.

"I can't believe it's March tomorrow!" she says excitedly. "One month closer to my birthday!"

The time sure passed by fast this month. We'd *definitely* still be in February if we were still doing online school.

"You think Dad's gonna make it over for my birthday?"

I nod encouragingly, even though we're not any closer to raising the money. Or getting Dad a job. Still, I don't want to deflate Lea's dream. We'll get there, one way or another.

"You think Cody's forgotten the way we smell?" Lea asks. "How long can dogs remember smell?"

I break out in a cold sweat, just thinking about it. Instead of answering, I try to distract my sister. I point to my feet, teaching her a soccer tip as I run with the ball.

"This is called the Cruyff turn." I tell my sister about the move invented by Dutch forward Johan Cruyff as I turn, switch directions, and cut across Lea on the grass at an angle.

"Cool!"

We play until we get tired and take a break. We walk back inside the kitchen to get some water. I stick my finger in the pancake batter, feeling the thick and gooey mix, as I listen to Mom's conversation.

"Oh my gosh, you're a lifesaver!" she says. "It's only for one day. I'm taking the red-eye from JFK right after my interview. Are you sure? I owe you one."

Lea and I look at Mom as she hangs up the phone.

"Auntie Jackie's agreed to take you guys while I'm in NYC!" Mom says, pouring the pancake batter onto the griddle.

Bowen stumbles into the kitchen in his usual groggy half-awake morning walk and grabs a muffin from the counter. "Auntie Jackie? She's picking me up from track?"

"Oh, track! That's right. I forgot," Mom says. "I suppose I can ask her to make two separate trips. First get Knox and Lea, drop them off at home, then come back and get you." Mom chews her lip. "That might be a lot, though."

"What if we took an Uber over?" I suggest.

"Oh no, you're not coming again," Bowen says, wriggling his finger at me.

"Why not?" I ask. "I can kick my ball around!" My soccer practice doesn't start for a few weeks.

"Good idea!" Mom says, taking Bowen's phone and programming Uber onto it. I lean over, worried Mom's going to see all of Bowen's emails to the country club people.

"Don't worry, I hid all of Dad's job stuff in a special email folder," Bowen whispers, reading my mind. "By the way, the interview's next week. I sent you all the info. Check your email."

Lea turns on the news as Mom hands Bowen's phone back and finishes the pancakes.

"As of this morning in Italy, there are now more than one thousand cases of the coronavirus, the most by far of any nation outside of Asia. The hardest-hit region is Lombardy, Italy, where residents have been on lockdown since February 23. So far, twenty-nine people have died," the newscaster says.

"More than a thousand cases?! How'd it jump so high in Italy all of a sudden??" I ask. I regret sticking my fingers in the pancake batter and immediately go and wash them.

"Here in the United States, a confirmed case is said to be in serious condition in Washington State, even as President Trump expressed optimism, claiming the coronavirus 'will disappear.' The World Health Organization, however, cautions that the virus has 'pandemic potential.'"

Pandemic? My eyes jump over to my mom, who switches off the TV and reaches for our last bottle of hand sanitizer.

"Calm down," she says, even though she herself is hugging the sanitizer like it's a life jacket.

"Should we still go to school??"

"Of course we're going to school," Lea says. "I want to see our baby trout grow, and I gotta show Stuart my new soccer moves!"

Mom puts the sanitizer down and assures us, "Don't worry. There are still only twenty or so cases in the US, not a big deal. Hardly a pandemic."

That's what she keeps saying, but every day, the number keeps inching up. First it was two, then it was five, now it's twenty. When will it finally be "a big deal"? And *then* what are we going to do?

After breakfast, I bike over to Christopher's restaurant so we can do our math homework together. As Christopher reads out the problems, I help him pack the take-out containers. Now that the restaurant's on Nextdoor, there are more orders! It's fun writing the names of the dishes on the boxes, along with smiley faces and messages like *Thanks for supporting our small business!*

When the last of the math problems are finished, Christopher and I take a break. We set up a bowling alley on the sidewalk with take-out containers and my soccer ball, and go "bowling."

"I don't know why my mom has to go so far away . . . especially *if* we're in a pandemic. What if something happens to her? We won't even be able to help her," I tell Christopher as we bowl.

"Can't she reschedule?" he asks.

I shake my head. "It's all set. She's leaving on Tuesday. She even got our auntie Jackie to agree to take care of us."

"Really?" Christopher asks, rolling the soccer ball. "I'd let you stay at my house, but it's the size of an Altoids tin. I have to share a room with my grandma."

I smile, thinking of how fun it would be if Lao Lao came. Then she could make us red bean *zongzi* wrapped in bamboo leaves after school. I make a note to send her a message when I get home. I hope she gets over her fear of flying soon . . . although now that we have more cases . . .

"It's okay. She should go. I hope she gets the job. If the

number of cases keep going up, we'll definitely need the health insurance," I tell Christopher. "We don't even have enough hand sanitizer."

He stops bowling.

"I can get you some hand sanitizer!" he says.

"How?"

"We can make some!" he suggests.

"*Make* some?"

"Sure, all you need is rubbing alcohol, aloe vera, and some peppermint oil! My mom's been doing it for years."

"Wow, that sounds amazing!" Then my face falls.

"What's wrong?"

"Rubbing alcohol," I tell Christopher. "I'll bet they're all out of that, too."

"We get ours from a special supplier," Christopher says. "Here, I'll get you his number."

I wait while he runs inside and scribbles down the number of one Matthew Madison.

I take the piece of paper with Matthew's number from him and stuff it into my pocket. "Thanks!"

I hop back on my bike and holler to Christopher, "You're a real friend!"

Chapter 66

---✈

We convince Mom to drop us off at the Oakland Public Library, across the street from Matthew's office, on Sunday.

"Tell me, why are you going to see this Matthew guy again?" Mom asks.

"To get some rubbing alcohol so we can make homemade hand sanitizer!" I say.

Lea claps her hands together. We had her at "homemade."

"Who is this Matthew?" Mom asks. "Do I need to come with you guys to meet him?"

"It's fine," Bowen assures Mom. "I'll be there. I got this."

"All right. Well, I'll pick you up at five p.m. I need to run some errands before my trip to New York on Tuesday," Mom says, pulling into the library.

At the mention of New York, Lea clutches her seat belt. "Do you have to go *so far away* for the interview?" she asks.

Gently, Mom switches off the car. She tries to explain to Lea. "Remember in *The Lion King* when the lionesses have to hunt?" she asks.

Lea nods. It's her favorite movie!

"Well, Mommy is a lioness. You three are my hungry little cubs. And right now, I've got to go and find some food to feed my cubs."

"I'd love some zebra," Lea says, putting her paws up, pretending to be Nala.

"Or an antelope!" I add.

Mom chuckles. "That's why I'm going to New York. There's a big juicy zebra there. All I have to do is fly over and do one short interview. And I'll be back before you know it!"

Lea looks down. I can tell she *really* wants to go along with the *Lion King* analogy. But still, the thought of Mom being so far away from the rest of her pack . . . when there might be something dangerous in the air, it cramps my throat.

I put a hand on my sister's shoulder. Maybe we'll feel better after making some hand sanitizer. "C'mon, let's go get some alcohol."

Mom shoots me an alarmed look.

"Sorry, that came out wrong!"

We finally find Matthew's office tucked behind the Safeway supermarket across the street. When we walk inside, we see him in a full hazmat suit, moving boxes. He looks like an astronaut!

"Hello?" I call out, waving my arms. I wonder if he can hear us in the suit. "Are you Matthew? I'm Knox. We spoke on the phone. . . ."

"Oh yes!" he calls out from under his suit.

He holds up a gloved finger and we wait for him to remove his helmet. When he gets it off, I see he has a surgical mask on underneath. Man, talk about overkill. The guy's dressed for a nuclear apocalypse!

"Gotta protect myself," he explains, pointing to his suit and mask.

I furrow my eyebrows. "From the virus? It hasn't officially been declared a pandemic yet."

Matthew gives me a look, like, *C'mon*, as he continues moving boxes. "Eighty-seven thousand cases around the world? You really think it will just skip the US? Why? Because we're so special?"

"So you think it might actually happen," I say.

"Oh, I know it will," he says. "The world's too globalized. It's wishful thinking, downright *arrogant* on our part, to think the virus won't come here. The question is not if, but when."

I shiver at my siblings. If what Matthew says is true, neither of our parents should be flying!

As Matthew digs out the bottles of rubbing alcohol for us, I tell him about our dad flying over soon from Hong Kong and our mom flying to New York this week. "You think we can get them hazmat suits?" I ask.

Matthew puts a gloved hand to his chin. "Your mom will be okay, but your dad . . . a long-haul international flight? He should definitely suit up."

"Can we buy one from you?" I ask.

"I wish I could help you, but I've sold all of mine to local hospitals. Everyone's stocking up on supplies, trying to brace themselves. Your best bet is to check directly with the hospitals. They might have one or two to spare."

I doubt the hospitals will have a spare hazmat suit. And if they did, we'd have to hold ten more garage sales just to afford it.

"Is there anything else he could wear that would protect him?" Bowen asks, reading my mind.

Matthew thinks for a minute. "He might be able to get

away with one of those full-body costume suits. Ever seen those people in inflatable shark suits at Halloween?"

"*That* protects you from the virus?"

"It's insulated. Better than nothing!" he says.

Bowen immediately starts googling.

"Found one!" he announces, showing us his phone. We all crowd around to look. Instead of a shark suit, it's a dinosaur suit. The idea of Dad running around the airport in a T-rex suit is so ridiculous, I burst out laughing.

"No *way* Dad's wearing that on a plane," I say. "How's he even gonna sit down? The tail's like two feet long!"

"Hmmmm . . . good point," Matthew says, handing us the rubbing alcohol. We take ten dollars from our garage sale money and hand it to him—luckily, he doesn't charge like the Taradippin brothers. "Check with the hospitals. Maybe they'll help you out."

As we thank Matthew and turn to leave, he throws us a box of surgical face masks.

"For your mom," he says. "On the house."

Bowen stares at the box in his hands. "Are you sure? These are worth more than liquid gold."

"Well, *people* are worth more than liquid gold in my book," Matthew calls back.

Bowen's speechless. He hugs the box in his arms as we walk back to the library. As he sits on the stoop, peering down at the masks, my sister and I try to make a TikTok with Bowen's phone.

"That guy was so nice," I say to Bowen, moving my arm up and across.

"Yeah, he really was," Bowen says.

He gazes at a homeless man picking through the recycling in the corner. He looks down at the box and pulls out a mask. I think he's taking one for himself, but instead he points to the homeless man. "He probably doesn't have one of these. You think we should give him one?"

I smile at my brother, never more proud of him.

That day, we distribute masks to the homeless in the library parking lot. It feels so good to give the liquid gold away to those who need it most . . . especially knowing we were once in their shoes.

Chapter 67

---✈

Mom picks us up at five and immediately nixes the idea of going to the hospital so we can ask for a hazmat suit. "No way," she says, pointing to the radio as she drives. "Do you know what I just heard?? A man died in Washington State of COVID! We're not going anywhere near the ER!"

My hands fly to my mouth at the tragic news of the first US death. I immediately open up one of the bottles of rubbing alcohol and start pouring it all over my hands, while Bowen barks at me, "Stop it! You're wasting it!"

I put the cap back. "Mom, you're not *still* going to New York, are you? There's got to be other interviews you can do here in SF!" *You can have my interview with the country club people this week,* I almost blurt out.

"I need to put food on our table, bao bao. I'm a lioness, remember?"

Yeah, and she's about to step into the most dangerous safari ever—SFO!

"I'll be fine," she says. "I've got my hand sanitizer and my disinfectant wipes. . . ."

"And surgical masks," Bowen says, pulling out a few we saved.

Mom glances at the masks. "Where on earth did you get these?? These are N95s!"

"You have to promise not to touch *anything*!" I say to her, repeating the words she once said to me.

Mom assures me, "Nothing's going to happen. New York City is perfectly safe, trust me."

Trust me. They're the words that got me here. That I've been holding close to my chest. Believing in them. Leaving Dad across the ocean for them. And now there are loads of cases. And a man *just* died. As the tears pool in my eyes, Mom pulls the car over.

"Hey, come here," she says, reaching for me. She can't quite hold me but our hands hug. As I hang on to Mom's hand, she explains what the last few weeks have been like for her. Not the cheery version. The *real* version. "I've been sending out my résumé everywhere. To every company on LinkedIn. I've been calling up people I went to college with, people I haven't seen for years. Begging them to find out if they know of anyone who's hiring. I've been doing everything I *humanly* can—" Mom's voice breaks. "And still no one wants to touch me."

Lea reaches out a hand to Mom. We've never seen her like this. So vulnerable. I hold a fistful of Mom's sweatshirt, clinging to it.

"Okay, you can go," Lea finally says. "But be careful, Mommy."

"You're all we've got . . . ," I add quietly.

Mom dabs a tear from her eye as she squeezes our hands back. She tells us she will and starts up the car again.

Chapter 68

On Monday, Christopher and I walk over to Mrs. Turner and present her with two big bottles of sparkling purple hand sanitizer that we made over the weekend.

"Where did you find these?? They're sold out *everywhere!*" Mrs. Turner gasps. "And they're so pretty!"

I smile at her proudly. "We made them!" As soon as we got back from Matthew's, we all went over to Christopher's restaurant, where we stirred up the ingredients in a humongous bucket Christopher's dad gave us. Lea had the brilliant idea of adding purple glitter.

"Well, we thank you!" Mrs. Turner says as she sets them down and announces to the class that we now have plenty of sanitizer to go around.

Christopher and I walk over to our mat together.

"Did you see your post on Nextdoor?" he asks. Christopher tells me someone's been replying, saying mean stuff.

I sneak out my iPad and scroll to look. Someone named CJ Axel replied to my post:

Are you kidding me?! Who still has an appetite for Chinese food when there's a virus from CHINA raging?

"Oh my God!" I shriek. I immediately scroll down to see the replies to his message.

The virus is also in Italy. You see anyone avoiding pizzerias?
—Thomas Eastman

THANK YOU, I mouth to Thomas's response. I keep scrolling.

Are you saying Chinese FOOD is to blame? —Rachel McKinlay
CJ Axel replied:
That's EXACTLY what I'm saying.

"Uh-oh." I scroll down and read CJ's long explanation, going on for *paragraphs.* He puts up a picture as "evidence" of an ice cream shop in Rome with a sign on its window: DUE TO INTERNATIONAL SECURITY MEASURES ALL PEOPLE COMING FROM CHINA ARE NOT ALLOWED TO HAVE ACCESS IN THIS PLACE. And another picture of a restaurant in Germany with a sign saying, NO CHINESE WANTED!!!

Christopher looks worriedly at me. "A thousand people have probably seen that comment. Now everyone will be too scared to order from us!"

I search for help on Nextdoor and tap on *report abuse.* "I'll write another post tonight saying how we need to support small businesses, now more than ever. And if people don't feel comfortable leaving their houses, we'll deliver."

"But how are we going to do that?" Christopher asks. "We don't have any delivery people, and Uber Eats is so expensive!"

Before I respond, Mrs. Turner announces that there's been a *second* case of locally spread COVID, just confirmed in Oregon.

"Oh no!" Jeff says, putting his arms over his head. "We're all going to get it."

My classmates start running around the classroom,

screaming. Tyler jumps up and pumps *twelve* pumps of my new homemade sanitizer and rubs it on his head.

"Back in your seats!" Mrs. Turner orders. "Everybody, stay calm!"

"I really have to go to the bathroom!" Simone says, wiggling in her seat. "Are bathrooms safe? Should we stop going to the bathroom??"

The question brings me straight back to the early days in Hong Kong, when we were all fretting over what to do. I raise my hand. Mrs. Turner calls on me.

"You can still go to the bathroom," I tell my classmates. "COVID-19 is mainly transmitted by people, through coughing and sneezing. That's why everyone in Asia wears face masks."

"Should *we* wear masks too?" Simone asks.

I hesitate before answering, wishing I still had face masks to give to all my classmates. But I gave them all away, except the two that Mom needs for her NYC flight. Christopher stands up next to me and has a suggestion.

"Since we don't have masks, we should move our desks apart. That's what my parents did with the tables at the restaurant," he says.

We look to Mrs. Turner, who nods. That afternoon, we work together to help our teacher clear away all the decorations and clutter from the four corners of our classroom and move our desks far apart.

It's sad to see our beloved Focus corner, Calm Down corner, and Tablet Reward corner disappear, and to have to sit so far away from my best friend. But I decide the distance is worth it to make our classroom a little safer.

Chapter 69

-- ✈

O n Tuesday, the morning Mom is supposed to go to New York City, I'm on Zoom with Dad, telling him all about our homemade sparkly sanitizer and how we spaced out our desks in our classroom, when I overhear Mom talking to Auntie Jackie on the phone. Her voice sounds panicked.

"Dad, I have to call you back," I tell him.

I click *leave meeting* and walk outside.

"I'm so sorry, but Maggie's got pink eye!" Auntie Jackie says on speakerphone downstairs. "She must have somehow gotten it this weekend when we went to Tahoe!"

"Oh my God!" Mom cries.

I walk down the stairs to the kitchen and take a seat next to Mom's recipe binder. Lately, she's been printing out more recipes from online. I start flipping through them, until Auntie Jackie says something that makes my head jerk up.

"Anyway, I took her to the doctor and he says it's highly contagious. I hate to bail on you, but I don't think it's a good idea for your kids to stay with us. . . ."

"We're not staying with them?" I blurt out, nearly snapping my finger as I close the recipe ring binder.

"Of course, I understand," Mom says to Jackie. "Poor Maggie. I'm so sorry. We'll figure something else out."

As Mom hangs up, my siblings walk into the kitchen. They heard the conversation too. *What are we gonna do?*

"Maybe we can stay at Christopher's?" I suggest out loud, then remember what Christopher said about having to bunk with his grandmother. I doubt he'd have the space for us.

"No, it's okay," Mom says with a heavy sigh. "I'm just going to have to cancel my interview."

"Wait!" Bowen says, jumping up. Mom's flight is in two hours. She's all packed and ready to go. "Maybe we can get a babysitter?"

I immediately start typing an ad on Nextdoor, but Mom reaches over to stop me. "I don't know how comfortable I feel letting a complete stranger take care of you three. Especially overnight," she says. "I'm going to cancel."

"No, *don't*," Bowen urges. He starts frantically googling on his phone. "Look! It says here there's no minimum age requirement in California for babysitting. You know what that means?"

"What?" I ask.

"*I* can babysit!" Bowen beams.

I look over at my sister. He's *kidding*, right?

To my disbelief, Mom takes Bowen's phone and reads from the website, actually *considering* this possibility. "Wow, you're right." She turns to me and Lea. "Are you two okay with that?"

Bowen beats me to answering. "It'll be great! I can call Uber to pick us up from school and we can Uber home from track practice!" he suggests. "And Uber Eats for dinner!"

"That's a lot of Ubers," Lea mutters. I can tell she's debating whether to pull a *you can't go* on Mom or negotiate for more TV time. She goes for the TV time.

"I'm going to need at least two hours of Netflix tonight," she tells Bowen.

"Fine," Bowen agrees.

"And chocolate chip ice cream with sprinkles," she adds.

"Done!" Bowen says. "Mom got some the other day from the store!"

"*Before* dinner."

"Really?" he asks Lea, frowning.

"And I'm going to require a proper tuck-in, with snuggles. One for each of my stuffed animals, too."

"Now you're just pushing it!"

Once all of Lea's terms and conditions are settled, Mom turns to me. She looks in my eyes to ask if I'm honestly okay with the arrangement.

I hesitate, torn between answering truthfully and not wanting to be the reason Mom can't get her job—*again*. So I nod.

Bowen grabs Mom's suitcase and wheels it to the car as we get our backpacks. "Go get 'em, lioness. We've got this!"

Chapter 70

--- ✈

Mom steps on the gas on the way to school, reminding us to listen to our brother. "Bowen's in charge now."

"Hear that?" Bowen grins.

Great. Now he's going to lord his new status over us. He probably gave Maggie pink eye. But maybe he doesn't have to be *in charge* in charge.

"Hey, what if we set up Dad in the living room like on virtual cleaning nights and he can watch us?" I suggest. Lea beams at the idea; she likes it too!

"Oh no, you can't Skype with Dad," Mom says, stepping on the brakes. The car jerks to a stop.

"Why not?"

"Because if he knows I left you three alone, he'd kill me! He can't ever know about this," Mom says.

Bowen warns me with his index finger. "That means you, Knox!"

"But what if he calls??" I ask, suddenly panicking. I don't like this whole lying-to-Dad thing.

"Hello, have you not heard of decline call?" Bowen asks.

For a whole day? I shake my head. No way. I can't do that. It's one thing to have Mom so far away, but to have to ghost Dad as well?

But it's too late to change course. As Mom pulls into the

parking lot of our elementary school and kisses us goodbye, I look at the desperation in her eyes and how badly she needs this. How badly *we* need this.

It's only one day. What can possibly happen?

I hug my mom back with all my might and wish her good luck on her interview, repeating everything she said to me when we flew from Hong Kong. "Don't touch anything on the flight. Disinfect everything. Don't go number two on the airplane!"

She repeats back with a wink, "Don't worry, I never go number two on the plane."

I smile.

"Bye, Mom," I tell her. "Good luck!"

Before she pulls away, I almost forget. I flex my arm up high in the air.

"Power of Mom!" I shout to her.

Mom mouths, *Love you*, and flexes her arm back at me. As I watch her drive out of the parking lot, I'm left with a hole in my heart so big, it's gonna take a *gallon* of chocolate sprinkles to fill it. Bowen better have enough.

Chapter 71

--- ✈

After school, Bowen picks us up in an Uber out front by the flag, right where he said he would. I look up from reading Nextdoor. I've been on it all day. Now that I'm more aware and on the lookout, I can't believe the number of racist posts on that thing! And not just about Asian Americans, but about Latinx and Black neighbors too! Many of them were coming from the same guy, CJ Axel.

"This CJ Axel guy, he's out of control!" I tell my brother, trying to show him some of the posts. In one post, he called the cops on a Black kid for walking around the neighborhood. That's it—just walking around!

"Show me later. Hurry up and get in!" Bowen orders, scooting over so we can all sit in the back. "I'm going to miss track!"

Lea and I scramble inside and Bowen changes the location in the app back to the middle school. Then he lowers his voice and says in Mandarin, "It was so hard to get an Uber. They just wouldn't pick me up."

I look at him, confused. Why's he speaking to me in Mandarin? "What are you talking about?" I ask.

"The drivers!" he replies.

"Were you using Mom's account?"

Bowen nods. "I had to finally change Mom's last name

from Wei-Evans to just Evans and change her profile picture."
He shows me a pic of some blond lady.

"Who's that?" I ask.

"Someone I found off the internet."

"Are you *serious*?" I can't believe our mom hasn't even been gone twenty-four hours and Bowen's already replaced her with an Old Navy model.

The driver hears us speaking Mandarin and calls out, "Hey, are you guys from China?"

We immediately stop talking. My mind flashes to the picture of the ice cream shop in Rome that CJ Axel put up.

"No! We just . . . we're learning Mandarin in school," Bowen quickly says.

I sit as still as I can, worried for a second that the driver might kick us out, like the other Uber driver did when we first arrived, but thankfully, he keeps driving.

For the next five minutes, Bowen, Lea, and I don't say another word. My leg jiggles nervously. It makes me think of what Bowen said about having to reject Lao Lao's calls in Hong Kong. When can we finally stop hiding who we are?

We arrive at the middle school and Bowen grabs his backpack and track stuff—he can't get out of the Uber fast enough. My sister and I get out but decide to walk instead of run after him.

"Where do you think Mom is right now?" Lea asks, gazing up at the sky as we walk toward the field.

"Probably somewhere over Chicago," I guess.

"I miss her," Lea says. She kicks at the grass under our feet. "It's weird being orphans."

I stop walking and turn to my sister. "We're not orphans."

I realize that as much as I'm struggling inside, I have to make my little sister feel better. "Nothing's going to happen to Mom. She'll be back tomorrow. In the meantime, I'll be here. And we have chocolate-sprinkled ice cream!"

That gets a smile out of Lea. She starts coming up with all types of ice cream sundae combinations as we walk.

"We can make a potato chip sundae!"

I shake my head. "No way, that's not a sundae."

"Sure it is! It's salty and crunchy on top and creamy and sweet underneath! That is totally a sundae!" she says. "Or how about a french fry sundae?"

I laugh. "What is it with you?"

Our laughter is cut off by Bowen's loud voice as he shouts to his track mates, "I did not!" I look up and see Coach Carter, hunched over, coughing, as he tries to separate the kids.

"Yes, you did!" one of the other kids shouts back, pointing to Coach Carter. "I saw him give you a water bottle! You got Coach sick. I'll bet you're the one who brought it over to the Bay Area!"

I gasp. Bowen's face turns fiery red. I turn to Lea, who covers her ears, looking like she's about to cry. I lead her away toward one of the soccer goals, trying to distract her with a soccer drill. Still, we can hear Bowen and his track mates loud and clear.

"I didn't give it to him!" Bowen says. "I don't have it! Just because I'm Chinese—"

"Well, how'd he get sick then?" the other kids ask as Coach Carter continues coughing and pushing on his chest to stop. All the kids look over at their coach, concerned.

I leave Lea doing free kicks and run over to Bowen.

"Hey! That's my brother!" I interrupt. "Stop it!"

The other track kids turn to look at me. One kid who's on the ground tying his shoelaces looks up. I should have said it last week, but I'm going to say it now.

"Just because we're Chinese doesn't mean we have the virus! The only thing my brother brought over was his super-fast legs, which are gonna beat all of you on the track!"

Coach Carter walks over and starts telling the other kids to cut it out, but his words are swallowed up by another bout of heavy coughing. As he blows the whistle, the other track kids get into position. I watch as my brother's long legs kick the turf. There's fire in his every step as he stares straight ahead.

Chapter 72

--✈

Bowen doesn't say anything about what happened at the track on the ride home. He just stares at the Uber app, watching the car zigzag through the city even though we all know the route by heart.

When we get back, there's a big box from Dad waiting for us! I run over and plop on the ground, trying to open it with my hands.

"It must be all our stuff!" I exclaim. "Finally!"

Bowen helps me drag the box inside. We crowd around the box in the living room. It feels like Christmas morning. Lea even draws a picture of a little tree and puts it up next to the box.

Bowen opens the box with scissors and pulls out the first item—Lea's stuffed bunny Bugsy. There's a collective "awww." Bugsy used to be Bowen's bunny, then it was mine, and finally Lea's. He's helped all three of us through some tough times, like the time I fell on the glass coffee table and had to get stitches. Or the time Lea had the chicken pox.

We take turns pulling out pieces from our childhood. Bowen thrusts his badminton racket in the air and I smile, thinking of the times we used to play down at the Sheung Wan Sports Center. Even though we both moved on to other sports, it was still fun taking the bus with Bowen every Sunday to go and hit birdies when we were little.

I pull out my special lockbox and am delighted to discover it's still locked! *Phew!* I take it upstairs and hide it in Mom's closet. I put in my secret passcode and open it just a peek to make sure all my red packets are still inside. They are. The *lai sees* are from all the big Chinese New Year dinners we had with my grandparents, before the pandemic started.

Bowen's pulling out Mom's work clothes, which Dad also sent, and a pair of track shoes Dad put inside, when I walk back downstairs. "Did those track kids ever apologize?" I ask my brother.

He puts the shoes down. He mutters from behind his badminton racket, "I don't want to talk about it."

Instead he gathers up all the wrapping paper and starts breaking down the box. I look inside one last time, to make sure that the last missing piece of my childhood isn't in there.

"Whatcha looking for?" Lea asks.

But sadly, Dad's not in the box.

As Bowen recycles the package, I fight the urge to call Dad. But I remember what Mom said.

"So what do we do now?" I ask, walking back to the staircase and sitting down.

The house is so still, you can hear the soft murmur of the refrigerator making ice. I never thought I'd say this, but I miss the sound of Mom nagging us to do our homework.

Lea claps her hands. "TV time!"

Chapter 73

As Lea searches Netflix and Bowen rummages through the fridge looking for things to cook for dinner (he insists it's cheaper than ordering out), I google *How to respond to racist comments.*

According to Google, when you hear a racist comment directed at someone, you should ICEE.

Wait, what? *We should get an ICEE from 7-Eleven?*

But as it turns out, that's not what the website means. ICEE stands for interrupt, correct, educate, and echo. Anytime someone says something intolerant, we should interrupt them, correct the thing they are saying, educate them on why it's wrong, and echo statements of support for the victim.

The echo part makes a lot of sense. Things have gotten so much better since me and Christopher started echoing each other. Now, when we stand up to Tyler, our voices carry the power of two. I think of what happened today on the track, glad I was able to be there to echo my brother. I smile and close my laptop and walk over to the kitchen.

"Can I help?" I ask Bowen as he pulls out old jars of pasta sauce and dumps them into the pot. I guess he's making spaghetti.

I reach for a loaf of french bread. "I'll make the garlic bread," I tell Bowen.

"Do you know how?" he asks with a skeptical tilt of his eyebrow.

"'Course! I've seen Dad do it a million times!" We work side by side. While I dice up the garlic, Bowen slices up mushrooms, carrots, onions, parsley, tomatoes, avocado, and whatever else he can find. He says it's all the same; it'll only make the sauce thicker and better.

Bowen turns on the news in the kitchen as he chops.

"Health officials in Contra Costa County today confirmed the first locally transmitted case of coronavirus," the newscaster says.

I nearly cut my finger with the knife when I hear that.

"Contra Costa County, that's here!" I say. *The virus is officially here!*

I reach for the house phone to call Mom, but Bowen grabs it and puts it back. "What are you doing?"

"Calling Mom!"

"We can't call her! She has to focus on her interview!" he says.

I put my garlicky fingers to my mouth, gulping at all the images of doctors in hazmat suits on TV. To think we came all the way over here, left our home *and* our dad to try to get away from this thing. And now it's here and there's *no one* to protect us, not either of our parents!

"I'm scared, gege . . . ," I tell my brother.

Bowen stops stirring and puts his tomato hands on my arms. "It's okay," he says. "It's just one case."

"You guys keep saying that," I say, shaking my head. "But it's not just one case. It's a whole *bunch* of cases now!" I pick up the slippery garlic in my hand and squeeze it, wishing Mom were here. "Mom shouldn't have gone!"

"Well, it's too late. She's already there. Nothing good can happen if we call her. You'll just ruin her interview *and* she'll still not be here!"

I frown at Bowen. I hate it when he gets all practical on me. Can't he just say, *You still have me. I'll protect us?* That's all I really want to hear.

Instead, he continues chopping and slicing. So I say the words for him in my mind as I gaze down at the spaghetti pot. Maybe the words are all in there. All finely diced up along with the olives.

Chapter 74

Bowen's everything spaghetti ends up tasting pretty good, I have to say. The pasta sauce is like a mini scavenger hunt: you never know what you're going to get. As I search around for a carrot, Bowen pours milk in our glasses, just like Dad used to do.

"Oh, I almost forgot!" I jump up from the table and serve up the toasted garlic bread I made.

Lea takes a piece of garlic bread gleefully as she tells us about her upcoming field trip. They're going to go to the river to release the baby trout they've been raising.

"Wow, that's cool!" I say to my sister. I'm glad she's having a better time at school.

"How about you?" Lea looks curiously at Bowen. "Those kids at track . . . are they in the same class as you?"

Bowen shakes his head, but I can tell what happened today is still bothering him. I take out my iPad and show him the racist posts that CJ Axel guy has been writing on Nextdoor about people of color.

"That's horrifying!" Bowen says. "I hope you reported him."

"I did! Five times!"

"Good."

I tap on my browser and pull up the site on ICEE.

"See, it says here when people are being racist, you have to interrupt and correct. That's what I did today," I say, smiling proudly at my big brother.

But instead of smiling back, Bowen just shrugs. "You don't *have* to. Sometimes it's better just to ignore them."

I furrow my eyebrows. "But you just said to report CJ Axel!"

"Yeah, but that's different."

"How's it different?" I ask.

"That's *online*," he says. "This is real life."

"So?"

"So I have to keep training with those kids!" he says. "I don't want to make it a *thing*!"

Oh, and ignoring racist remarks is so much better? I shake my head at him. I can't believe *I'm* the one he's mad at. "I was standing up for you!" I say, throwing my fork down.

"Well, I wish you hadn't," he mutters as he gets up and dumps the rest of his garlic bread in the sink uneaten. I stare at all that wonderful bread, not sure what hurts more—him wasting my bread or wasting my words.

Lea holds up a snow pea from her sauce, in a desperate attempt to keep the peace. "Look, I'm eating snow peas!" she cries, popping one into her mouth.

But neither Bowen nor I say anything. I get up with my own plate and dump my everything spaghetti in the sink too. Even though I'm still hungry. I don't care what my brother says. It was absolutely the right thing to do.

Chapter 75

✈

After dinner, Lea shovels gobs of her chocolate-sprinkled ice cream into her mouth while watching *Turbo*. *Turbo* used to be one of me and Bowen's favorite rituals. We'd rewatch all the scenes of snail brotherly love when we were little. It was our thing. I wonder when it became just a movie to Bowen.

I tell myself maybe it's okay that we don't get along. I think about the Taradippin brothers. Then I remind myself there are other options besides hating each other and starting an evil empire together.

Lea offers me one of her sprinkles as Bowen busies himself loudly washing dishes, and I shake my head, *No thanks*.

"Why do you look so down?" Lea asks.

I google *CJ Axel*, ignoring the question. Who is this guy? But all that comes up is a bunch of ads for car axles.

Bowen rummages through the kitchen. One of the cabinets makes a *bang* sound. "Argh! This handle!"

"Want some help?" I ask.

"Nope! Found the popcorn!"

Soon the smell of buttery popcorn wafts from the kitchen as Bowen microwaves the bag. My sister and I close our eyes and breathe it in.

"Hey! Is there any Parmesan? Maybe you can sprinkle some on the popcorn like Dad does!" I call out.

Bowen bangs around in the kitchen, then disappears into the garage.

When he walks into the living room, I turn around, expecting to see a giant bowl of cheesy popcorn in his hands, only to see Bowen's nostrils flaring as he clutches his headphones.

"WHAT. IS. THIS?" Bowen demands, holding up the Bose headphones. *Uh-oh.*

I hide under the sofa throw for cover. But Bowen pulls the blanket off me in one violent jerk.

"I can explain," I say, putting my hands up.

Bowen thunders toward me. "I can't believe you *stole* these from me! This was my birthday present from Dad! You have any idea how much these headphones mean to me??" he asks, shaking them so hard, they rattle. "And you just *sat there* while I freaked out looking for them!"

His anger burrows deep into my bones. I look around for Mom, but she's thousands of miles away, unable to protect me. She might as well be on the moon.

"I'm sorry . . . ," I say. "I was gonna give them back—"

"No, you weren't! You were going to pawn them!" Bowen says. "Admit it! You don't care about me."

"Of course I do," I say, standing up. Tears spill out of my eyes. "Why do you think I echoed you on the track? Because you're my brother." Now I'm full-on crying. "And I will always echo for you. Even if you don't even appreciate it!" I shoot out the words from the rawest part of me. "It's like you don't even want me for a brother!"

There, I said it. The painful shard of truth that has been poking me through the mattress of our bunk bed ever since we got here. I squeeze my eyes shut, thinking of the deep wounds that can't be patched up with a few days of nice. All the times my brother has called me Knot over the years. Made fun of my disability. Yelled at me to stay far, far away from him on the track field. "It's like you're ashamed of me. . . ."

I run up the stairs and fly into our room. *That's it, I've had it!* I grab my sleeping bag and stuff it into my backpack along with my iPad and some of Bowen's CLIF bars for track. Then I run downstairs and I bolt out the door. I don't know where I'm going. I just know I can't be here anymore.

"Knox, wait!" my sister calls out.

But I charge up the hill as quickly as I can, toward the horses, and don't look back. I can't handle one more minute with my brother, who will never love me the way I love him. Not in a million years. Not even if I stand on the top of the mountain and echo him until the valleys shiver and my lungs collapse.

So I run.

Chapter 76

I hike and hike and hike up the muddy trail, lugging my huge backpack on my achy back. I've never been this far up the trail. I have no idea where I'm going. Part of me is tempted to turn around and bike over to Christopher's restaurant, but I don't want to bump into Bowen on my way down. He's probably called Mom by now. And they're probably both mad at me. I think about their joint angry faces and I charge forward. I can never go back. They'll skewer me!

I hike until the soles of my feet are blistering raw, and finally collapse at the base of a tall oak tree on top of the hill. The tree is so vast and big, its leaves form a snug roof. I drop at its feet and lie on the ground.

Gazing out at the gorgeous view, I can see the entire bay, stretching as far out as Marin to the right and my namesake beach to the left. This was the picture I imagined in my head before we left for America. A postcard of green rolling hills and pink sunsets. This was the picture that got me on the plane.

And now I'm here and everything's falling apart.

I take my iPad out to call Dad. In my mind, the no-calling-Dad rule went out the door when I did. But there's no Wi-Fi, so I take a picture instead.

As I curl up in my sleeping bag, I record a message to Dad on my iPad.

Hey, Dad, it's me. I just want to you to know, I'm safe and well. I'm in the canyon behind our house. Don't worry, I hiked WAY past the wild horses, so they can't bother me in the middle of the night. I'm under a tree right now, looking out at this great view. I wish you could see it. I wish you were here with me, and we were camping together. If you were here, maybe none of this would have happened.

I'm sorry I took Bowen's headphones. I'm sorry that I ran away, but I just couldn't take it anymore. I hope Mom doesn't blow her interview because of this. Bowen's probably told her at this point and she's probably freaking out in New York right now. I don't mean to cause problems for our family. But I'm tired of feeling like the purple Goldfish. I know I do things differently, but I'm trying hard. I wish people could see me and love me for who I am.

I really miss you, Dad. You're the only one who understands. Anyway, I'm sorry. I hope you're not mad at me too.

The wind blows as I press send, and I wrap my sleeping bag firmly around me. I know Dad can't get it just yet because there's no Wi-Fi. But I imagine him getting it anyway and I imagine what he'll say.

I record another message, this one from Dad to me:

Hey, Knox, it's Dad. No need to apologize. I'm sorry about Bowen getting so mad at you. We all love you very much. And I know Mom and Lea will want you to come home. But you take all the time in the world that you need right now. I promise if you go back, Bowen will not get mad at you. You running off has taught him a HUGE lesson—trust me. (Also

I am taking away his headphones, because they were too expensive for him to begin with.) He loves you. He misses you as a brother. And he NEEDS you. Come home soon, son. Love, Dad.

Somewhere between "huge lesson" and "come home," I get sleepy. I dream of many things as I curl myself into a ball to warm myself against the chilly, breezy night . . . the snuggle of Mom when she wakes me up, my grandmother's homemade dumplings, which she pan-fries just for me, my sister's long, funny stories, which she tells her imaginary friends whenever she's combing her hair. All the things I have to go back for . . . if I ever go back.

Chapter 77

-- ✈

My brother's and sister's faint voices wake me up the next morning.

"Knox? Where are you??" Lea calls.

Her voice gets louder and louder. What do I do? My first instinct is to lie frozen and not make a peep. Bowen is probably still boiling mad. If he finds me, I'm deader than the branches by my feet.

Then I hear another voice.

"Knox, *please*. If you're out there, say something!"

It's Mom! Her voice cracks as she pleads. I immediately jump up, wanting to know how her New York trip went.

"Mom! I'm over here!" I cry out to her.

The look on her face when she sees me, happiness engulfed in relief, makes me forget all about Bowen, all about the fight last night. Mom runs toward me, galloping like a wild horse, jumping over dandelions and wood chips until she crashes into my arms. She hugs me so tight, no words can escape.

"Don't ever do that again, bao bao," she cries, tears streaming from her eyes.

I cry too. Not just for last night but for everything . . . all the tears I've been hanging on to, trying to be so brave in front of my big brother. Trying to be like him and step out from his shadow.

"I'm sorry, Mom," I say, when we finally pull away. "Did I screw up your interview?"

Mom runs her fingers through my hair. "No," she assures me. "Bowen didn't call me until it was already over. I was scared sick. I flew back as soon as I could."

"I was worried sick too," Bowen says. "I *lost* a person!"

I sneak a glance at him, standing sheepishly in the grass.

"Not just any person," Lea adds, tugging at my hand with hers. She dabs her eyes as she whimpers, "I thought I was never going to see you again." It hits me that by leaving Bowen, I also left Lea. I put my arms around my mei mei.

"I'm sorry, Lea," I say to her.

As Lea hugs me back, Bowen picks up my sleeping bag off the leafy ground. "C'mon, let's go home," he says.

Mom sits me and Bowen down in our room when we get back. I peek out from behind the wooden guardrails on the top bunk, dreading the heart-to-heart. I just know Bowen's gonna roll his eyes. While I lay out my feelings and feel all naked, even though I'm covered with blankets, he'll act like what happened was all my fault.

Instead, Mom starts off with a question. "What's one thing you wish your brother knew about you?"

I blurt out "I'm sorry I took your headphones" at the same time that Bowen says, "I'm glad you echoed me."

I look over to Bowen at his desk in surprise. *WHAT?* I stare into his eyes, at the rawness of the confession. He squirms like he's naked too.

Mom holds out a hand to us both. "You two are the only brother you'll each ever have, you know that?" she asks. "You need to protect each other, and love each other."

Bowen doesn't say anything.

"The world is hard enough as it is," Mom continues. "Did you know on my flight, there were people wearing pantyhose over their heads, because they didn't have a mask? We never know what life's going to throw at us. But one thing we *can* control is how we treat each other. Here in this house. The love and support we give to one another, that's what will get us through the tough times."

I nod, feeling every single one of her words. I glance at Bowen to see if he's ready. I've *always* been ready.

"Now come down here," Mom orders. Gently, I lift my covers and start climbing down.

As I climb, Mom admits tearfully, "When Bowen called me, my heart dropped to the pit of my stomach. You're the light of my life, you know that?"

Mom pulls me in for a hug when I get down. I close my eyes and feel the love she has for me. It's enough to launch a rocket to the moon.

"Promise me you'll never do that to me again, bao bao," Mom says.

A lump forms as I promise Mom I won't.

In a small voice, Bowen adds, "Or to me."

I look over at my brother. Even though it's just three little words, it means the world.

The fog lifts as I run over to Bowen's desk and give him a hug.

Lea comes in with the home phone as we're hugging. "It's Daddy," she says, handing Mom the phone. "He knows about Knox!"

Mom knits her eyebrows. *How?*

I gaze down at my iPad—my voice message! It must have automatically sent when I walked into the house!

Chapter 78

--- ✈

Bowen, Lea, and I lean against Mom's door, trying to listen as she takes the call with Dad.

"What are they saying?" I ask.

"Shhhh!" Lea says. "I can't hear!"

I look over at Bowen, expecting him to huff, *It's all your fault. Why'd you record a message for Dad?* Instead, he says, "I'm not going to mention the headphones if he asks."

Which is generous. I take it.

"I won't either," I say.

My head jerks up at the sound of Dad's booming voice on speaker, "I want you all to come home!"

Our faces turn ashen white. I immediately scramble up and reach for the doorknob. "I don't want to go back. I like it here!" I blurt out as I run inside my parents' room.

"Knox, I need to talk to your mother about this alone," Dad says back on speaker.

"No!" I'm done having my parents make decisions about my life and keep me out of the conversation. I run to my room and grab my iPad and play back the message I *want* Dad to say—the one from him to me.

As everyone listens to my message as Dad, telling me everything's fine, that he understands why I ran away, and assuring me how much he loves me, I beg Dad, "Please,

Dad, I have a life here now! I have friends! I have school!"

"Me too!" Lea chimes in. "I finally did the Cruyff turn with Stuart! And we have rainbow trout that we have to release back in the river! And DAD, yesterday I ate a snow pea!"

"And I finally have time to do stuff, like bike around town! Not just do my homework all day!" Bowen says.

Our pleas are not enough to melt Dad's anger, though.

"Well, you're still coming home," Dad says. "I can't believe your mother left you by yourselves overnight. Julie, what were you thinking? My God, when I think about what could have happened . . ."

Bowen grabs the phone. "It's not Mom's fault. I was the one who told her to go." He takes a deep breath. "And I was the one who drove Knox away."

My head swivels as Bowen accepts full responsibility for what happened. It's so unexpected, even Lea's jaw hangs open. And yet. The guilt nibbles at me.

"Actually," I confess, "I took his headphones. I wanted to pawn them and use the money to get you here, Dad." I suck in a breath, waiting for his response. *Please, please say you'll come.*

"Well, that's not happening. You're all coming home," Dad replies.

As Dad delivers his verdict, I drop onto the floor. All I wanted was to talk to Dad under the stars. I never thought the sky would collapse.

guess we better start packing," Lea mumbles, wiping her eyes and walking back to her room with her stuffed bunny in her hand.

Bowen and I follow Lea to her room, while Mom continues pleading with Dad on the phone, telling him how well her interview went, and how she'll hear back in just a few days. *Please, just give her a few more days!*

As Lea starts pulling out the suitcases, I glance timidly at my brother.

"Do you really mean what you said? About how you liked me echoing you?" My voice lingers. "Because if you don't, I can stop."

Bowen looks down for a long time at the frayed carpet.

"No, I don't want you to," he finally says. "What I really want . . . is for them to stop."

I plop down on the floor cross-legged, gazing up at my brother.

"But they won't on their own. It takes all of us to stand up to them," I say.

"Yeah!" seconds Lea.

"There are too many of them, and there's only one of me," Bowen says, shaking his head.

I get up and reach my arm out, placing it side by side with

his arm. Even though mine is a shade lighter than his, we're made of the same blood inside. We have the same hopes and dreams. And fire in our step. "You've got me," I say.

"And me," Lea adds. She puts her stuffed bunny down and flexes her arm. "Power of family."

Bowen beams, his eyes glassy.

"Thanks," he says.

I smile at him.

"What about Dad?" Lea asks. "How are we gonna get him to let us stay?"

"Maybe if he has a job offer here . . . ," I think out loud. At the thought of Dad's job, I scramble up and run to my room to double-check the time of Dad's interview at Oakhill Country Club. It's this afternoon after school!

That day in school, my sister and I arrive late. Thankfully, Mom tells the school it's because she was in New York, not because I ran away and slept in the hills because I was mad at my brother.

In class, I finish my math early and then spend my ten minutes of earned gadget time secretly googling everything there is to know about Oakhill Country Club. It has a dining room, a golf course, a badminton court, and a pool. I wonder if Dad works there, if we get to go for free. Maybe Bowen and I can play badminton again. Mrs. Turner interrupts my daydreaming with an announcement.

"Boys and girls, can I please have your attention? Governor Newsom has just announced that California is in a state of emergency due to the coronavirus."

Christopher immediately pulls out his organizer and

scribbles two Post-its—one for him and one for me: *Go to the grocery store!!!*

"Why?" I ask.

"Before all the rice, pasta, and flour get snapped up! It's a state of emergency!!!"

I make a *yeah right* face. The last time we were at Safeway, there was *plenty* of flour. Then I remember what Dad said about the toilet paper in Hong Kong and how it all disappeared so quickly that people were getting into fistfights over it.

"Do you guys have a second fridge?" Christopher asks.

I shake my head. We barely have a first fridge! Ours is tiny!

"Well, if you run out of space, you can always come over and use ours. We have five big fridges in the restaurant," Christopher tells me. "Now we're *really* not going to need all of them."

"Hey, don't worry, we'll think of something together!" I say to him. My face falls. That is, *if* Dad lets us stay.

Christopher studies my worried expression. "What's wrong?"

"Nothing." Now's not the time to tell him about Dad. I can't abandon my echo buddy in a state of emergency.

I take the Post-it note from Christopher and staple it to my backpack. "Grocery store—on it!"

Chapter 80

-- ✈

I tell Mom and my siblings what Christopher said about the grocery store when she picks us up. We should go as soon as my country club interview is over, which Mom hopefully won't overhear.

"I highly doubt all the food will be gone," Mom says, skeptical. "But if you really want to go, we can go a little later. I have to send off some emails, then I need to FedEx my college transcript over to the company in New York. I can drop you three off at the store and come back to pay."

"Later works!" I tell Mom, glancing at my siblings. "I have something important . . . er . . . to do for school before then anyway."

"So when are they gonna decide? The company in New York?" Bowen asks.

"Any day now!" she says.

I cross my fingers and my toes. It's one thing not to have healthcare in normal times; it's another thing altogether not to have it in a pandemic. That reminds me. "*Are* we officially in a pandemic?" I ask Mom.

"If we are, we can't fly back, right?" Lea asks. "We'd have to get those dinosaur suits!"

Mom raises an eyebrow in the mirror. She doesn't confirm that we're in a pandemic, but she doesn't unconfirm it either. Instead, she tells us not to worry, she's going to talk to Dad again tonight. We're staying put for now. I race out of the car when we get back, determined to land Dad his first job offer before the situation gets even worse.

"You *sure* you want to do this?" Bowen asks me one last time as I hold his phone, ready to make the call to Oakhill Country Club. "Because I'll totally do it."

"Or me! Why can't I do an interview?" Lea says, jumping up and down for the phone.

"I got this," I say. I wipe my sweaty palms on my jeans and press call. Mr. Anderson from the Oakhill Country Club answers on the second ring. *Here goes . . .*

"Hello? Mr. Anderson? Hi, I'm Andrew Evans," I say, clearing my throat and putting on my Star Wars Jedi voice. I put Mr. Anderson on speakerphone.

"Thanks for calling, Andrew," Mr. Anderson says. "I'm looking at your résumé and it says here you are currently a lawyer. Is that right?"

"Yes."

"So why do you want to be a country club supervisor?"

Bowen gestures to me, *Go on.* "Uh . . . well, I love countries," I laugh nervously. "And clubs!"

"But have you had any experience working in one?"

My siblings' heads jiggle up and down. But I decide to answer honestly.

"No," I say. "But I have experience working with tight deadlines and managing my time. And dealing with very demanding clients." I glance at Bowen. "And very demanding kids."

The last part makes Mr. Anderson chuckle. "You too, huh? Mine are a handful," he says. "The other day my son ate all the cereal, then filled the box up with paper clips."

"Mine decided to hold a garage sale and sold my wife's anniversary earrings!"

"Oh no!"

"For a quarter!"

Mr. Anderson laughs.

"And what was your reaction, just out of curiosity?" he asks.

"I told them they had to find them and get them back."

"And did they?"

"Yup!" I say proudly, smiling at my siblings. "They're real smart kids." It's fun pretending to be Dad, bragging about us.

"Well, I applaud you. I wish everyone who worked here was as calm and even-keeled as you. Lord knows we certainly have some clients who can be pretty difficult sometimes," Mr. Anderson says. "Tell you what, why don't you come in for an interview, face-to-face."

"Really?" I ask, then quickly correct myself. "I mean, great. Thank you so much." I turn to my siblings. Lea's got her hand over her mouth like she's trying hard not to squeal. Bowen gives me a thumbs-up sign.

"I'll have my secretary, Martha, set something up. Looking forward to meeting you, Andrew," Mr. Anderson says before he hangs up. "And good luck with your kids!"

I throw my arms up when I get off the phone. I DID IT!!!

Chapter 81

Y ESSSS!" Bowen, Lea, and I cheer. "Dad's gonna get a job!"
As I toss Bowen back his phone, he holds out his hand
to me. "Guess you're better at interviewing than me," he
offers. I look up in surprise.

"Not everything's a competitive sport," I tell my brother as
I shake his hand.

It takes Bowen a second to digest my words. When he
does, his whole body relaxes and he smiles.

Lea throws us a pillow. "But you guys! How are we going
to get Dad here for the interview?" she asks.

I crawl under our bunk bed to retrieve our Ziploc bag of
money from the garage sale. As I count out the money, Bowen
gets on his computer to see what the cost of a flight is now.

"Good news! I found a one-way ticket from Hong Kong
for only a thousand dollars," Bowen says. "*But* Dad has to go
through LA."

"Through LA??" I ask. "What happened to the flights to
SFO?"

"They're all cancelled."

Things are changing so quickly. We better hurry or pretty
soon there will be no planes to anywhere!

"We have a hundred and ninety dollars here," I tell my
siblings, visualizing the math in my head—1,000 airplane

parking spaces and 190 planes. "We'll need eight hundred ten dollars if we want to get Dad over here!"

"How are we going to do that?" Bowen asks as Mom calls out to us that it's time to go to Lucky's.

Bowen hollers back, "We'll be right there."

"We could hold another garage sale!" Lea suggests. I shake my head. At those prices, we'd have to hold five, and besides, Mom is running out of shoes.

"I have a better idea," I say.

Chapter 82

--- ✈

After Mom drops us off in front of Lucky's, I tell my brother and sister my idea of helping Christopher deliver food. We have bikes and nothing to do after school. We could be his delivery crew and make tips for our Dad fund!

"But what about the virus?" Lea asks. "We can't be biking all over town!"

"Hear me out," I say as we push our cart into Lucky's.

But before I can explain my plan, I crash my cart into the stampede of people inside the store. Lucky's is packed! The shelves are completely empty. Almost *everything* inside the store is gone!

"Lea, you get the pasta! Grab whatever you can get!" Bowen calls out, jumping into action and getting another cart. "I'll get the pasta sauce and the rice. Knox, you grab the toilet paper, soap, and trash bags!"

"What about meat?" I ask Bowen, gazing over at the crowd of people in the meat section.

Bowen thinks for a second, then decides, "Nah. Meat's not gonna last. Besides, it's too expensive. Let's just get stuff we can keep for a long time."

"On it!" my sister says, bolting for the pasta aisle.

I head toward the toilet paper section, staring at the line of customers, which stretches from the cashier counter all the way to the meat section! There are people with entire carts full of cheese. I've never seen so much wine! Or eggs—cartons and cartons of eggs, like someone's about to make an omelet the size of a strip mall.

"Grab whatever you can!!!" people scream throughout the store. "Go! Go! Go!"

"But all that's left is SPAM!!!" one woman says.

"GET THAT SPAM!!! I DON'T CARE!!!" her husband calls back.

I push my cart toward the toilet paper aisle, squeezing in between all the people. I hope there's still some left.

But the aisle is completely cleared out. Not a single roll of toilet paper is left. Not even a square.

I look around and spot a woman hugging ten giant packages of toilet paper rolls in her cart. They're stacked so high, they go up *way* past her head. I walk up to her and ask, "Excuse me, could I maybe have one of those?"

"No!" she says. "These are mine!"

"You need *this* much toilet paper?" I ask her.

The woman pushes her cart away from me in anger, without answering.

I turn and scan the rest of the aisle. *Think.* Christopher's voice pops into my head—*Sometimes you just need to look at a problem a different way to solve it.* What else can we use? I roll my cart up and down the aisles, grabbing gift-wrapping tissue paper, baby wipes, even coffee filters. Hey, if it's wipe-able, I'll take it!

By the time I'm finished, Bowen and Lea are already standing in line. I look down at their carts. Lea managed to grab fifteen packages of pasta, though most of them are alphabet pasta. Bowen made off with a bag of rice and eighteen jars of peanut butter. I'm slightly worried about how much all the stuff is going to cost—Mom still hasn't gotten her new job yet—but mostly excited we're not going to starve.

"There was no more pasta sauce," Bowen sighs. He looks in my cart. "What happened to the toilet paper?"

"They were all out."

He reaches into my cart. "So you got coffee filters?!"

"Hey! It's better than nothing! We don't know how long the situation's going to last!"

Mom comes in through the double doors and spots us in line. "I'm back! Oh my goodness, look at this line!" she exclaims.

The weirdest thing happens when Mom gets in line with us. The two people ahead of us both get out of the line and push their cart all the way to the back of the line. One guy uses his baseball cap to cover his mouth and nose until he's safely around white people again.

Mom's jaw drops. "Oh my God, are you serious?" she asks. "You'd rather start *all over* waiting in line than stand in front of us?" She loses it at this point. "Look around you! We are literally contemplating a future of wiping our butts with coffee filters." She reaches into my cart and grabs the coffee filters. "And *I'm* the scariest thing to you right now?"

"We just want to be on the safe side," the man in the baseball cap calls from the back.

"You want to be on the safe side?" Mom asks. "Don't be mean and racist. Try that."

To our surprise, several people in line start clapping for Mom. I look up to see African American and Latinx families clapping, echoing my mom. A Black woman calls out that she stands with her. One Latinx mother tells Mom someone in her community got turned away from a grocery store and it's not right. Mom gets so emotional, she reaches for a coffee filter to wipe her eye.

I glance over at my brother, who looks around at all the people standing up against racism. We might not have gotten any toilet paper today. But we filled up on the knowledge that we were not all alone.

Chapter 83

- ✈

Later in the car, after all the groceries have been loaded, Mom is quiet.

"Are you okay?" Lea asks.

Mom nods, even as she lets out a sob. There are no tears. Just the dry swell of hurt.

"I'm so sorry, you guys," she says. "I really thought bringing you three over here would keep us safe. If I had known all this was going to happen—"

"It's okay," we say to Mom.

"No it's not okay. I wanted so badly for things to be different for you. I'm supposed to keep you safe and secure," she says. "That's my *job*. To protect you from having to experience what you just did."

I bite my lip, looking over at Mom. I know how much it pains her that we had to see those people rush to get away from us because of the color of our skin. But what she doesn't know is we've already experienced it. In our own way. And we found the courage to stand up and ICEE it, just like she did.

"You can't protect us forever, Mom," I say. "No offense, but you're not that powerful."

Mom lets out a small smile.

"And *look* at all those people who echoed us!" my brother says, smiling at me.

"It was something, wasn't it?" Mom agrees. "I never told you this, but remember the restaurant Lao Lao and Lao Ye worked at? It was vandalized once. Someone graffitied racist slurs on the walls."

We gasp. Lea reaches for my hand. No wonder Lao Lao and Lao Ye wanted to go back to Beijing.

"It was heartbreaking," Mom says. "But you know something? A cleaning crew showed up the next day and helped wash away the graffiti—for free. A local rabbi came and put down flowers. Local singers and musicians started performing outside, to show their support." Her eyes glisten. "Words of hate will always be overpowered by words of love."

I smile.

"Well, I have *lots* of words of love." Lea beams, shaking up a box of alphabet pasta.

Mom turns to us and stretches out her arms to give us a hug from her seat. "I'm so proud of you guys. I wish your dad could be here to see how much you've grown. Thanks for being such troopers in a tough situation, even when we have no toilet paper."

"Well, thankfully we have these," Bowen says, pulling out the boxes of coffee filters. I laugh through my tears.

Chapter 84

--- ✈

O ver the next few days, as we try and conserve our toilet paper and Mom waits anxiously for the company in New York to tell her whether she got the job, I think about what Mom said about how the vaccine for racism is love. I decide to flood Nextdoor with kind messages.

To my surprise, so many strangers online echo my words, expressing their thanks and appreciation for the small businesses in our community, especially Black, Latinx, and Asian American small businesses affected by the pandemic. And giving their love and support to all the workers on the front lines of the pandemic, risking their lives so that we can all stay safe.

I copy and paste some of the messages and send them to Dad. He calls me later that week.

"I talked to Mom," he says. "I understand the situation. You kids might be scared to fly right now. . . ."

"It's not just that." I shake my head into the phone. I take a deep breath. "I don't want to leave. My best friend's here! I'm finally doing well in school, and I love my teacher. . . ."

"But buddy, California is in a state of emergency. I'm worried about you all over there," Dad sighs. "And I just . . . I really miss you guys. You're all I have in the world."

Dad's voice breaks slightly, and it dawns on me that as hard as the last few weeks have been for us, moving countries, starting a new school, and trying to find a job, it's even harder for Dad going through a pandemic alone.

"But if you don't want to come back right now because of the virus, I understand," he says.

I swallow hard. I wish Dad would understand it's not because of the virus. It's because I refuse to give up on us all being together. Here. In our homeland. As flawed as it is. As hard as it is. This is still my country. And I don't want to just give up on it. I want to stay and make it better.

"I miss you, too, Dad," I say, gripping the phone with all my might.

Chapter 85

-- ✈

B owen is in the kitchen early Saturday morning, disinfect-
ing the rice package and the peanut butter jar, as the
news blasts that the number of coronavirus cases in the
US has jumped to 444, with nineteen people dead.

"This thing is spreading so fast!" Bowen says as he rubs
sanitizer on the last jar of peanut butter. "Thank goodness we
bought all that rubbing alcohol!"

"There's something else we gotta buy!" I say, sitting down
at Mom's computer and trying to guess her Amazon password.

Before I can log in, Mom bursts into the kitchen with her
phone in her hand. "Guess what, you guys?? I got the job!!!"

Our house is rich with celebration and laughter that weekend
as Mom makes us peanut butter cookies, Bowen and I clean
the house, and Lea steams Mom's old work clothes that Dad
sent over, so she'll have the nicest blouses on Zoom. Dad Face-
Times with Mom to say congratulations.

"I'm glad the NYC trip paid off, though it was *such* a huge
risk to go," Dad says. "But I'm proud of you. When do you
start?"

Mom tells him she's starting on Monday. Though the

company has a small San Francisco office, due to the virus concerns she'll be working remotely.

"What about when school closes?" Dad asks. "Have you thought about that?"

"Schools are not going to close," Mom tells him, even though the rumors are getting louder and louder. Just last week, we had a substitute because Mrs. Turner had to go to meetings to help the district plan for remote learning.

"I hope schools don't close again," I say to my brother. "I don't want to have to go back to doing online homework."

I think about my A– test on the wall next to my bed. *Just when I was starting to do well!*

Then Bowen says something that knocks the socks off me.

"I'll help you," he says. "It'll be different this time. We'll make a schedule."

Lea and I share a glance—*Who are you and what have you done with our brother, Bowen?* We follow Bowen upstairs, where he puts on "Survivor" from his computer.

As the song blasts from the speaker, I smile. Maybe we can survive online school.

Mom hears us as we're singing and gets off the phone with Dad. She walks upstairs.

"Does this mean we get to stay?" I ask her.

"We get to stay, bao bao!" Mom smiles.

"And we finally have health insurance?"

"YES!"

At the confirmation that we'll finally be able to see a doctor in this country, I let out a breath I didn't know I was holding. All this time, I have been blocking out in my head what would happen if any of us got sick. Trying not to think about it. Trying to convince myself it's not going to happen, while secretly worrying life is going to Cruyff turn us. As the relief washes over me, Lea dances to "Survivor." I watch from the top of the staircase, too emotional to dance. I rock my body back and forth with relief.

Chapter 86

O n Mom's first day at her new job, she wakes us up at the
crack of dawn.

"Hurry up!" she says, getting us out of bed, wearing
a crisp white shirt and black slacks. Her hair's all up in a bun
and she's got makeup on. I never thought I'd say this, but I'm
glad Winter Mom's back.

Lea comes bouncing into our room, all dressed up herself. She nods approvingly at Mom's work outfit. "Girl, you
look *great!*" she says.

Mom laughs. "Thanks for steaming my shirt yesterday.
Now hurry up, you guys need to get to school!"

Bowen points to Mom's dress pants. "Why are you wearing
those pants?" he asks. "You realize no one can see your pants
on Zoom."

"Well, *I* can," Mom says. She claps her hands. "All right,
let's go! I can't be late!"

I jump out of bed. As I'm brushing my teeth, I tell my
siblings about my idea for staying safe while delivering take-
out. When I talked to Christopher about it online, he was so
excited!

But Bowen balks. "You want to order those dino suits and
ride around town in a T-rex costume? No way!"

"You heard the guy—they're completely insulated. We

311

won't get the virus. They're practically the same as wearing a hazmat suit," I say to him.

"Yeah, and everyone's going to *stare* at us!" Bowen says.

I roll my eyes. "So??" I ask. I cross my arms and remind him what Mom said about Lao Lao and Lao Ye's restaurant—and how the community came together to support it. "This is our chance to help *our* community!" I tell my brother. "Besides, how else are we going to raise eight hundred ten dollars??"

Bowen hesitates. "How would we even collect the money in that thing?" he says.

I hold up a foamy toothbrush. "I have an idea for that, too!"

Bowen and Lea follow me to the garage, where I dust off the old skateboard Dad bought me two summers ago.

"We can use this to push the food and the money back and forth from a safe distance!" I tell my siblings. "Pretty cool, huh?"

I nudge the skateboard to Bowen.

"Errr . . . ," Bowen says, pushing it back. "What if they take the food and just close the door on us?"

"Then they'll have three angry T-rexes on their back! C'mon, guys! Work with me here!"

Mom walks into the garage. As we all pile inside the car for school, she answers her phone on speaker.

"Good morning, El Tercera families. Out of an abundance of caution, the school district will be closing our campuses to avoid the spread of COVID-19. To be clear, there have been no cases of COVID-19 on our school campuses or in any of the families in our community. That being said, the health and safety of our staff and students is our top priority, so we will be closing school at noon today."

Mom takes a deep breath as she absorbs the news that this is happening. On the first day of her new job!

"Don't worry, Mom," Bowen says. "We'll get an Uber home. And we'll manage ourselves when we get back. Right, guys?"

Mom gazes at Bowen appreciatively. "Thanks, but I'll pick you up," she says. "If you can just stay real quiet while I'm on Zoom calls in my room . . ."

"You won't even see us. It'll be like we're not even there," I promise, glancing at my siblings.

"Like we're out delivering things in dinosaur—" Lea starts to say. I give her a little kick with my leg.

Mom, thankfully, doesn't catch on. As she backs the car out, Bowen reaches into her purse and slips me her phone. Heart pounding, I pray that the app doesn't ask for Mom's password and order us three dinosaur suits from Amazon.

Chapter 87

--- ✈

I t is total chaos as everyone cleans out their desks and bombards Mrs. Turner with a million questions about how online school is going to work.

"How long will schools be closed? Do you know?" Simone asks.

"At this point, it's hard to tell. I've put enough assignments and worksheets in this packet to last you for two weeks. If it extends beyond that, we'll have to figure it out. For now, I want you all to know that the most important thing is that you keep reading."

Jonathan raises his hand. "But Mrs. Turner, the library has also closed! What if we have no books at home to read?"

Mrs. Turner puts her hand over her heart, like it pains her to hear the words. "If you don't have any books at home, please send me a message. I promise I'll bring books to your house and put them on your porch."

When Mrs. Turner says that, I feel a lump in my throat. Never in my entire education in Hong Kong, and certainly not during COVID-19, has any teacher ever offered to bring a book to my house. I'm going to miss Mrs. Turner so much.

As the other kids and I scribble down our addresses for Mrs. Turner, Alan raises his hand timidly. "Mrs. Turner, what about school lunch?"

"Oh, that reminds me!" she says. "We will continue giving out free school lunches at Del Rey High School. All you have to do is drive over and pick it up."

Alan exhales in relief.

I raise my hand. "What about you, Mrs. Turner?"

"What about me?" she asks.

"Who's going to tell you every day that you're making a difference in our lives?" I ask shyly.

All my classmates put their pencils down. "Yeah," Jonathan adds. "Who's going to tell you that I like reading now?"

"And that I'm getting better at math because you make it fun?" Kimmy chimes in.

"And that I'm just as capable. I just learn a little differently than everyone else," Christopher echoes.

"Me too," I stand up and say proudly.

"Me too," Tommy adds.

"Me too!" Simone yells.

Before I know it, the entire class is echoing me, even Tyler, who pipes up, "Me too. Thanks for making learning fun." Tears stream down Mrs. Turner's cheeks as she promises each and every one of us that she'll meet us online and we'll carry on, just as if we were here. We nod bravely, even though in our hearts we all know there are some things online school can never give us—like the joy of a teacher telling you to your face she thinks you have potential.

And Mrs. Turner sure was good at that.

Chapter 88

---✈

"All right, here's how it's gonna work," Bowen says when we get back home. I help my brother move his desk to the living room. I was so surprised when he said he'd rather do his homework downstairs next to me. We helped Lea moved her desk down too. It feels good knowing that I'll have some company this time. That things are going to be different.

"Every morning, we'll do our homework. I'll help you guys. Then we'll go over to the restaurant at eleven," Bowen says, plugging his computer cord into the living room wall.

I grin. Christopher was *over the moon* when I told him!

"What do we tell Mom?" Lea asks.

"I'll tell her I made a picnic and we're having it up on the hill behind the house."

That works! "We can tell her it's for PE!" I suggest.

Bowen points to me. "Good thinking!"

"When are our dino suits coming again?" Lea asks.

"Tomorrow," I tell her. "Gotta love next-day delivery!"

Mom walks downstairs at half past five to see how we're doing. We show off our desks, in three corners of the living room. It almost feels like a real classroom!

"Looks great!" Mom says, grabbing her keys. "C'mon, we

need to go over to the middle school track. They're handing out refunds."

"Refunds??" Bowen asks, getting up from his desk.

"It's not a school-funded program, so I had to pay three hundred dollars when you first joined."

"So that's it? The season's over?"

My face falls slightly at the realization that soccer's probably cancelled too.

"I'm sorry, honey," Mom says, putting a hand on his shoulder. "I knew you wanted to race on a real American track, but with everything going on, it makes sense not to have crowded meets."

Bowen nods. I can tell he's super disappointed.

I glance at the timer app on my iPad. "Hey, just because the season's over doesn't mean you can't keep training . . . ," I say to my brother.

"Yeah!" Lea says, jumping up from her desk. She sprints from one side of the living room to the other. "We can race you!"

Bowen looks over at us and chuckles. He's trying hard not to show his disappointment, even though the news falls pretty solidly in the *this stinks* camp.

"Or at the very least, time you," I offer.

He gives me a slight smile.

"That's a great idea!" Mom says as we follow her to the car.

There's a crowd of mothers around the coach when we get to the middle school track. Mom quickly joins the line. One of Bowen's teammates walks over, shaking his head.

"Hey, Bowen," he calls out.

"Hey, Jackson," Bowen calls back. I recognize Jackson as the kid who sat on the ground tying his track shoes when the other kids said the mean thing about Bowen last practice.

"Can you believe this?" Jackson asks. "This is the *worst*. Now I can't go to the Junior Olympics this year!"

Bowen looks over at him.

"Yeah, it's pretty bad . . . ," Bowen says. "But at least we can keep training."

Jackson gazes at him, confused.

"How do you figure?"

"Well, track is an individual sport," Bowen tells Jackson. "All we have to do is keep running." He turns to me. "My brother here plays soccer, and that's a lot harder to keep doing by yourself."

I suck in a breath. I can't believe my brother's talking about me. And acknowledging *my* problems.

"I never thought about it that way," Jackson says. He falls quiet for a long while before adding, "Sorry about last week, by the way. What those other kids said, that was mean."

Now Bowen's the one sucking in a breath. I'll bet he never expected *that* to come out of Jackson's mouth.

Jackson extends a hand. Bowen reaches to shake it. Then stops and offers his elbow instead.

"Maybe we can train together sometime," Jackson says as his mother calls his name.

Bowen nods. "Maybe . . . in the open air . . . in a dinosaur suit."

Jackson furrows his eyebrows. "What?"

Bowen laughs. "Never mind."

I smile as my brother waves goodbye to his new friend.

Chapter 89

---✈

The next morning, we sit impatiently in the living room doing our homework while Mom's upstairs on a Zoom call. Unlike the schools in Hong Kong, our schools don't have any live Zooms yet. We just have to do a bunch of assignments on our own.

When Lea gets confused on the math, Bowen teaches her.

"April has thirty days, see," Bowen tells Lea, making a fist and holding it out. "You can count it here on your knuckles. Lao Lao taught me."

I still can't believe Bowen's actually serious about helping us with our homework. As he shows Lea an old Chinese way with his hand, I marvel at him. He sure has changed.

"Cool! Where did Lao Lao learn that?" Lea asks.

"We should ask her the next time we Skype!" I suggest. It's been a while since we last Skyped, and I've been itching to talk to my grandparents again. I wonder how they're holding up in Beijing . . . are they still hibernating or have they ventured outside?

"Let's do it tonight!" Bowen says. "How about you? You need any help?"

I look down at my homework. I'm having trouble remembering the difference between an acute triangle and an obtuse triangle. So Bowen teaches me a trick.

"An acute triangle is smaller than ninety degrees. Remember, it's always smaller because it has the word 'cute' in it," Bowen says. "Things that are small are usually cute."

"You got that right!" Lea chimes in.

"Usually," Bowen says.

Before I know it, the pile of homework disappears. What would have taken me *days* to do when we first got here takes me only an hour. Plus I actually feel like I learned something! When the last of the assignments is completed, Lea and I hand them over to "teacher" Bowen, who takes pictures of them and helps us submit our work via Google Classroom.

As Bowen's uploading, I walk over to the door and check on the dino suits.

"Did they come yet?" Bowen calls from the kitchen.

"Not yet," I say, walking back inside.

"All right, I'm going to go for a run up the hill," Bowen says, putting on his sneakers.

"Want me to time you?" I ask. I expect him to say, *Nah, I've got it.* Or that he'd rather have a Zoom race with his new friend Jackson. But instead he says, "Sure."

I scramble over to my desk to grab my iPad, excited to be Bowen's new coach!

"Maybe later we can play soccer?" Bowen asks as we walk outside.

I beam like I've scored ten goals.

Chapter 90

An Amazon truck comes by as we're playing soccer in the backyard. I hear the *ding-dong* of the bell and bolt for the back gate. "Our dino suits!" I squeal to my brother and sister. We run out to the delivery truck.

The deliveryman chuckles behind his face mask as he hands us the box.

"Here you go, guys!" he says. "What's in it?"

"Our dad!" we reply as we take the box that's going to reunite our family and run off to try on our suits.

"I can't feel my toes," my sister says, wiggling in her inflated T-rex suit in the kitchen. She twists and turns, knocking over the bottle of soy sauce on the counter with her tail.

I try and wipe up the soy sauce, but my little dinosaur arms are too short.

"Feel your toes, I can't even *see* my toes!" Bowen says. He puts up his claws, looking like a beast about to raid the fridge!

Mom walks into the kitchen. "What are you guys doing??" she asks.

"Nothing!" we exclaim.

"We, uh . . . we're just trying out our Halloween suits," I say to Mom.

She points at the inflatable dino suits. "Did you guys get

those from Amazon? I was wondering who ordered three dino suits from my account. I thought it was Dad." She smiles. "You three look so cute! Let me take a picture!" She reaches for her phone. "But isn't it a little early for Halloween?"

"It's *never* too early for Halloween." Lea grins her T-rex teeth at Mom.

When Mom's safely back in her room, Bowen, Lea, and I shuffle over to the garage in our suits. Bike time!

Clumsily and slowly, we ride our bikes over to Christopher's restaurant. It's hard biking with one claw and a skateboard. He nearly drops all the single-use chopsticks and plastic forks in his hands when he sees us wobble in.

"You guys look . . ."

"Hot," Bowen tells Christopher, taking off his giant T-rex costume for a second and fanning himself. "It's like a hundred degrees in there!"

"Here," Christopher says, handing us cups of freshly brewed iced tea. "Drink this!"

I unzip my costume a little to let some air in and mumble from under my face mask (Mom picked up a few extras from NYC), "So what do you got for us?"

Christopher points to the take-out containers on the table, neatly organized into plastic bags. He hands me a list of addresses and a package of Clorox wipes.

"Make sure you disinfect the cash," he says, helping me and Bowen move the containers to our bike baskets. "Thanks again for doing this. You guys are literally saving the restaurant!"

I wave to Christopher's dad in the kitchen. "No problem. Thanks for letting us make some extra money!"

I zip up my dino suit, take the list of addresses from my friend, and hop on my bike—here we go!

Chapter 91

---✈

That day, we deliver Chinese takeout to stressed-out parents, construction workers, and young couples who don't want to cook.

A few people scream when they open the door, but when they realize we're *friendly* dinosaurs, with chow mein, they immediately calm down.

And they tip us generously, especially the distressed parents!

"You guys are lifesavers!" one mom says, pushing the skateboard back with a twenty-dollar tip. Her screaming brood runs up and down the stairs behind her. "Let me tell you, this whole homeschooling thing is *not* easy!"

"Thanks!" We disinfect the money with the Clorox wipes and get back on our bikes.

To my surprise, the next house on the list is Mr. Brady's!

"Baby T-rexes!" he greets us when he opens the door. Jokingly, he asks, "Am I in Jurassic Park?" I poke my head out of my T-rex suit for a second so he can see it's us, as Bowen rolls his order to him on the skateboard.

"Knox! Bowen! Lea!" he laughs. "How wonderful to see you guys!"

"How've you been?"

"Lonely," he says. "My grandkids haven't been able to

come by because of the virus. They don't want to get me sick, which I understand . . . but . . ." He looks down, his eyes heavy. "It's so hard when you're my age and you have no human interaction. . . ."

My heart falls into the pit of my stomach when I hear Mr. Brady's words, for I know how it feels not to be able to see your loved one.

Bowen puts a claw on his dinosaur chin, thinking.

"Do you have Zoom or Skype?" he asks. "I can set it up for you. It's not the same as seeing your grandkids face-to-face, but . . . it's better than nothing."

"We use it with our dad!" I tell him.

"Sure, go ahead!" Mr. Brady says, letting us inside.

Lea and I follow Bowen's enormous tail into the living room.

While Bowen disappears to Mr. Brady's den to install Zoom for him on his computer, Lea and I sit on Mr. Brady's couch, scratching through our thick, rubbery suits. It sure is hot in this thing. I can feel my eczema flaring, but I remind myself it's all for Dad.

The TV in the background reports, "As the number of coronavirus cases in the US surges past one thousand, many experts are saying that the true tally of coronavirus could be far greater. Several states are expected to issue a shelter-in-place order as early as Monday, asking all residents to remain in their homes except for *essential* workers," the newscaster says.

"What's an essential worker?" we ask Mr. Brady.

"I think it's someone whose job is absolutely critical in order for society to function, like healthcare workers, emergency services, food and grocery store staff. . . ."

I suddenly panic, worried we'll have to stop delivering food!

"Food delivery employees should count too," Mr. Brady says, reading my mind. "But do you guys really need to be doing this? You heard the newscasters—we're up to a thousand cases now."

"We have to! Before it's too late and they stop all the flights!" Lea says, desperately explaining how hard we've worked and how far we've come to try to get Dad here. We're *so* close!

"Well, I'd call that pretty essential work you kids are doing," Mr. Brady says as Bowen walks out of the den and announces to Mr. Brady that his Zoom is all installed.

Mr. Brady's face lights up.

"You mean I can see my grandkids again?" he asks.

"Yup!"

"Thank you kids so, so much," Mr. Brady says, getting a hundred-dollar bill out of his wallet.

Our eyes boggle at the cash. More than the money, though, the knowledge that we've helped a neighbor fills me up inside.

Walking back outside, Bowen, Lea, and I high-paw as Lea takes the hundred dollars and adds it to our stash of tips. I help my little sister count it all up.

"Just six hundred seventy-eight dollars more to go!" I squeal. Lea gazes up at the vast blue sky overhead, pointing with her claw. "I can almost see Daddy's plane. . . ."

Chapter 92

-- ✈

Mom's just getting off her last Zoom call of the day by the time we get home and finish setting the table. Bowen puts his phone down. He and Jackson have been trading Usain Bolt videos ever since we got back.

Mom's eyes widen when she sees the dining table, all wiped and shined, with plates of scrumptious sweet-and-sour chicken. Christopher's dad gave us a humongous bag of take-out to thank us for delivering all the food.

"Surprise!" we say, pulling out a chair for Mom.

"This is . . . amazing!" she says. "Thank you guys so much!"

"Christopher gave us all the food." I beam.

"And some toilet paper!" Lea giggles, holding up a roll.

"Awww, well, tell Christopher we appreciate it!" As she reaches for her first piece of sweet-and-sour chicken, Mom asks me about my day. "Did you get all your homework done, Knox? Want me to work on it with you after dinner?"

"Actually I finished everything," I reveal, glancing at my brother. "Bowen helped me."

"*Really?*" Mom asks, shocked. She turns to Bowen, who pours her a glass of Fresca in her UC Berkeley glass. "Watch out, you'll be getting this glass soon!"

Bowen smiles.

"Tell us again how you got it from the chancellor. Did he

give it to you at graduation for having the best grades?" my brother asks.

Mom chuckles, admiring her glass. "He did give it to me at graduation," she says. "But it wasn't for having the best grades."

"It wasn't??" Bowen asks.

Mom shakes her head, peering at the glass. "It was for my public service. I started an advocacy group for immigrant students and students who are the first in their family to go to college. To help them combat professor bias."

I form an O with my mouth.

"That's why the chancellor recognized me. It was for my efforts to help others," Mom says. "*That's* the true marker of success."

I smile, thinking back to the warm feeling of helping Mr. Brady today. And helping save a small family restaurant. Mom's right. It really *is* the true marker of success.

As Mom passes her glass around, we all take turns holding it and admiring it.

I look over at Bowen, who seems the most surprised. But then again, he shouldn't be. If we've learned one thing this year, it's that we're all connected to each other. We all breathe the same air into our lungs. None of us are immune to each other's problems. That's why we have to care about each other.

Chapter 93

--- ✈

Fueled by Mom's words, Bowen, Lea, and I deliver takeout every afternoon for the rest of the week, racking up tips. As we get closer and closer to hitting a thousand dollars, I picture Dad's face when we tell him the good news.

The glow of Bowen's phone wakes me up on Friday. "Jackson just invited me to run at the track—with masks on. You wanna go and kick some balls around?"

"Sure," I mutter. It comes out a low murmur.

I try to get up but my body is slow and sluggish. I put my hand up to my neck. Why does my throat suddenly feel so painful and dry? And my hand so cold?

I start coughing.

"Oh no . . . ," Bowen cries. "MOM!!!!"

Mom runs into our room.

"What's wrong?" she asks.

Before I can respond, she puts her hand to my scorching hot forehead. As she dashes into the bathroom for a thermometer, I shiver in my blanket. My sister walks in. She sees my face and the stuffed bunny drops from her hand.

"You think it's . . . ," Bowen starts to say.

"No!" Mom exclaims. "You guys haven't been going out, except to have picnics up the hill. We haven't been exposed. . . ."

"Um." Bowen swallows hard.

As the thermometer in Mom's hand takes my temperature, Bowen tells her what we've been doing. The blood drains from her face.

"You've been running around town doing *what*?!?" Mom asks.

"We wore dino suits! We were fully protected!" Bowen insists.

Mom picks up Bowen's deflated rubber suit in the corner of our room. "You call this fully protected?"

"We didn't just deliver takeout! We also helped Mr. Brady install Zoom!" Lea tells Mom.

But Mom doesn't care. She scolds Bowen for letting us go out and taking such reckless risks. Their argument is interrupted by the loud beeping of the thermometer: 100.7 degrees.

"You definitely have a fever," Mom declares as I huddle in my blanket, coughing in the direction of the wall so I don't get my siblings sick.

She asks me if I have any difficulty breathing. I shake my head. I don't *think* so, although now that she mentions it, it does hurt a little in my chest every time I move. Like a baby T-rex foot is lightly stepping on me.

"No, no!" Mom says. "We have to get you to a hospital." She chews her lip. "But going to the hospital right now, with everything going on . . ."

"To the hospital?" I gasp.

Mom weighs the risks in her head. "I don't want to take any chances," she finally says.

I plead with her. "I'm *fine*!" I tell her. I start getting out of bed to show her, only to fall off the bunk. I land on the floor with a thud.

Lea screams. "Are you okay??"

Mom scoops me up and takes me to her bed. While she calls the doctor we went to a few summers ago when Bowen had an ear infection, my brother sits by my side, putting blankets on me.

"You should sit farther away," I tell him. "Just in case."

Bowen shakes his head. "I'm fine where I am," he insists.

I close my eyes. I should have listened to Mom; *I should have stayed inside.* A whimper builds in me as I think of Dad. All I wanted was for him to come home to us. Tears trickle down from the corners of my eyes. For once, I don't bother hiding them from Bowen.

Chapter 94

--✈

Mom presses on the gas, zipping down the streets toward Alta Bates in Berkeley. The doctor told us that based on my symptoms, he can't see us at his clinic. We need to go to the hospital. When we arrive, three doctors in hazmat suits greet us by the entrance. I'm relieved the hospital is still open—according to the radio, the whole county will start sheltering in place on Monday. The doctors help get me into a wheelchair.

"Where are you taking him?" Mom asks.

"To an isolation room," one of the doctors tells her. "All our suspected COVID-19 cases have to be put in isolation rooms to avoid possible contamination and spread, until the tests come back."

"Isolation room??" I glance over at Mom, panicking. "NO!!" I don't want to be separated from my family!

"Can I go with him?" Mom pleads with the doctor. "Please. I understand the risk of getting COVID and I'm willing to take the risk."

"I'm sorry, it's our hospital policy," the doctor says. "We're going to do everything we can to help your son, but you have to let us do our job."

"Mom . . . I don't want to go," I whimper, coughing in between words.

Mom nods and kneels down to look into my eyes. "Bao bao," she says. "I know you're scared. But it's going to be okay. The doctors are going to make sure you get all better. And we'll be right here in the waiting room the entire time."

"It could be a while," another doctor says. "We're currently low on tests."

I turn to Bowen. "Will you let Christopher know what happened and that I'm so sorry we can't help him today?"

Bowen tells me not to worry about Christopher, he'll take care of it. He hands me his cell phone. "Here," he says. "So you can FaceTime us. And Dad."

At the thought of Dad, I start bawling uncontrollably. If something happens to me, I won't even get to see him. I'll be stuck in the isolation room. I won't even get to say goodbye. Lea wraps her arms around me, despite the doctor's warning not to touch me. She puts her beloved Bugsy the stuffed bunny into my hands. "Don't die, gege," she whispers into my ear. And I promise her, for her sake and for Dad's, "I won't."

As the doctors push me through the double doors, Mom crumples onto the floor. I hold one arm out to her and flex my other arm up high, trying to stay strong.

Chapter 95

- ✈

I t's cold and noisy inside the isolation room. There are all
sorts of machines beeping and buzzing as the doctors put
long wires and tubes in me. Down the hall, I can hear the
ooooof of oxygen machines. I gulp, hoping I don't need one.

"Hey, buddy, I'm going to stick this swab up your nose to
do some tests. I need you to hold real still, okay?" the doctor
asks.

I muster a brave nod, even though I'm really scared. The
swab he's holding is as long as a pencil.

"Here we go," he says, holding my face back with his
gloved hand. On the count of three, he sticks the swab *way* in.
I imagine it coming out of the other side of my skull. It kind
of feels . . . like I've eaten too much wasabi. It makes my eyes
water slightly.

When he's done, he puts it in a container and shows me
my name on the sticker to make sure it's accurate.

"Knox Wei-Evans," he says. "Like the beach?"

I nod, wondering if I'll ever get to see it again.

"Now tell me where it hurts in your chest," the doctor says
to me. I point to the spot where it aches if I hold my breath
for too long, and he puts his stethoscope over it. He tells me
to inhale and exhale. I try and do it without coughing.

"Your air passageways seem clear when I listen to them,"

he says. "But I'm going to schedule a CT scan just in case." He walks out of the isolation room as my phone rings.

I smile when I see Dad's face on FaceTime.

"Hey, Dad," I say to him, coughing. I reach out and touch the screen with my finger.

"How do you feel?" he says. "Are you okay? Did they give you anything?"

I tell Dad the doctors gave me some medicine for my fever. But just seeing him, I feel my toes warming up. Softly, I whisper, "I'm so sorry, Dad."

"It's not your fault," Dad says.

"But it is." Tears drip down onto my hospital bed. Amid all the beeping machines in the isolation room, I finally tell Dad what the last few weeks have been like for me. About the Taradippin brothers. The dinosaur suits. The takeout. Goose bumps of regret spider up my arms as I think about how careless we were.

"I'm sorry," I say. "I didn't mean to get sick. All I wanted was to get you over here."

Dad wipes at his own wet eyes.

"*I'm* sorry," he says. "I should have listened sooner when you said you wanted me over. I should have found a way. But I'm going to figure it out now. You just hang in there, buddy."

I shake my head. I'm done putting my family in danger. "No. They won't let you see me even if you come," I tell him. I close my eyes, thinking back to that fateful airplane trip and how I thought we were getting on the lifeboat to safety. And now . . .

"I don't want you to get sick, Dad," I whimper.

My eyelids grow heavy from the fever. I whisper "I love you, Dad" one last time and fall asleep.

Chapter 96

--- ✈

It's the middle of the night when I finally wake up. I'm in another room. Did they move me? I gaze up at the monitor, shocked to see it's Monday, March 16. I've been in the hospital three days. The fever must have knocked me out cold. I watch my heartbeat on the monitor, relieved to see it is still pumping strong.

I reach for my phone, but there's no more battery. Bowen gave me his phone but he forgot to give me a charger.

The hospital hallways are quiet. I try to call out for a doctor, but no one responds. Did they get the results back from my test? Do I have COVID? I feel my nose with my finger, at the place where they probed me. It still hurts a little when I touch it.

Wide awake and with no phone or iPad, I decide to compose recordings for my brother and sister in my head—in case I have COVID.

> Dear mei mei,
> I know I don't always tell you this, but you're pretty cool. Thanks for always making me feel better even when you didn't have to. I hope you always remember the soccer moves I taught you . . . and that you have a gege who loves you very, very much.
> Love,
> Knox

And for my brother, Bowen . . .

Dear gege,
In case anything happens to me, I want you to know that
the combination to my lockbox is 1-4-6. It's the months of
our three birthdays. I want you to have my stamps and give
Lea my soccer match cards (you'll have to teach her how to
collect them and trade them).

Okay, this is kind of embarrassing, but you'll also find
a bunch of your old certificates for "Best at Reading" and
"Best at Chinese" from elementary school in my lockbox.
You might be wondering what they're doing in my lockbox.
You didn't want them, but I kept them for you.

I always thought that if something happened to you,
it sort of happened to me, too. But now something has
happened to me that I hope never happens to you. I
know you'll be blaming yourself as the oldest for "letting
it happen"—please don't. You couldn't have stopped me
even if you wanted to, because when I put my mind to
something, I hyper-focus. And you know what? I wouldn't
trade the memories of us running around town in our dino
suits for anything else in the world. We finally bonded,
which is all I ever wanted.
Love,
Knox

When I'm done, I press send in my head and hope my
siblings get my messages telepathically. I gaze out the window
at the silvery moon, hoping they're looking at it too . . . and
thinking of me.

Chapter 97

---+

Knox . . . Knox . . . ?"

The sound of my brother's voice wakes me up the next morning. I open my eyes and see my brother sitting on my bed. Is he really here, or am I dreaming it? I look around, not recognizing the room I'm in.

"Bowen?" I ask.

"Guess what??" He smiles at me. "The test came back. It's negative! You're not in the isolation room anymore! You don't have the coronavirus!"

I sit up. Is he messing with me?

"I'm serious. Mom just talked to the doctor. She's signing your discharge papers right now. You just have the flu."

"The flu—that's it?" I ask. Bowen nods. I punch the air with my arms in my hospital bed. A nurse comes in and checks on my pulse and temperature.

"Ninety-eight degrees, all normal," she says. I exhale a sigh of relief.

Bowen waits until after the nurse leaves before getting something off his chest. "I was so worried these past few days. . . . I really thought I was going to lose my best friend."

I stare at him. Is he feeling okay? Does *he* have a fever?

But Bowen doesn't just stop there. "I'm sorry for not always being nice to you the last few years."

"It's okay . . . ," I start saying.

"No," Bowen says, his eyes full of determination. "I'm sorry for calling you Knot. It was mean. The truth is . . . I have impulsivity issues too. And I just . . . sometimes . . ." He clutches my hospital bedsheet, unable to describe it.

"Lose control?"

"Yeah."

I get that.

"It felt so weird looking up at our bunk and not having you there," Bowen confesses.

"Same here . . . ," I tell him. "I kept waiting for you to yell, 'Stop tossing and turning!'"

Bowen chuckles at my imitation of him. "Seriously, though, I'm sorry for being so hard on you. I just wanted to be 'the man' and step up because Dad wasn't around."

I prop myself up with a pillow. Gently, I remind Bowen, "Being the man doesn't mean being harsh. It means you're kind to those you love."

As he reaches to give me a hug, a familiar voice echoes my statement.

"Knox is right. Being the man means you're there for the ones you love."

My brother and I spin around.

"DAD!!!!!" we exclaim.

Chapter 98

I leap off my hospital bed and run toward our dad, the wires and monitors on my body beeping and flying every which way. But I don't care! Dad's here! I hug him in the flesh, never wanting to let go of him again.

"How did you get here?" I ask, breathing him in. Dad smells like disinfectant wipes and granola bars.

"I took the first flight out," he says. "Told you I'd be here."

"But what about your work??" I ask.

"They'll survive for a few days," he says, reaching up with his hand to feel my temperature. "How do you feel? Are you all right?"

I put my hand in his. "I am now."

Dad turns to Bowen and tells him to "get in here." It's a hamburger hug with me in the middle, until Lea runs into the room and I become the ketchup. We laugh and cheer, jumping up and down in the hospital. We finally did it! Turns out, we didn't even need a thousand dollars! All I needed was to get the flu!

Mom walks in.

"Andrew!" she cries, just as surprised to see him standing there as we are. I guess he didn't tell her he was coming. "You're here! But . . . how?"

"Let's just say, I'm not winning Employee of the Year anytime soon," Dad chuckles. He frees himself from our hamburger hug and holds his arms out to Mom. "But God, it feels good to see you guys. I've missed you so much."

"Not as much as I've missed you," Mom replies, putting the hospital discharge papers down and walking into his arms.

As my parents hug, Lea climbs onto my hospital bed and throws "confetti" cotton balls onto them. At long last, we're together. We're a family again.

Walking out of the hospital, I hold Mom's hand in one hand and Dad's hand in the other. It's amazing: when you haven't seen both your parents in the same place for a long time, the sight of them together is like a shooting star. You just can't stop looking at it.

A doctor walks over and hands Mom the records from our COVID tests on our way out. While I was in the isolation room, Mom got everyone tested for COVID just in case. The results came back negative for all of us.

As I thank the doctor for taking care of me, I can't believe the mask he's wearing. It's a cloth mask, like it's made from a T-shirt.

"Your mask . . . ," I say, pointing at it.

"Yeah, sadly we don't have enough surgical ones here," he says. "So my wife made this at home. It's not quite the same thing. . . ."

Bowen and I share an angry look. *Those Taradippin brothers!*

As I walk into the parking lot, thinking of how to get those greedy brothers to donate their loot, a bark interrupts my thoughts. I look up at Dad's rental car from the airport. It's Cody!!! My dog jumps out of the open window of Dad's car and gallops toward me.

"I thought you'd like the fur ball back," Dad says. "He was getting too cooped up in my tiny apartment."

Bowen, Lea, and I hug Cody as he jumps on us, licking us and barking with excitement. Oh, how I missed my dog!

I turn to Dad. "Does this mean you're going to stay!?" I ask.

Dad hesitates for a second. "No . . . I'm afraid I've got to get back to my job, buddy," he says. "I fly back in a couple of days. My office needs me."

So do we. I glance at my siblings, wishing we could change Dad's mind. I can tell from the looks on their faces they're thinking the same thing too. A couple of days—can we do it?

Chapter 99

get home to see a bunch of posters in our living room. They're posters my brother and sister made for me while I was in the hospital. They say *GET WELL SOON, WE LOVE YOU!* and *BEAT COVID.* There are a few others, too, like *STOP ASIAN HATE, BLACK LIVES MATTER,* and *WE ARE NOT A VIRUS.*

Mom explains to me that while I was in the hospital, an African American woman named Breonna Taylor was shot dead in her home by the police. She was an innocent emergency room technician who had plans to be a nurse.

My breath chokes in my throat when I hear the news.

"The racism in this country affects all of us," Mom says as she puts a tissue to her eyes, unable to find the words to express the injustice. The sorrow. "Black, brown, Asian, Indigenous. And it's not okay!"

We huddle together as a family. That day, we cry for Breonna Taylor, the heroic frontline worker who will never get to be a nurse. We cry for the Asian Americans who have been spit on and assaulted. For the Latinx essential workers getting turned away from grocery stores. We cry for the double whammy of fear—fear of the virus itself and fear of racism, a pandemic just as terrifying.

I pick up the beautiful posters my brother and sister made.

"When can we put these up around town?" I ask, hugging the Black Lives Matter poster and the Stop Asian Hate poster.

"As soon as you get better, buddy," Dad says, putting a hand on my forehead.

As I recover from the flu upstairs, reading the *Get Well Soon* card from Christopher on my desk, I check my email to see if Mr. Anderson's secretary reached out for that in-person interview. She didn't. I try Mr. Anderson at the country club on Bowen's phone.

C'mon, pick up, pick up!

But it just goes to voicemail. I put the phone down and glance out the window at Bowen and Lea setting up a special date night for Mom and Dad in the backyard. It was Lea's idea. Watching my siblings decorate the backyard with Christmas lights and play romantic jazz music on Mom's little portable speakers, I smile and open my window. I can smell Bowen's burgers wafting from the kitchen. Lea waves at me in her black-and-white waitress uniform as she sets Mom and Dad's table.

"Wow," Mom says, stepping out into the backyard in a white flowing dress and gold strappy heels. Ohhhhh. So *that's* what the heels are for.

"You look great." Dad smiles.

Bowen and Lea decide to give our parents some privacy and come upstairs to my room, where we can spy on our parents from my bunk.

"You think he's going to stay?" Bowen asks.

"How could he not? Did you *see* the dress she's wearing?" Lea asks, kicking her feet next to me. Bowen let me have the lower bunk, saying it'll be easier for me to get up and go to the bathroom while I recover.

I'm still not used to Nice Bowen. It's like when you've been wearing shorts your whole life and you suddenly start wearing pants. You don't know what to do with all that extra fabric. I don't know what to do with all that extra nice. But I like it. I like having pants.

"Listen! They're saying something!" Bowen says. We get real quiet and press our ears to the screen window to hear our parents' conversation.

"I was watching Bowen help out Lea with her homework today," Dad says. "It was really something. And Lea, the way she put her mind to transforming this backyard into an upscale restaurant."

Mom looks around at the glimmering lights. "She did a beautiful job!"

"And Knox, how strong and brave he was in the hospital," Dad says. "They've all matured so much." He holds up a glass to Mom. "Thanks to you. I'm proud of you."

Mom clinks Dad's glass with her Berkeley glass. "Thanks. It hasn't been easy without you," she tells Dad. "There are some days when I feel like I have no idea how to do this—be a mom *and* a career woman—and I feel like I'm failing on both fronts."

Mom? Failing?? I guess I'm not the only one in the family who feels that way sometimes.

"But then I look at the excitement in their eyes when they tell me that they've been helping a restaurant stay afloat. Or a senior citizen set up Zoom. And I think . . . I must be doing something right." Mom smiles.

"You're doing everything right," Dad tells her. "I'm sorry for insisting they come home. It's clear how much the kids have grown."

Mom reaches a hand across the table. "Do you really have to leave the day after tomorrow?"

"You know I'd love to stay, but my boss will fire me in two seconds if I don't get back."

"What about getting a job here?"

"In this economy? While we're going through a pandemic?"

"I did it," Mom reminds him.

"You're *you*. The strongest, most courageous woman I know. It's what I love about you," Dad says. His eyes gaze down at the white tablecloth. "But I'm not like you. It's taken me a *long* time to establish myself as an immigrant in Hong Kong. And then there's the matter of our finances. . . . I don't know if it's practical for me to just reinvent myself and start all over again here . . . or if I even can."

I lean up against the window, wanting to shout, *Of course you can! We're already reinventing you, Dad! We're doing it!!!*

"You won't know until you try . . . ," Mom says gently. She reminds Dad that before we came, none of us knew how to do this. And now look at us—learning on Zoom and closing deals in our fuzzy bedroom slippers! "The only thing stopping you is fear, Andrew."

As Mom tries to convince Dad, I reach for Bowen's phone again.

"Where is that Mr. Anderson at the country club?? We're running out of time! We gotta find him!"

Chapter 100

--✈

Mr. Anderson finally calls us back the next day, but unfortunately, it's bad news. Due to the shelter-in-place order, the country club is closed and they're no longer hiring.

"I'm so sorry," he says. "I really wish I could give you a chance, but I myself may be out of a job soon. Stay safe."

Bowen and I get back on LinkedIn after we finish our online homework. We write job applications all day long. This time, I even make myself read the small text of the boring "Careers" pages. I tell myself I have to hyper-focus! Dad's leaving tomorrow! We can't give up! But the shelter-in-place order is more powerful than my focusing skills, wiping out most of the job opportunities, even the undercover shopper job.

Cody whines at my brother's feet as we close our laptops.

"We should walk him," I say, scratching and rubbing Cody's head. I'm feeling a lot better and could use some fresh air. "Let's take him to the dog park!"

At the mention of the dog park, Bowen shakes his head. "I don't know . . . ," he says.

I gaze at my brother, wanting to tell him he can't let that mean racist man win! At the same time, I understand how it's different for me. I wasn't the one the man yelled at and called a racist slur. Bowen has the right to take all the time he needs.

But Cody is less patient. He whimpers at my brother's feet. Finally, his big brown puppy eyes convince Bowen.

"Maybe we can go for five minutes," Bowen says. "He's probably not even going to be there."

I smile and grab Cody's leash.

"Let's go."

We take one last drive as a family, making a stop along the way to the dog park, to put up our *STOP ASIAN HATE*, *BLACK LIVES MATTER*, and *WE ARE NOT A VIRUS* posters. They look amazing on the corner of our main street. I hope lots and lots of people see the signs, that they never get taken down from our streets or from our minds.

Bowen looks up from his phone next to me—it's nice having him in the back again with me and Lea—as my parents turn into the dog park.

"Hey, look at this! Alta Bates hospital just received two thousand surgical face masks from two anonymous donors!" Bowen reads from his phone.

I beam proudly.

Bowen looks at me, lifting an eyebrow. "Did you have something to do with this . . . ?"

"I might have put something up on Nextdoor," I giggle.

"Nice!" He high-fives me as Mom unlocks the car and lets Cody out. Dad hands us extra masks he brought over from Hong Kong and we put them on.

Cody runs and runs between the tall eucalyptus trees, wagging his tail. The cool Northern California wind ripples through his soft fur. I'm so glad we came.

I turn to my brother, who looks around the park, a little

uneasy at first, then relaxes when he sees the park is pretty empty. He throws a tennis ball at Cody, and Cody jumps up so high to get it, Bowen laughs.

As he plays fetch with Cody, Dad kicks a soccer ball around with Lea.

"You're getting good, Lea. Keep your body over the ball!" Dad says.

"Like this?" Lea asks.

"Like that exactly!" Dad says.

I run toward them, positioning myself between the tall trees, pretending to be the goalie. Lea uses her side foot, just like I taught her, to shoot the soccer ball in. She scores! Dad and I clap wildly for her while she does a somersault on the grass. I close my eyes and take in the moment, imagining for a second that it could be like this all the time. That Dad didn't have to leave tomorrow.

Dad's loud whistling draws the attention of a labradoodle, who comes galloping over from the other side of the dog park.

"Charlie, come back here!" a cranky voice calls.

When I turn around to look at the owner, I freeze.

Chapter 101

--✈

Bowen comes face-to-face with the man who called him a racist name, his face hot with humiliation. As if that's not bad enough, the man's not even wearing a mask! I stiffen, drenched in regret for asking my brother to come. I start leashing Cody up so we can go home, but Bowen stays right where he is.

"No, we're not leaving," Bowen says. "He should leave!" He points a finger at the owner, who looks completely shocked.

"I should leave?" the man asks. "Why should *I* leave?"

"What's going on?" Dad asks, walking over with the soccer ball.

"This man called me an oriental," Bowen tells Dad.

Mom turns to the man, her eyes full of fury.

At first, the old man denies what happened. "I don't know what you're talking about," he says.

I immediately jump in. "Yes, you do. You wouldn't let my brother pet your dog! You said it was unhygienic. But you let me and my sister pet him."

"Hey, listen, it's *my* dog," the owner says, pointing to Charlie with his finger. "*I* decide who gets to pet him."

"Not based on the color of my skin!" Bowen says.

Curiously, Charlie goes up to smell Cody and I kneel down and try to hold Cody back. That's when I notice the other tag on Charlie's collar—*CJ Axel (510) 555-2828.*

"*You're* CJ Axel??" I jump up and turn to my siblings. "He's the guy on Nextdoor writing horrible racist posts!"

"I think you better get out of here," Dad says, pointing toward the parking lot.

"Not without an apology," Mom demands. She tells Mr. Axel that his cowardly actions traumatized Bowen and he ought to be ashamed of himself.

"I'm not apologizing for the truth," the man says simply, shaking his head and yanking hard on his dog's leash. "C'mon, Charlie, let's go home."

That afternoon, we drive back to our house in silence. It's so disappointing that CJ Axel could not find it in himself to apologize to my brother. Still, I'm proud of Bowen for standing up to racism and letting the man know that what he did was not okay.

As Dad packs that night, he has a conversation with us about racism. He tells us of America's long, painful history of racism, which goes all the way back to the country's inception, and how it lingers to this day.

"It's something we have to work hard at every day to stamp out," Dad says. "Even though we don't always succeed, it takes consistent courage, and through our small heroic acts of bravery, we *will* turn the tide."

I think of all the little things we did this year to right wrongs, and I smile. *Consistent courage.*

"Speaking of . . . ," I say to Dad, glancing at my brother and sister. We hand him the folder of all the job applications we filled out for him. He might as well have it, since he's leaving tomorrow. He should know how hard we tried, even though we didn't succeed.

"You guys did all this?" he asks, looking through all the various applications and cover letters.

"We *almost* got you a job at the country club," I brag.

Dad's eyes pop when he sees the résumé we wrote for him. "Tried my hardest at Berkeley. Wow . . . That's . . . very true!" He smiles at us, holding the folder in his hands. "I don't know what to say."

"Say you'll stay," Lea begs. My sister takes Dad's ticket from his passport pouch and hides it behind her back.

Dad puts the folder into his carry-on and kneels in front of Lea. "You know I want to. I really do. But I have to be responsible. What if something happens with your mom's job? Things are so uncertain right now. I need to be able to provide for all of you." He reaches out a hand and touches Lea's cheek. "You understand, don't you, mochi?"

With a heavy sigh, Lea hands back Dad's ticket.

"I did get you something for your birthday, though," Dad says, pulling out a light-up tracing pad and a framed picture of our family from his luggage.

Lea takes the picture and puts her finger on Dad's smiling face. I know what she's thinking. It's beautiful, but it'd be more beautiful *for real.* Still, she hugs Dad and thanks him.

"We'll FaceTime every day," he promises as he kisses all of us on the head.

Mom stands at the doorway, with a tissue to her nose, as Bowen and I run into Dad's arms too. I try to memorize this feeling, counting down the days until I can have it all the time.

Chapter 102

‑‑‑✈

I listen to the low hum of the refrigerator the next morning as Bowen, Lea, and I sit in the kitchen, staring at our cereal bowls. Dad left at six a.m. for the airport, and even Cody's sad. He leaves his dog food untouched.

"Why don't we finish our homework later?" Bowen suggests. "I gotta train so I can race Jackson next weekend at the track!"

I smile, excited to hear that's still on. As I reach over for my stopwatch, Bowen puts his hand over mine.

"Forget the stopwatch," he says. "Let's all run together."

I blink with surprise, wondering if my brother read my note. Last night, as we were printing out all the job applications for Dad, I finally wrote out my "If I get COVID" messages to my siblings and put them under their pillows.

Lea slips her hand in mine—she *definitely* read my note. We grab our shoes and our face masks. As we're walking out, we see a taxi pull into our driveway.

"Dad!!!" we yell.

"What happened? Did you forget something?" I ask. His flight was supposed to take off an hour ago.

Dad nods. "Yes, I forgot something very important." His eyes smile back at us. "Something I said back at the hospital. That being the man means you're there for the ones you love."

I hold my breath with anticipation.

Dad pulls out his folder of job applications. "As I was waiting for my flight, I thought to myself . . . if you three rascals managed to *almost* land me a job pretending to be me, I think I owe it to myself to *actually* give it a shot."

"All right, Dad!!!" We run over and give him a hug.

Dad laughs as he hugs us back. "Thanks for saying such nice things about your old man in the applications."

At the sound of Dad's voice, Mom comes running down the stairs. She takes out her conference-call AirPods, and Dad spins her in his arms.

"What changed your mind?" Mom asks.

"You were right. The only thing stopping me is fear. But I realized this week"—Dad winks at us—"maybe I can be consistently courageous too."

Mom interlaces her fingers with Dad's. "You won't have to do it alone."

As my parents embrace, Bowen, Lea, and I cheer. We did it!!!

Hand in hand, we walk up the hill in our face masks with our parents. Things might be completely unpredictable. One day, we might be in the middle of a pandemic. The next day, we might be swimming in toilet paper. But somehow, we'll pull through it all as a family.

Author's Note

In January 2020, when I told my children to pack their bags for America with three days' notice, I never thought that the world would change so dramatically or that our family would be split up across two continents for more than a year (and counting!).

There we were, packing up fifteen years' worth of memories in Hong Kong into five big suitcases, trying to escape the novel coronavirus that hadn't yet been named, not knowing what fate would await us on the other side of the ocean. We were Americans living in Asia. We had been through SARS, which had devastated Hong Kong, and thought it would be safer to bring our children back to the United States. There was just one problem—my husband couldn't come. He had to stay behind for work.

As we hugged Dad goodbye and I hurried toward one of the last United flights from Hong Kong to San Francisco, my children, Eliot, Tilden, and Nina, tried their hardest to be brave behind their face masks. Still, I could see the tears soaking my son Tilden's mask. Dad was his best friend. It felt like we were boarding a lifeboat on the *Titanic* without him. It didn't hit me until I actually sat down on the plane that this would be the first day in our ongoing, sometimes hilarious, deeply emotional struggle as a long-distance family.

In the months that followed, life threw one curveball after another at us, as we navigated distance learning, ADHD, medical insurance (and lack thereof), a volatile toilet paper situation (and lack thereof), and surging racism and anti-Asian hate. I had immigrated to America once before as a young girl. But immigrating to America the second time, during a pandemic, tested me like never before.

During the COVID-19 pandemic, the number of anti-Asian hate crimes skyrocketed. From March 19, 2020, to February 28, 2021, there were 3,795 hate crimes reported to the Stop AAPI Hate reporting center. They've ranged from verbal abuse to physical assault to murder. A horrific number of Asian American elderly citizens were shoved, stabbed, or set on fire by people spewing hatred, including eighty-four-year-old Thai American Vichar Ratanapakdee and seventy-five-year-old Chinese American Pak Ho, who did not survive. And in March 2021, six Asian American women died in three connected shootings in Atlanta.

Like so many Asian Americans and people of color, I felt the terror of the mounting hate. Early in the pandemic, I was verbally assaulted at the park in front of my children, called a racial slur, and told to go back to where I came from. My children were forced to play coronavirus tag at school and be "It." As a mother, I wanted so desperately to shield my children from the idea that they were unwelcomed here. But, unfortunately, there is no face mask for racism.

All there is, is truth. And I wanted to write ours as honestly as I could. I wanted to write about my sons' brotherly love for each other, in all its complexities. I wanted to write about the challenges with navigating ADHD, based on my son's experience. I wanted to write about separation and the worry of growing up, a world apart. Most of all, I wanted to celebrate family. Ours may not be a conventional one—we're one big intercontinental, interracial, and intergenerational bunch, and there are some days when it feels like the sky is crashing down and all I have to hold it up is a Popsicle stick—but we're a loving one. And it's that love that's gotten us through all the curveballs.

Ultimately, love is the only vaccine for hate. It's love that gets us through the hard times. And it's love that will bind us back together as a community, nation, and world.

Kelly and her children leaving Hong Kong.

Kelly Yang writing *New from Here* in her closet (the only quiet place she could find in her home) during quarantine.

Acknowledgments

I would like to thank my three kiddos, Eliot, Tilden, and Nina, for trusting me when I said, "Pack your bags, we're going to America." I still remember sitting on the plane as we departed Hong Kong, squished together in the few remaining seats left. My kids were firing away questions at me: How long are we going for, Mom? Are we ever going to see Dad again? Will the virus be in America too? I didn't have any answers to their questions. All I knew was that we were going.

And when we landed, I didn't know what fate would await us. What schools would welcome us. Whether I could even get us health insurance. How to make the whole long-distance intercontinental family thing work. All I knew was I had to write this story, because what I'd just gone through was the most dramatic experience in my life. So I called up my literary agent, Tina Dubois, and told her I would like to write about a family separated, trying to put itself back together, during a pandemic.

At the time, the pandemic was not in the United States yet. I am so grateful to Tina for not balking, for recognizing immediately that this was so much more than a pandemic book, it's a book about family. About siblings growing apart. About a mom trying to hold it together, trying to infuse her kids with love, hoping the love will be enough to combat all the hate and uncertainty. Thank you, Tina, for embracing this book with your whole heart and encouraging me every step of the way. We submitted this book during the first week of lockdown in New York City, when every publishing house was scrambling to put into place work-at-home schedules. Against this chaotic backdrop, Tina calmly led an auction in her apartment. And when Krista Vitola at Simon & Schuster wanted to publish it, tears of joy streamed down my face.

That night, my family celebrated over Zoom and ice cream. We were all so proud, especially my son Tilden, who has ADHD and whose journey is reflected in Knox's story. There was a feeling that everything we'd gone through was not in vain, that the world would know our story—that other children navigating ADHD would not feel so alone. My deepest gratitude to Krista for approaching Knox's story with such loving care. Her brilliant editorial input made this book sing. Thank you, Krista, for encouraging me to write a story packed with my heart, and for championing this book every step of the way! To the entire Simon & Schuster team, Justin Chanda, Lisa Moraleda, Chantal Gersch, Lucy Cummins, thank you for believing in me. It's an honor to be an S&S author, and Knox and I could not have found a better home!

To Maike Plenzke—it's my great luck in life to have you as my cover illustrator for all my middle-grade books! Your talent continues to blow my mind! Thank you for bringing Knox, Lea, and Bowen to life!

To Alicia Gordon and Ava Greenfield at ICM—it's such an honor working with you every day. Thank you for supporting this book, and all my books. To Roxane Edouard and the Curtis Brown team, thank you for bringing my stories to the world! My thanks as well to Tamara Kawar and John Burnham as well as my lawyer, Richard Thompson.

To my husband, Stephen, I love you so much. The last year and a half have not been easy, with all of us being separated. Thanks for believing in me, for always validating my dreams as equal to yours, and for cheering me on, even from the other side of the world. Much love and gratitude to my parents, particularly my mom, who was diagnosed with pancreatic cancer as I was writing this book. . . . You're my hero, Mom. You inspire me every day with your courage.

My deepest thanks to the teachers and librarians who worked tirelessly during this impossible time. I love you, I see you, and I thank you.

And to all the children who have persevered despite all the curveballs—thanks for being so resilient and so strong. I hope this book brings you comfort, laughs, and hope.

A READING GROUP GUIDE TO
New from Here
by Kelly Yang

About the Book

Ten-year-old Knox Wei-Evans doesn't want to move to California without his dad and dog, but his parents decide that leaving Hong Kong will keep him and his siblings safe from the new virus that is spreading like wildfire across China and Europe. Almost overnight, Knox, his mom, and his two siblings are living in a small house in San Francisco. At school, he feels the impact of being the new kid. In addition to worrying about his dad and learning he has ADHD, Knox experiences the hostility directed toward Asians and Asian Americans that is skyrocketing during the pandemic. Can Knox keep his family together during a pandemic *and* find the sense of belonging in his new country?

Discussion Questions

1. The first line of *New from Here* by Kelly Yang reads: "My name is Knox and sometimes I just blurt words out." Knox has ADHD (attention deficit hyperactivity disorder), a common condition including attention difficulty, hyperactivity, and impulsiveness. When he hears his mother tell the school assistant that he has ADHD, Knox is shocked. How does the knowledge of his condition help him to better understand himself? How does learning that Christopher also has ADHD help Knox feel less alone? Knox's father suggests that Knox think of his ADHD as a "superpower." How does his condition work in positive ways?

2. At the start of the story, cases of the coronavirus have begun to appear in Hong Kong, and Knox, his siblings, and his mother prepare to relocate temporarily to San Francisco, in an attempt to escape the virus. The family lived through the SARS epidemic and they are afraid that this new virus could be worse. Discuss specific examples of how fear is one of the story's dominant themes. When the family arrives in the US, their Uber driver makes the family get out of the car because he assumes, as Asians, they could be infected with the virus. How is this a fear-based example of discrimination? Discuss other examples of how fear drives people's decisions. When Knox notices a homeless woman pushing a shopping cart, he asks Bowen, "'You think that's ever going to happen to us? If Mom doesn't get a job . . .'" Afterward he compares the thought to a "big and terrifying boa constrictor." How is this simile a powerful one to describe Knox's fear, given his mother's struggle with finding work?

3. Describe the siblings' relationship in the book. How are their tensions and bonds common among siblings? How does each sibling cope with the pandemic and the experience of being "the new kid"? Why do you think that no one invited Lea to play while she was sitting on the friendship bench at school? Why is Knox so thrilled when Ms. Turner gives him a Trader Joe's bag of valentines? How do you think Bowen was feeling when he saw the bag after school that day? Bowen confesses to Knox that he misses "'not being the only Asian kid'" in his class. In what ways were the siblings there for each other? Identify and discuss a scene in the book where you wished they'd said something to one another to help ease the pain? Why do you think it's so difficult sometimes for siblings to say they're thinking of each other?

4. Almost immediately after Knox, his siblings, and their mom leave Hong Kong for the United States, they confront the anti-Asian discrimination and racism that would quickly grow and spread alongside the virus. How did you feel as the family approached the customs agent at the airport? How did you feel after they were allowed entry into the country? Discuss why Bowen wonders if the family should tell people they are from Asia, and his mother's response: "'If you want, you can tell them you're new from here. I mean we sort of are.'" Do you think this was an appropriate thing for her to say? Why might she worry about her children just saying they come from Hong Kong? Some of the kids at Knox's school have created a game called coronavirus tag, and they make Knox and Christopher be "it" because they are Asian. How is this game basically comparing the boys to a disease? If you could, what would you say to those kids if you saw this happening during recess? Discuss some of the most extreme examples of anti-Asian hate that appear in the story. Also, discuss some of the examples that reflect the best in people who stand up for those being targeted because of their race. After the scene in the grocery store, Knox is left with the feeling that they are "not alone." In your own words, describe what you think Knox is feeling. What does Knox's mother mean by "'You know what the vaccine for racism is? Love.'"

5. Above all else, *New from Here* is the story of a family that loves and supports one another even when faced with serious challenges: discrimination, separation, loss, and financial, food, and health insecurity. Even though Bowen is tough on Knox at times, Knox does small acts of kindness for his big brother. Discuss ways in which Knox is there for Bowen. Discuss ways the family bonds. How did your family bond during the pandemic? Discuss examples from the story that illustrate Bowen's reply to Knox: "'Family beats virus, any day.'"

6. Knox has never been great at making friends, and as he begins his new school in America, he hopes that he can make at least one. Discuss how Knox and Christopher bond after the coronavirus tag game. Knox worries that Christopher won't want to be his friend once he learns that Knox came from Hong Kong. "Instead, he walks over, takes a seat, and squeezes my green apple squishy toy. His eyes smile back at me." If Christopher's eyes could talk, what do you think they would say to Knox? How does the knowledge that Knox and Christopher both have ADHD further bond their friendship? Discuss examples from the story that illustrate how these two friends truly care for and support each other.

7. What is an "assumption"? [An assumption is a thing that is accepted as true or as certain to happen without proof. Source: Oxford Languages.] People make all kinds of assumptions about Asians and Asian Americans in the story, most of them ethnicity-based. Discuss an assumption that you can recall from the book that felt particularly unfair or mean. In chapter 13, Knox and his mom discover some family photographs from the period of the 1918 flu pandemic. Knox points out that it killed 50 million people, to which his mother replies, "'It's okay. This time it's different. We've evolved. We learned. And now we take these things very, very seriously. You'll see, this virus is going to be over superfast.'" How is this statement an example of an assumption? Why do you think that early in the pandemic so many people assumed that the virus wouldn't affect the United States as much as it did Asian and European countries? Why does Bowen assume that the homeless lady will want all the money if offered only a part of it in chapter 49? Why are so many people in the book willing to assume that Asians or Asian Americans either caused or have COVID-19? Imagine if you were targeted and blamed for being the cause of an infectious disease that has caused millions of deaths. How do you think it would affect your life and sense of well-being? How can assumptions be dangerous?

8. Knox worries about a lot of things, and for good reason: he is starting a new school, his family has just moved to the United States at the start of a pandemic, his father and dog are back in Hong Kong and he doesn't know when or if they will be reunited, his mother has lost her job and is having a difficult time finding a new one, and Bowen seems to hate him. As the cases of COVID-19 rise across the world, so does Knox's anxiety. How does his mom withholding information from Knox and his siblings make him more tense? What aspects of Knox's experience relate to your own worries over the pandemic and the future?

9. There are many examples in the story of people behaving in horrible, ugly ways as the pandemic begins to take root: from the Taradippin brothers taking advantage of a desperate situation for profit to people selfishly overbuying items like toilet paper, to implicit and explicit hostility against Asian Americans and other people of color. But the opposite is also evident in the story. Discuss examples of how Knox and his siblings bring kindness and generosity into the community, despite experiencing discrimination and scapegoating. What does Knox mean when he realizes: "If we've learned one thing this year, it's that we're all connected to each other. We all breathe the same air into our lungs. None of us are immune to each other's problems." (chapter 92)?

10. All three siblings demonstrate empathy, kindness, and compassion to their parents, their friends, their neighbors, and to each other. Discuss examples of how Knox, Bowen, and Lea show their capacity for caring. How does Knox's reaction to the hateful man in the dog park show empathy for his brother's pain? Reread chapter 31. How do the siblings show compassion and kindness for their lonely neighbor, Mr. Brady? Share examples of compassion, kindness, and empathy that you have given or experienced during the pandemic.

11. Throughout the book, you probably made connections to Knox, Bowen, and Lea as children who are living through a pandemic. How does the decision to move to San Francisco without Dad bring about unforeseen changes to the Evans family? In chapter 68, Knox and his classmates help Mrs. Turner move the classroom desks to create social distancing, losing areas of the room that Knox loved, such as the Calm Down corner. How is this scene symbolic of the changes you've had to make at home and at school? Discuss how the characters' experiences, such as online school and practicing protocols (such as mask wearing, hand sanitizing, and social distancing), as well as the many changes they had to make in their daily lives, compare to what you experienced and may still be experiencing during this time. How has the pandemic affected your family, friendships, and daily lives?

12. Discuss what health insurance is and why it is so important to have. In chapter 17, after the IKEA shelving unit arrives, Lea nearly drops one of the heavy wood shelves on her foot, to which Mom exclaims, "'Careful! We don't have any health insurance here yet!'" Why is Mom so worried that the children might need to see a doctor or go to a hospital? For the many people who lost their jobs during the pandemic, the stress of worrying about buying food, paying rent and bills, and covering the cost of health care (especially for people without insurance) created stress and anxiety. Discuss how the financial insecurity the family experiences affects their daily lives and relationships.

13. Knox displays remarkable fortitude over the course of the story. Discuss examples of how Knox demonstrates "consistent courage." Share examples of how you have had to be brave during the pandemic.

Suggestions for Classroom Activities

1. 1918 Flu to COVID-19. In 1918, the world was seized by a pandemic caused by a virus that became known as the Great Influenza epidemic or the 1918 Influenza pandemic. In late 2019, the world first began to hear of a novel (new) virus that originated in China and began to rapidly spread across the world. On March 11, 2020, the World Health Organization officially declared COVID-19 a global pandemic. Guide students in learning about the 1918 pandemic that killed an estimated fifty million people, and how it compares to the current pandemic. Encourage students to focus their research on the similarities and differences between the two outbreaks, particularly around public health and discrimination, and what lessons we have applied and also ignored.

2. Poetry of a Pandemic. Perhaps no people have been more affected by the changes brought about by the pandemic than children. Millions of children stopped going to in-person school because of lockdowns. Students without access to computer technology didn't go to school at all. After the Wei-Evans family moves to San Francisco, the kids have to continue going to school online before starting in-person school. Knox is supposed to write a haiku, but is confused on how to proceed and writes this instead:

I want to learn,
From a human, not a box.
Because a human cares,
And a box stares.

Begin a series of brainstorming sessions encouraging students to share their personal experiences with online school and/or in-person school during the pandemic. As a culminating activity, guide students to write haikus or quatrain poems about their experiences.

3. Survivors. Knox's mom's favorite song is "Survivor" by Destiny's Child. Lea asks her mother why she likes the song so much, to which she replies, "'Because it's all about the ups and downs of life. And how there are challenges, but if you work hard, you can survive anything!'" Place students into pairs or small groups. Have students select a popular song to which they will write original lyrics about facing life's challenges head-on. Give each group an opportunity to perform the song for the class.

4. A Note to Future Me. In chapter 27, Knox describes how Christopher has a habit of writing things down on Post-its: "I got the idea of writing notes to myself from Christopher . . . It's kind of cool. Like Old Me talking to Future Me." Give each student five Post-it notes. After reading *New from Here*, have each student write down one thing they learned from the story; something that they want to remember in the future. (Students should write only one item per note). Have students place all their notes onto a sheet of paper, fold it, and mail it to themselves in a self-addressed stamped envelope. Encourage students to put the notes in a safe place for future reference.

5. ICEE in Action. After the ugly scene at the track where Bowen is scapegoated for his coach's cough, Knox googles *How to respond to racist comments*. What he discovers is the acronym ICEE: interrupt, correct, educate, echo. Reread chapter 37. Discuss the components of this strategy. Place students in pairs or groups of three. Give each group time to write a short script based on some of the scenes in *New from Here* that involve racism, discrimination, or scapegoating, or students can create original scenarios. Direct students to incorporate ICEE into their scripts. Give each group an opportunity to perform their piece for the class.

6. Your Message to the Future. The lessons from those who lived through the 1918 pandemic have informed how people today are navigating life with the COVID-19 pandemic. Reading first-person accounts of people who experienced the last great pandemic can be comforting to those living through similar circumstances today. Imagine the world in one hundred years. A child your age discovers a buried time capsule. Inside the time capsule the child discovers a bound book, a journal written by a student living through the COVID-19 pandemic. Imagine you are the writer of that journal. Create a series of reflections about how you have coped during this difficult and frightening time. Share your thoughts, fears, and advice for those who will endure the next great pandemic.

This guide was created by Colleen Carroll, literacy educator, content creator, and children's book author. Learn more about Colleen at www.colleencarroll.us.

TURN THE PAGE FOR A SNEAK PEEK AT
Finally Seen

#1 NEW YORK TIMES BESTSELLING AUTHOR
KELLY YANG

Finally Seen

listen to the quiet hum of the plane and the not-so-quiet flutter of my heart in my chest. *This is it.* Another six hours and I will finally see my parents and my sister again! I try to picture Mom's and Dad's faces when I land. Except I keep picturing Marge and Homer Simpson. Only Asian. With shorter hair. And a less smart Lisa. (Hopefully.)

I guess that's what happens when you haven't seen your family in five years (and you've watched a *lot* of subtitled *Simpsons*). I was starting to give up on the whole going-to-America thing, until my mom called six weeks ago.

"Lao Lao told me you're doing your middle school applications," Mom said. "And you're writing an essay on your parents being in America?"

I nodded, coiling the phone cord around my fingers.

"Is that not a good topic?" I asked.

"No . . . ," she said, "it's just . . . what are you going to say?"

I shrugged. I like writing, but not as much as I like drawing pictures. But art's a sure way to get kicked out of any school in Beijing, let alone Beijing Normal Middle School #3, where I was applying. It was my aunt Jing's middle school. She now has a fancy tech job in Shenzhen. She says there's no future for artists in China. Beijing Normal would get the art out of me . . . and turn me into a steady workhorse. Just like her.

"Well?" Mom asked.

I felt a rush of heat spread across my forehead. Here was my chance to tell her how I really felt about being left behind all these years. I was only five years old when she left. I thought she was going on a *work* trip. I didn't even understand. Most of all, how could she take Millie, my baby sister, and not me? My sister got to grow up with my parents. Me? I grew up with postcards from my parents.

But as usual, my voice was locked in the chamber of my throat.

It's like my throat has a word catcher to catch all my hard feelings. Grabbing them before they pass through. Making sure they don't get out for anyone, well, except Lao Lao.

My grandmother, Lao Lao, is my moon and my Wilson. Like the volleyball in *Castaway* (another movie I binged), she is my companion in my waiting city. That's what Beijing feels like, just me and Lao Lao waiting. It used to be me, Lao Lao, and Lao Ye. But last year, when Lao Ye passed away . . . our trio of tea leaves went down to two. Now I am Lao Lao's human alarm clock (I wake her up every day at 6 a.m.), dumpling steamer, pu'er brewer, flower waterer, and medicine fetcher.

I know how much she needs me. I'm all she's got left. Which is why some feelings are too hard to even tell her.

Instead, I catch them with my word catcher and tuck them behind my cheek.

There are a lot of word catchers in China, starting with the official one from the government.

Every morning, Lao Lao reminds me: go to school, make your parents proud, and watch your words, lest they label you a bad apple. She grew up in the era of the Cultural Revolution, and her father was thrown in jail for being a "bad apple." Even though that was a long time ago, the memory of it never really left. She's always telling me to sew up half my mouth. I imagine an invisible thread running along my mouth, my lips stitched like a sock.

But the thing about some feelings is . . . they just won't go away. Instead, they form a tight ball at the base of my throat. Where they sit and they wait, planning their escape from the thread. And one day, just when you least expect it, they shoot out like a rocket.

That's exactly what happened that rainy Beijing spring day when Mom called.

"Do you really want to go to Beijing Normal #3?" Mom asked.

I looked over at my lao lao, craning her head eagerly to catch snippets of our conversation. She put her knitting needles down, massaging her hand. Her arthritis had gotten so much worse since Lao Ye passed, she could hardly keep knitting. The doctors in China had warned her that this day would come. They told her to do more acupuncture, to get out and exercise. But Lao Lao was born in the Year of the Ox. She does not like anyone telling her what to do.

I turned away from Lao Lao, held the phone close to my face, and cupped a hand around my mouth.

"No," I whispered. "I want to go to school in America. Please, Mama. I want to come."

And with that, I chose my future over my past.

A hand on my arm pushes me awake.

"Lina Gao?" the flight attendant asks. I rub my eyes awake.

She smiles and says to me in Chinese, "We're moving you up to first class. So you can get out first when we land!"

I blink in confusion. I reach for my sketch pad. I was in the middle of working on a sketch of Lao Lao gardening, but as I look up, my eyes nearly pop when I see the flight tracker on the screen. We're almost *there*!

"Your escort will be waiting as soon as we get to LAX to take you to your parents."

I leap up from my seat. *Let's gooooo!!!*

I follow the flight attendant up the long aisle to first class, staring at all the people stretched out in *beds* with their noise-canceling headphones and cotton candy slippers. These are airplane *apartments*.

I take a seat in one of the cabins and reach for the fancy first-class cotton slippers. I'm so saving these for Lao Lao. I wonder if she likes her new nursing home.

I feel a tug of guilt thinking about it, but Aunt Jing said it was necessary. She and Uncle Hu both live in Shenzhen, which is about twelve hundred miles away from Beijing, and they both have 9-9-6 tech jobs. A 9-9-6 job means you work from 9 a.m. to 9 p.m. six days a week. They're the envy of the country, because they make the most money. But it also means there's no *way* my aunt can be a tea brewer for my lao lao.

So they took me and Lao Lao to visit the nursing home. I remember the floors were very shiny, almost like you could go Rollerblading on them. I pictured a bunch of elderly folks Rollerblading, and then had to bite on my cheeks to stop myself from giggling. Because it wasn't funny.

The rooms were bright, with big windows that allowed the team of nurses to look in at all times. Aunt Jing said she got

Lao Lao the biggest room of all—a private room. It was the nicest room in the entire nursing home. But to Lao Lao, it was like living inside a fishbowl. She didn't like the idea *at all*.

"*No way!*" *she said, stomping her walking cane down on the ground.* "*Not happening! I am a free spirit—I need to be able to roam around the park and go to see my friends!*"

"*They can come see you!*" *Aunt Jing insisted.* "*That's why we're putting you into a retirement home in Beijing—so your friends can come visit. Anytime!*"

Lao Lao has two good park friends: Chen Nai Nai, a grandma who loves to dance, and Wang Nai Nai, whose daughter is also in America. I've never seen either of them come to our house, though.

"*Why can't I just stay by myself?*" *Lao Lao asked, peeking at my aunt.*

"*Because, Ma, your arthritis and osteoporosis, it's all getting worse. And now that Dad's gone . . . Frankly, you should have gone into a retirement community a long time ago,*" *Aunt Jing said.* "*But you had Lina—*"

"*And I loved every minute of it, sweet child,*" *Lao Lao said, patting my hand.*

I felt a tear escape. This was all my fault.

"*No, don't you cry,*" *Lao Lao told me. She nodded to my aunt, and with a shaking hand, she signed the papers.*

I put my hand to the airplane window and whisper with all my heart:

"I'm so sorry, Lao Lao. I promise I will find a way to bring you over. I will find a way to get you out of the waiting city, too."

"Fifteen minutes to landing!" the captain announces on the speaker.

I immediately grab the stash of free goodies next to the cotton candy slippers. I stuff as many as I can into my backpack. Socks, sleeping masks, you name it. I add the stash to my collection of Chinese snacks I've brought over for my (almost) new family. I've packed wheat flour cake, hawthorn flakes, pumpkin chips, and White Rabbit candies for them, hoping the candies will fill them with sweet guilt for leaving me behind.

I gaze out the window at the wispy clouds. The Los Angeles houses sprawl across the land, stretching all the way to the shimmering blue sea! I've never seen the ocean before. Before Lao Ye passed, we talked about going to Beidaihe, the closest beach to Beijing. But it was always too hard, with Lao Ye's work and health. He was a magazine editor. Even after he "retired" he kept going into the office. He said working was the best way to stay young, but Lao Lao secretly suspected it was so he could keep eating lunch at his favorite fried dumpling place next to his office.

My lao ye had heart disease and diabetes. He used to joke that at his age, heart disease and diabetes were like stamps in a passport—signs of a life well lived.

I wish Lao Ye had had actual stamps in his passport, though, and more time to get them. But at seventy-two, he had a stroke in the taxi on his way home from work.

We didn't believe it even when we were sitting in the hospital waiting area. Lao Lao and I were still talking about going to the beach and pushing Lao Ye to actually retire after this. When the doctor delivered the news, all I remember is my grandma falling to the ground, pounding the cold stone floor, crying, "You get back here, you old goat! Don't you dare leave me!"

But her beloved goat was already gone.

Lao Lao's voice comes burrowing into my head as the plane starts to descend.

This is different. Remember, we may be six thousand miles apart, but I'm right there in your heart. Anytime you want to talk to me, just put your hand over your chest and I'll feel it, sweet child.

As the turbulence jiggles my butt, I open my mouth, like I'm about to eat a gigantic baozi, the tears running down my cheeks. *This is it, Lao Lao! I made it!!!*

We touch down at 9:58 a.m. As the plane taxis, a flight attendant comes up to me. "Are you ready?"

"I'm ready!" I announce.